NOVA 2

NOVA 2

edited by

HARRY HARRISON

WALKER AND COMPANY
New York

First published in the United States of America in 1972 by the Walker Publishing Company, Inc.

Published simultaneously in Canada by Fitzhenry & Whiteside, Limited, Toronto.

Printed in the United States of America.

CONTENTS

INTRODUCTION vii

ZIRN LEFT UNGUARDED,
THE JENGHIK PALACE
IN FLAMES,
JON WESTERLY DEAD 1
by Robert Sheckley

"EAST WIND, WEST WIND" 6
by Frank M. Robinson

THE SUMERIAN OATH 30
by Philip José Farmer

NOW + n NOW − n 36
by Robert Silverberg

TWO ODYSSEYS INTO THE CENTER 53
by Barry N. Malzberg

DARKNESS 63
by André Carneiro, translated by Leo L. Barrow

ON THE WHEEL 80
by Damon Knight

MISS OMEGA RAVEN 86
by Naomi Mitchison

THE POET IN THE HOLOGRAM
IN THE MIDDLE OF PRIME TIME 91
by Ed Bryant

CONTENTS (*continued*)

THE OLD FOLKS 107
by James E. Gunn

THE STEAM-DRIVEN BOY 123
by John Sladek

I TELL YOU, IT'S TRUE 131
by Poul Anderson

**AND I HAVE COME UPON
THIS PLACE BY LOST WAYS 149**
by James Tiptree, Jr.

THE ERGOT SHOW 167
by Brian W. Aldiss

INTRODUCTION

Science fiction is as American as apple pie. Or at least it used to be. This is no longer true. There has been an international upsurge of interest in the medium that is very heartening to anyone involved in it.

Of course the father of modern science fiction, H. G. Wells, was English, and there have always been a good number of British writers working in the field ever since. But, until recently, their primary markets were American magazines and publishers. Kingsley Amis, in one of his more penetrating moods, was heard to remark that "science fiction is written by Americans and Britons and not by women and foreigners." There is just enough truth in this to make it relevant as well as funny. There are some excellent female science fiction writers, but all too few of them writing all too little. (Though we are lucky enough to have a Naomi Mitchison story in this *Nova*, as well as one in the first.) And, until quite recently, there were just no other science fiction writers of international caliber outside of the English speaking countries. However, it must be admitted that an exception can be made for the Soviets who have produced an indigenous form of science fiction that seems very fusty and old-fashioned by our standards. There is hope that they will improve.

Then very suddenly, within the past decade, a number of countries discovered science fiction. *Discovered* in this context means that publishers around the world became aware that they could make money by selling this particular brand of fiction. Since there were no home-grown writers whom they could turn to, they were forced to buy translation rights from the American and British publishers. It is interesting to note that they knew just what to buy since there were science fiction enthusiasts eagerly waiting to advise them in every country. These were fans who read science fiction in English and who were as enthusiastic and knowledgeable as any American fan. Soon the major writers could count upon a steady trickle of income from foreign sales, plus occasional decorative copies of their works in exotic bindings and languages. (They could also count upon the occasional outright theft of a book since a number of countries take a much more lenient view of copyright laws than America and Great Britain. The Soviet Union is not a member of the Universal Copyright Convention so they pirate our books just as we pirate theirs—legally. Not that this in any way cheers the writers or fattens their bank accounts. I recently obtained a copy of an anthology in Latvian containing one of my stories. The entire book, containing only American stories, had been translated from the Russian. This means that not only had all of these stories been stolen and reprinted in Russian, but the crooks had sold the rights all over again and made more money for themselves.)

These publishing successes of translated books encouraged local writers to try their hands at science fiction, so local German, Italian and Japanese schools sprang up. In the beginning they disguised their national character and pretended to be true American Anglo-Saxon writers. Roberta Rambelli, who later became one of Italy's leading editors and translators, wrote her first science fiction under the pen name of "Robert Rainbell." It consisted of stories all about great guys named Milton Woodrich and Morton G. Moore. This is all part of the past now and indigenous writers are proud of their work and the distinctive difference that national culture supplies.

Yet the familiar, popular science fiction authors all over the world are still the same as they always were. The truth of this was driven home to me by the First Brazilian Science Fiction Film Festival that was held in Rio de Janeiro last spring. A number of foreign writers and film makers were guests of the festival, and the writers participated in a science fiction forum held in conjunction with it. Among the people there were Robert Sheckley, Philip José Farmer, Damon Knight, Poul Anderson and Brian W. Aldiss. Robert Silverberg was invited but was in Africa and could not make it. If these names seem strangely familiar it is because they all have stories in this volume. André Carneiro was chairman of the science fiction sessions and his work is represented here as well.

Rio was an experience not soon forgotten. Brazil is a country bigger than the United States, busy, throbbing, vital—and fascinated by science fiction as this festival proved. Yet home-brewed science fiction is still new on the scene there. Dr. Leo L. Barrow, translator and close student of Brazilian letters, writes:

"With notable exceptions like André Carneiro, Fausto Cunha, and Dinah Silveira de Queiroz, few Brazilians write science fiction. Perhaps more should. Brazilians with their rich African heritage, and their jovial optimistic way of not facing the harsh realities that surround them, have a natural gift for the blending of reality and phantasy.

"André Carneiro sees little difference between science fiction and other good literature. He feels that science fiction may be the type of literature most closely linked to the evolution of humanity, since it studies man's problematical side projected into the future. All Brazilian literature tends to see reality and the human essence through a very special lens, with a strong touch of native stigmatism, which gives them a fascinating new dimension."

What I find of particular interest is that Carneiro's writing is concerned with the approach to reality, J. G. Ballard's "inner space." (Ballard was also in Rio—as were many American writers.) More than one author in this anthology writes a story concerned with an approach to reality. This is either a complete coincidence, a virus caught in Brazil, or a new thing on the wing in science fiction. I prefer to believe the latter. (Ed Bryant caught the infection and he was safe in his stirrup buckle factory while the others were sweating and sipping beer on the beach in Copacabana.)

There is a new awareness in science fiction. It is a product of the same awakening that is producing student interest in ecology and Presidential attention to pollution. It is a slippery feeling that all is not quite so right with this perfect world, that the superpatriotic bumper sticker *Love America or Leave It* is too simplistic, in addition to being downright stupid. It is a suspicion that the sticker, *Change America or Lose It,* is much closer to the truth, and a feeling that the governor is missing from our run-away technology and that a new one had better be fitted. At once.

This new-found awareness of science fiction writers is reflected in this anthology. Perhaps they are being churlish to scrutinize so closely the science half of their craft, but I do not think so. Science is not being doubted—just questioned. And there is a world of difference between these two words. The efficacy of big science, unplanned and uncontrolled science, is being looked at, not the basic concepts. Accepted values are being questioned and goals—planned or unplanned —examined from all sides. That this is a good cause goes without saying.

Yet these writers are still entertainers; they have not forgotten that important aspect of their art. In looking at the world with new eyes and asking new questions they still write good stories. Better stories perhaps because they are looking at problems vital to continued existence on this spaceship Earth.

And they are also laughing. At least seven stories in this collection are sparked with wit—and two of these are downright funny. This is a wonderful change that I hope continues. There is little enough around to laugh at these days and all contributions are gratefully accepted.

Harry Harrison

Zirn Left Unguarded,
The Jenghik Palace
in Flames, Jon Westerly Dead

by Robert Sheckley

*There is a noble tradition of great and epical adventure in science
fiction. Beginning, perhaps, with Edgar Rice Burroughs, it continues
through the wide screen space opera epics of E. E. Smith, Ph.D., on
through Jack Williamson, and even the very young John W. Camp-
bell, Jr. Lately it has begun to be called "sword and sworcery," but
this is just the most recent protean form the continuing epic tradition
has taken. I record this all historically because here, that exceedingly
fine writer and wielder of a mordant typewriter, Robert Sheckley, has
finished off the up until now endless saga, written finis to those
mighty tomes, killed the entire literature dead. Read on—if you dare!*

The bulletin came through blurred with fear. "Somebody is dancing
on our graves," said Charleroi. His gaze lifted to include the entire
Earth. "This will make a fine mausoleum."

"Your words are strange," she said. "Yet there is that in your manner which I find pleasing . . . Come closer, stranger, and explain
yourself."

I stepped back and withdrew my sword from its scabbard. Beside
me, I heard a metallic hiss; Ocpetis Marn had drawn his sword, too,
and now he stood with me, back to back, as the Megenth horde approached.

"Now shall we sell our lives dearly, Jon Westerley," said Ocpetis
Marn in the peculiar guttural hiss of the Mnerian race.

"Indeed we shall," I replied. "And there will be some more than
one widow to dance the Passagekeen before this day is through."

1

He nodded. "And some disconsolate fathers will make the lonely sacrifice to the God of Deteriorations."

We smiled at each other's staunch words. Yet it was no laughing matter. The Megenth bucks advanced slowly, implacably, across the green and purple moss-sward. They had drawn their *raftii*—those long, curved, double-pointed dirks that had struck terror in the innermost recesses of the civilized galaxy. We waited.

The first blade crossed mine. I parried and thrust, catching the big fellow full in the throat. He reeled back, and I set myself for my next antagonist.

Two of them came at me this time. I could hear the sharp intake of Ocpetis's breath as he hacked and hewed with his sword. The situation was utterly hopeless.

I thought of the unprecedented combination of circumstances that had brought me to this situation. I thought of the Cities of the Terran Plurality, whose very existence depended upon the foredoomed outcome of this present impasse. I thought of autumn in Carcassone, hazy mornings in Saskatoon, steel-colored rain falling on the Black Hills. Was all this to pass? Surely not. And yet—why not?

We said to the computer: "These are the factors, this is our predicament. Do us the favor of solving our problem and saving our lives and the lives of all Earth."

The computer computed. It said: "The problem cannot be solved."

"Then how are we to go about saving Earth from destruction?"

"You don't," the computer told us.

We left sadly. But then Jenkins said, "What the hell—that was only one computer's opinion."

That cheered us up. We held our heads high. We decided to take further consultations.

The gypsy turned the card. It came up Final Judgement. We left sadly. Then Myers said, "What the hell—that's only one gypsy's opinion."

That cheered us up. We held our heads high. We decided to take further consultations.

You said it yourself: "'A bright blossom of blood on his forehead.' You looked at me with strange eyes. Must I love you?"

It all began so suddenly. The reptilian forces of Megenth, long quiescent, suddenly began to expand due to the serum given them by Charles Engstrom, the power-crazed telepath. Jon Westerley was hastily recalled from his secret mission to Angos II. Westerley had the supreme misfortune of materializing within a ring of Black Force, due to the inadvertent treachery of Ocpetis Marn, his faithful Mnerian companion, who had, unknown to Westerley, been trapped in the Hall of Floating Mirrors, and his mind taken over by the renegade Santhis, leader of the Entropy Guild. That was the end for Westerley, and the beginning of the end for us.

The old man was in a stupor. I unstrapped him from the smoldering control chair and caught the characteristic sweet-salty-sour odor of manginee—that insidious narcotic grown only in the caverns of Ingidor—whose insidious influence had subverted our guardposts along the Wall Star Belt.

I shook him roughly. "Preston!" I cried. "For the sake of Earth, for Magda, for everything you hold dear—tell me what happened."

His eyes rolled. His mouth twitched. With vast effort he said, "Zirn! Zirn is lost, is lost, is lost!"

His head lolled forward. Death rearranged his face.

Zirn lost! My brain worked furiously. That meant that the High Star Pass was open, the negative accumulators no longer functioning, the drone soldiers overwhelmed. Zirn was a wound through which our life-blood would pour. But surely there was a way out?

President Edgars looked at the cerulean telephone. He had been warned never to use it except in the direst emergency, and perhaps not even then. But surely the present situation justified? . . . He lifted the telephone.

"Paradise Reception, Miss Ophelia speaking."

"This is President Edgars of Earth. I must speak to God immediately."

"God is out of his office just now and cannot be reached. May I be of service?"

"Well, you see," Edgars said, "I have this really bad emergency on my hands. I mean, it looks like the end of everything."

"Everything?" Miss Ophelia asked.

"Well, not *literally* everything. But it does mean the destruction of us. Of Earth and all that. If you could just bring this to God's attention——"

"Since God is omniscient, I'm sure he knows all about it."

"I'm sure he does. But I thought that if I could just speak to him personally——"

"I'm afraid that is not possible at this time. But you could leave a message. God is very good and very fair, and I'm sure he will consider your problem and do what is right and godly. He's wonderful, you know. I love God."

"We all do," Edgars said sadly.

"Is there anything else?"

"No. Yes! May I speak with Mr. Joseph J. Edgars, please?"

"Who is that?"

"My father. He died ten years ago."

"I'm sorry, sir. That is not permitted."

"Can you at least tell me if he's up there with you people?"

"Sorry, we are not allowed to give out that information."

"Well, can you tell me if *anybody* is up there? I mean, is there really an afterlife? Or is it maybe only you and God up there? Or maybe only you?"

"For information concerning the afterlife," Miss Ophelia said, "kindly contact your nearest priest, minister, rabbi, mullah, or anyone else on the accredited list of God representatives. Thank you for calling."

There was a sweet tinkle of chimes. Then the line went dead.

"What did the Big Fellow say?" asked General Muller.

"All I got was double-talk from his secretary."

"Personally, I don't believe in superstitions like God," General Muller said. "Even if they happen to be true, I find it healthier not to believe. Shall we get on with it?"

They got on with it.

Testimony of the robot who might have been Dr. Zach:

"My true identity is a mystery to me, and one which, under the circumstances, I do not expect to be resolved. But I was at the Jenghik Palace. I saw the Megenth warriors swarm over the crimson balustrades, overturn the candelabra, smash, kill, destroy. The governor died with a sword in his hand. The Terran Guard made their last stand in the Dolorous Keep, and perished to a man after mighty blows given and received. The ladies of the court defended themselves with daggers so small as to appear symbolic. They were granted quick passage. I saw the great fire consume the bronze eagles of Earth. The subject peoples had long fled. I watched the Jenghik Palace—that great pile, marking the furthest extent of Earth's suzerainty, topple soundlessly into the dust from which it sprung. And I knew then that all was lost, and that the fate of Terra—of which planet I consider myself a loyal son, despite the fact that I was (presumably) crafted rather than created, produced rather than born—the fate of divine

4

Terra, I say, was to be annihilated utterly, until not even the ghost of a memory remained.

"You said it youself: 'A star exploded in his eye.' This last day I must love you. The rumors are heavy tonight, and the sky is red. I love it when you turn your head just so. Perhaps it is true that we are chaff between the iron jaws of life and death. Still, I prefer to keep time by my own watch. So I fly in the face of the evidence, I fly with you.

"It is the end, I love you, it is the end."

END

"East Wind, West Wind"

by Frank M. Robinson

The first time I experienced a Los Angeles supersmog I simply would not believe it. People could not go on living in this kind of poisonous soup without doing everything possible to change it. I was wrong. Just how wrong and why is explained by Frank M. Robinson in this singularly chilling story.

It wasn't going to be just another bad day, it was going to be a terrible one. The inversion layer had slipped over the city four days before and it had been like putting a lid on a kettle; the air was building up to a real Donora, turning into a chemical soup so foul I wouldn't have believed it if I hadn't been trying to breathe the stuff. Besides sticking in my throat, it made my eyes feel like they were being bathed in acid. You could hardly see the sun—it was a pale, sickly disc floating in a mustard-colored sky—but even so, the streets were an oven and the humidity was so high you could have wrung the water out of the air with your bare hands . . . dirty water, naturally.

On the bus a red-faced salesman with denture breath recognized my Air Central badge and got pushy. I growled that we didn't *make* the air—not yet, at any rate—and finally I took off the badge and put it in my pocket and tried to shut out the coughing and the complaints around me by concentrating on the faint, cheery sound of the "corn poppers" laundering the bus's exhaust. Five would have gotten you ten, of course, that their effect was strictly psychological, that they had seen more than twenty thousand miles of service and were now absolutely worthless. . . .

At work I hung up my plastic sportscoat, slipped off the white surgeon's mask (black where my nose and mouth had been) and filled my lungs with good machine-pure air that smelled only faintly of oil and electric motors; one of the advantages of working for Air Central was that our office air was the best in the city. I dropped a quarter in the coffee vendor, dialed it black, and inhaled the fumes for a second while I shook the sleep from my eyes and speculated about what Wanda would have for me at the Investigator's Desk. There were thirty-nine other Investigators besides myself but I was junior and my daily assignment card was usually just a listing of minor complaints and violations that had to be checked out.

Wanda was young and pretty and redhaired and easy to spot even in a secretarial pool full of pretty girls. I offered her some of my coffee and looked over her shoulder while she flipped through the assignment cards. "That stuff out there is easier to swim through than to breathe," I said. "What's the index?"

"Eighty-four point five," she said quietly. "And rising."

I just stared at her. I had thought it was bad, but hardly that bad, and for the first time that day I felt a sudden flash of panic. "And no alert? When it hits seventy-five this city's supposed to close up like a clam!"

She nodded down the hall to the Director's office. "Lawyers from Sanitary Pick-Up, Oberhausen Steel, and City Light and Power got an injunction—they were here to break the news to Monte at eight sharp. Impractical, unnecessary, money-wasting, and fifteen thousand employees would be thrown out of work if they had to shut down the furnaces and incinerators. They got an okay right from the top of Air Shed Number Three."

My jaw dropped. "How could they? Monte's supposed to have the last word!"

"So go argue with the politicians—if you can stand the hot air." She suddenly looked very fragile and I wanted to run out and slay a dragon or two for her. "The chicken-hearts took the easy way out, Jim. Independent Weather's predicting a cold front for early this evening and rising winds and rain for tomorrow."

The rain would clean up the air, I thought. But Independent Weather could be bought and as a result it had a habit of turning in cheery predictions that frequently didn't come true. Air Central had tried for years to get IW outlawed but money talks and their lobbyist in the capital was quite a talker. Unfortunately, if they were wrong this time, it would be as if they had pulled a plastic bag over the city's head.

I started to say something, then shut up. If you let it get to you, you wouldn't last long on the job. "Where's my list of small-fry?"

She gave me an assignment card. It was blank except for *See Me* written across its face. "Humor him, Jim, he's not feeling well."

This worried me a little because Monte was the father of us all—a really sweet old guy, which hardly covers it all because he could be hard as nails when he had to. There wasn't anyone who knew more about air control than he.

I took the card and started up the hall and then Wanda called after me. She had stretched out her long legs and hiked up her skirt. I looked startled and she grinned. "Something new—sulfur-proof nylons." Which meant they wouldn't dissolve on a day like today when a measurable fraction of the air we were trying to breathe was actually dilute sulfuric acid. . . .

When I walked into his office, old Monte was leaning out the window, the fly ash clinging to his busy gray eyebrows like cinnamon to toast, trying to taste the air and predict how it would go today. We had eighty Sniffers scattered throughout the city, all computerized and delivering their data in neat, graphlike form, but Monte still insisted on breaking internal air security and seeing for himself how his city was doing.

I closed the door. Monte pulled back inside, then suddenly broke into one of his coughing fits.

"Sit down, Jim," he wheezed, his voice sounding as if it were being wrung out of him, "be with you in a minute." I pretended not to notice while his coughing shuddered to a halt and he rummaged through the desk for his little bottle of pills. It was a plain office, as executive offices went, except for Monte's own paintings on the wall—the type I liked to call Twentieth Century Romantic. A mountain scene with a crystal clear lake in the foreground and anglers battling huge trout, a city scene with palm trees lining the boulevards, and finally, one of a man standing by an old automobile on a winding mountain road while he looked off at a valley in the distance.

Occasionally Monte would talk to me about his boyhood around the Great Lakes and how he actually used to go swimming in them. Once he tried to tell me that orange trees used to grow within the city limits of Santalosdiego and that the oranges were as big as tennis balls. It irritated me and I think he knew it; I was the youngest Investigator for Air Central but that didn't necessarily make me naive.

When Monte stopped coughing I said hopefully, "IW claims a cold front is coming in."

He huddled in his chair and dabbed at his mouth with a handkerchief, his thin chest working desperately trying to pump his lungs full of air. "IW's a liar," he finally rasped. "There's no cold front coming in, it's going to be a scorcher for three more days."

I felt uneasy again. "Wanda told me what happened," I said.

He fought a moment longer for his breath, caught it, then gave a resigned shrug. "The bastards are right, to an extent. Stop garbage pick-ups in a city this size and within hours the rats will be fighting us in the streets. Shut down the power plants and you knock out all the air conditioners and purifiers—right during the hottest spell of the year. Then try telling the yokels that the air on the outside will be a whole lot cleaner if only they let the air on the inside get a whole lot dirtier."

He hunched behind his desk and drummed his fingers on the top while his face slowly turned to concrete. "But if they don't let me announce an alert by tomorrow morning," he said quietly, "I'll call in the newspapers and. . . ." The coughing started again and he stood up, a gnomelike little man slightly less alive with every passing day. He leaned against the windowsill while he fought the spasm. "And we think this is bad," he choked, half to himself. "What happens when the air coming in is as dirty as the air already here? When the Chinese and the Indonesians and the Hottentots get toasters and ice-boxes and all the other goodies?"

"Asia's not that industrialized yet," I said uncomfortably.

"Isn't it?" He turned and sagged back into his chair, hardly making a dent in the cushion. I was bleeding for the old man but I couldn't let him know it. I said in a low voice, "You wanted to see me," and handed him the assignment card.

He stared at it for a moment, his mind still on the Chinese, then came out of it and croaked, "That's right, give you something to chew on." He pressed a button on his desk and the wall opposite faded into a map of the city and the surrounding area, from the ocean on the west to the low-lying mountains on the east. He waved at the section of the city that straggled off into the canyons of the foothills. "Internal combustion engine—someplace back there." His voice was stronger now, his eyes more alert. "It isn't a donkey engine for a still or for electricity, it's a private automobile."

I could feel the hairs stiffen on the back of my neck. Usually I drew minor offenses, like trash burning or secret cigarette smoking, but owning or operating a gasoline-powered automobile was a felony, one that was sometimes worth your life.

"The Sniffer in the area confirms it," Monte continued in a tired voice, "but can't pinpoint it."

"Any other leads?"

"No, just this one report. But—we haven't had an internal combustion engine in more than three years." He paused. "Have fun with it, you'll probably have a new boss in the morning." *That* was something I didn't even want to think about. I had my hand on the doorknob when he said quietly, "The trouble with being boss is that you have to play Caesar and his Legions all the time."

It was as close as he came to saying good-bye and good luck. I didn't know what to say in return, or how to say it, and found myself staring at one of his canvases and babbling, "You sure used a helluva lot of blue."

"It was a fairly common color back then," he growled. "The sky was full of it."

And then he started coughing again and I closed the door in a hurry; in five minutes I had gotten so I couldn't stand the sound.

I had to stop in at the lab to pick up some gear from my locker and ran into Dave Ice, the researcher in charge of the Sniffers. He was a chubby, middle-aged little man with small, almost feminine hands; it was a pleasure to watch him work around delicate machinery. He was our top-rated man, after Monte, and I think if there was anybody whose shoes I wanted to step into someday, it would have been Dave Ice. He knew it, liked me for it, and usually went out of his way to help.

When I walked in he was changing a sheet of paper in one of the smoke shade detectors that hung just outside the lab windows. The sheet he was taking out looked as if it had been coated with lampblack.

"How long an exposure?"

He looked up, squinting over his bifocals. "Hi, Jim—a little more than four hours. It looks like it's getting pretty fierce out there."

"You haven't been out?"

"No, Monte and I stayed here all night. We were going to call an alert at nine this morning but I guess you know what happened."

I opened my locker and took out half a dozen new masks and a small canister of oxygen; if you were going to be out in traffic for any great length of time, you had to go prepared. Allowable vehicles were buses, trucks, delivery vans, police electrics and the like. Not all exhaust control devices worked very well and even the electrics gave off a few acid fumes. And if you were stalled in a tunnel, the carbon monoxide ratings really zoomed. I hesitated at the bottom of the locker and then took out my small Mark II gyrojet and shoulder holster. It was pretty deadly stuff: no recoil and the tiny rocket pellet had twice the punch of a .45.

Dave heard the clink of metal and without looking up asked quietly, "Trouble?"

"Maybe," I said. "Somebody's got a private automobile—gasoline—and I don't suppose they'll want to turn it in."

"You're right," he said, sounding concerned, "they won't." And then: "I heard something about it; if it's the same report, it's three days old."

"Monte's got his mind on other things," I said. I slipped the masks into my pocket and belted on the holster. "Did you know he's still on his marching Chinese kick?"

Dave was concentrating on one of the Sniffer drums slowly rolling beneath its scribing pens, logging a minute-by-minute record of the hydrocarbons and the oxides of nitrogen and sulfur that were sickening the atmosphere. "I don't blame him," he said, absently running a hand over his glistening scalp. "They've started tagging chimney exhausts in Shanghai, Djakarta and Mukden with radioactives—we should get the first results in another day or so."

The dragon's breath, I thought. When it finally circled the globe it would mean earth's air sink had lost the ability to cleanse itself and all of us would start strangling a little faster.

I got the rest of my gear and just before I hit the door, Dave said: "Jim?" I turned. He was wiping his hands on a paper towel and frowning at me over his glasses. "Look, take care of yourself, huh, kid?"

"Sure thing," I said. If Monte was my professional father, then Dave was my uncle. Sometimes it was embarrassing but right then it felt good. I nodded good-bye, adjusted my mask, and left.

Outside it seemed like dusk; trucks and buses had turned on their lights and almost all pedestrians were wearing masks. In a lot across the street some kids were playing tag and the thought suddenly struck me that nowadays most kids seemed small for their age; but I envied them . . . the air never seemed to bother kids. I watched for a moment, then started up the walk. A few doors down I passed an apartment building, half hidden in the growing darkness, that had received a "political influence" exemption a month before. Its incinerator was going full blast now, only instead of floating upward over the city the small charred bits of paper and garbage were falling straight down the front of the building like a kind of oily black snow.

I suddenly felt I was suffocating and stepped out into the street and hailed a passing electricab. Forest Hills, the part of the city that Monte had pointed out, was wealthy and the homes were large, though not so large that some of them couldn't be hidden away in the canyons and gullies of the foothills. If you lived on a side road or at the end of one of the canyons it might even be possible to hide a car out there and drive it only at night. And if any of your neighbors found out . . . well, the people who lived up in the relatively pure air of the highlands had a different view of things than those who lived down in the atmospheric sewage of the flats. *But where would a man get a gasoline automobile in the first place?*

And did it all really matter? I thought, looking out the window of the cab at the deepening dusk and feeling depressed. Then I shook my head and leaned forward to give the driver instructions. Some places could be checked out relatively easily.

The Carriage Museum was elegant—and crowded, considering that it was a weekday. The main hall was a vast cave of black marble housing a parade of ancient internal combustion vehicles shining under the subdued lights; most of them were painted a lustrous black though there was an occasional gray and burst of red and a few sparkles of old gold from polished brass head lamps and fittings.

I felt like I was in St. Peter's, walking on a vast sea of marble while all about me the crowds shuffled along in respectful silence. I kept my eyes to the floor, reading off the names on the small bronze plaques: *Rolls Royce Silver Ghost, Mercer Raceabout, Isotta-Fraschini, Packard Runabout, Hispano-Suiza, Model J Duesenberg, Flying Cloud Reo, Cadillac Imperial V16, Pierce Arrow,* the first of the *Ford V8s, Lincoln Zephyr, Chrysler Windsor Club Coup.* . . . And in small halls off to the side, the lesser breeds: *Hudson Terraplane, Henry J., Willys Knight,* something called a *Jeepster,* the *Mustang, Knudsen,* the 1986 *Volkswagen,* the last *Chevrolet.* . . .

The other visitors to the museum were all middle-aged or older; the look on their faces was something I had never seen before—something that was not quite love and not quite lust. It flowed across their features like ripples of water whenever they brushed a fender or stopped at a hood that had been opened so they could stare at the engine, all neatly chromed or painted. They were like my father, I thought. They had owned cars when they were young, before Turn-In Day and the same date a year later when even most private steam and electrics were banned because of congestion. For a moment I wondered what it had been like to own one, then canceled the thought. The old man had tried to tell me often enough, before I had stormed out of the house for good, shouting how could he love the damned things so much when he was coughing his lungs out. . . .

The main hall was nothing but bad memories. I left it and looked up the office of the curator. His secretary was on a coffee break so I rapped sharply and entered without waiting for an answer. On the door it had said "C. Pearson," who turned out to be a thin, over-dressed type, all regal nose and pencil moustache, in his mid-forties.

"Air Central," I said politely, flashing my wallet ID at him.

He wasn't impressed. "May I?" I gave it to him and he reached for the phone. When he hung up he didn't bother apologizing for the double check, which I figured made us even. "I have nothing to do with the heating system or the air-conditioning," he said easily, "but if you'll wait a minute I'll—"

"I only want information," I said.

He made a small tent of his hands and stared at me over his fingertips. He looked bored. "Oh?"

I sat down and he leaned toward me briefly, then thought better of it and settled back in his chair. "How easy would it be," I asked casually, "to steal one of your displays?"

His moustache quivered slightly. "It wouldn't be easy at all—they're bolted down, there's no gasoline in their tanks, and the batteries are dummies."

"Then none ever have been?"

A flicker of annoyance. "No, of course not."

I flashed my best hat-in-hand smile and stood up. "Well, I guess that's it, then, I won't trouble you any further." But before I turned away I said, "I'm really not much on automobiles but I'm curious. How did the museum get started?"

He warmed up a little. "On Turn-In Day a number of museums like this one were started up all over the country. Some by former dealers, some just by automobile lovers. A number of models were donated for public display and. . . ."

When he had finished I said casually, "Donating a vehicle to a museum must have been a great ploy for hiding private ownership."

"Certainly the people in your bureau would be aware of how strict the government was," he said sharply.

"A lot of people must have tried to hide their vehicles," I persisted.

Dryly. "It would have been difficult . . . like trying to hide an elephant in a playpen."

But still, a number would have tried, I thought. They might even have stockpiled drums of fuel and some spare parts. In the city, of course, it would have been next to impossible. But in remote sections of the country, in the mountain regions out west or in the hills of the Ozarks or in the forests of northern Michigan or Minnesota or in the badlands of the Dakotas. . . . A few would have succeeded, certainly, and perhaps late at night a few weed-grown stretches of highway would have been briefly lit by the headlights of automobiles flashing past with muffled exhausts, tires singing against the pavement. . . .

I sat back down. "Are there many automobile fans around?"

13

"I suppose so, if attendance records here are any indication."

"Then a smart man with a place in the country and a few automobiles could make quite a bit of money renting them out, couldn't he?"

He permitted himself a slight smile. "It would be risky. I really don't think anybody would try it. And from everything I've read, I rather think the passion was for actual ownership—I doubt that rental would satisfy that."

I thought about it for a moment while Pearson fidgeted with a letter opener and then, of course, I had it. "All those people who were fond of automobiles, there used to be clubs of them, right?"

His eyes lidded over and it grew very quiet in his office. But it was too late and he knew it. "I believe so," he said after a long pause, his voice tight, "but. . . ."

"But the government ordered them disbanded," I said coldly. "Air Control regulations thirty-nine and forty, sections three through seven, 'concerning the dissolution of all organizations which in whole or in part, intentionally or unintentionally, oppose clean air.' " I knew the regulations by heart. "But there still are clubs, aren't there? Unregistered clubs? Clubs with secret membership files?" A light sheen of perspiration had started to gather on his forehead. "You would probably make a very good membership secretary, Pearson. You're in the perfect spot for recruiting new members—"

He made a motion behind his desk and I dove over it and pinned his arms behind his back. A small address book had fallen to the floor and I scooped it up. Pearson looked as if he might faint. I ran my hands over his chest and under his arms and then let him go. He leaned against the desk, gasping for air.

"I'll have to take you in," I said.

A little color was returning to his cheeks and he nervously smoothed down his damp black hair. His voice was on the squeaky side. "What for? You have some interesting theories but. . . ."

"My theories will keep for court," I said shortly. "You're under arrest for smoking—section eleven thirty point five of the health and safety code." I grabbed his right hand and spread the fingers so the tell-tale stains showed. "You almost offered me a cigarette when I came in, then caught yourself. I would guess that ordinarily you're pretty relaxed and sociable, you probably smoke a lot—and you're generous with your tobacco. Bottom right hand drawer for the stash, right?" I jerked it open and they were there, all right. "One cigarette's a misdemeanor, a carton's a felony, Pearson. We can accuse you of

14

dealing and make it stick." I smiled grimly. "But we're perfectly willing to trade, of course."

I put in calls to the police and Air Central and sat down to wait for the cops to show. They'd sweat Pearson for all the information he had but I couldn't wait around a couple of hours. The word would spread that Pearson was being held, and Pearson himself would probably start remembering various lawyers and civil rights that he had momentarily forgotten. My only real windfall had been the address book. . . .

I thumbed through it curiously, wondering exactly how I could use it. The names were scattered all over the city, and there were a lot of them. I could weed it down to those in the area where the Sniffer had picked up the automobile, but that would take time and nobody was going to admit that he had a contraband vehicle hidden away anyway. The idea of paying a visit to the club I was certain must exist kept recurring to me and finally I decided to pick a name, twist Pearson's arm for anything he might know about him, then arrange to meet at the club and work out from there.

Later, when I was leaving the museum, I stopped for a moment just inside the door to readjust my mask. While I was doing it the janitor showed up with a roll of weatherstripping and started attaching it to the edge of the doorway where what looked like thin black smoke was seeping in from the outside. I was suddenly afraid to go back out there. . . .

The wind was whistling past my ears and a curve was coming up. I feathered the throttle, downshifted, and the needle on the tach started to drop. The wheel seemed to have a life of its own and twitched slightly to the right. I rode high on the outside of the track, the leafy limbs of trees that lined the asphalt dancing just outside my field of vision. The rear started to come around in a skid and I touched the throttle again and then the wheel twitched back to center and I was away. My eyes were riveted on Number Nine, just in front of me. It was the last lap and if I could catch him there would be nothing between me and the checkered flag. . . .

I felt relaxed and supremely confident, one with the throbbing power of the car. I red-lined it and through my dirt-streaked goggles I could see I was crawling up on the red splash that was Number Nine and next I was breathing the fumes from his twin exhausts. I took him on the final curve and suddenly I was alone in the world of the straightaway with the countryside peeling away on both sides of me, placid cows and ancient barns flowing past and then the rails lined with people. I couldn't hear their shouting above the scream of my car. Then I was flashing under banners stretched across the track and thundering toward the finish. There was the smell of burning rubber and spent oil and my own perspiration, the heat from the sun, the shimmering asphalt, and out of the corner of my eye a blur of grandstands and cars and a flag swooping down. . . .

And then it was over and the house lights had come up and I was hunched over a toy wheel in front of me, gripping it with both hands, the sweat pouring down my face and my stomach burning because I could still smell exhaust fumes and I wanted desperately to put on my face mask. It had been far more real than I had thought it would be—the curved screen gave the illusion of depth and each chair had been set up like a driver's seat. They had even pumped in odors. . . .

The others in the small theatre were stretching and getting ready to leave and I gradually unwound and got to my feet, still feeling shaky. "Lucky you could make it, Jim," a voice graveled in my ear. "You missed Joe Moore and the lecture but the documentary was just great, really great. Next week we've got *Meadowdale '73* which has its moments but you don't feel like you're really there and getting an eyeful of cinders, if you know what I mean."

"Who's Joe Moore?" I mumbled.

"Old time race track manager—full of anecdotes, knew all the great drivers. Hey! You okay?"

I was finding it difficult to come out of it. The noise and the action and the smell, but especially the feeling of actually driving. . . . It was more than just a visceral response. You had to be raised down in the flats where you struggled for your breath every day to get the same feeling of revulsion, the same feeling of having done something dirty. . . .

"Yeah, I'm okay," I said. "I'm feeling fine."

"Where'd you say you were from, anyway?"

"Bosnywash," I lied. He nodded and I took a breath and time out to size him up. Jack Ellis was bigger and heavier than Pearson and not nearly as smooth or as polished—Pearson perspired, my bulky friend sweated. He was in his early fifties, thinning brown hair carefully waved, the beginning of a small paunch well hidden by a lot of expensive tailoring, and a hulking set of shoulders that were much more than just padding. A business bird, I thought. The hairy-chested genial backslapper. . . .

"You seen the clubrooms yet?"

"I just got in," I said. "First time here."

"Hey, great! I'll show you around!" He talked like he was pro-

16

grammed. "A little fuel and a couple of stiff belts first, though—dining room's out of this world. . . ."

And it almost was. We were on the eighty-seventh floor of the new Trans-America building and Ellis had secured a window seat. Above, the sky was almost as bright a blue as Monte had used in his paintings. I couldn't see the street below.

"Have a card," Ellis said, shoving the pasteboard at me. It read *Warshawsky & Warshawsky, Automotive Antiques,* with an address in the Avenues. He waved a hand at the room. "We decorated all of this—pretty classy, huh?"

I had to give him that. The walls were covered with murals of old road races, while from some hidden sound system came a faint, subdued purring—the roaring of cars drifting through the esses of some long-ago race. In the center of the room was a pedestal holding a highly-chromed engine block that slowly revolved under a baby spot. While I was admiring the setting a waitress came up and set down a lazy Susan; it took a minute to recognize it as an old-fashioned wooden steering wheel, fitted with sterling silver hors d'oeuvre dishes between the spokes.

Ellis ran a thick thumb down the menu. "Try a Barney Oldfield," he suggested. "Roast beef and American cheese on pumpernickel."

While I was eating I got the uncomfortable feeling that he was looking me over and that somehow I didn't measure up. "You're pretty young," he said at last. "We don't get many young members —or visitors, for that matter."

"Grandfather was a dealer," I said easily. "Had a Ford agency in Milwaukee—I guess it rubbed off."

He nodded around a mouthful of sandwich and looked mournful for a moment. "It used to be a young man's game, kids worked on engines in their backyards all the time. Just about everybody owned a car. . . ."

"You, too?"

"Oh sure—hell, the old man ran a gas station until Turn-In Day." He was lost in his memories for a moment, then said, "You got a club in Bosnywash?"

"A few, nothing like this," I said cautiously. "And the law's pretty stiff." I nodded at the window. "They get pretty uptight about the air back east . . ." I let my voice trail off.

He frowned. "You don't *believe* all that guff, do you? Biggest god-damn pack of lies there ever was, but I guess you got to be older to know it. Power plants and incinerators, they're the ones to blame, always have been. Hell, people, too—every time you exhale you're polluting the atmosphere, ever think of that? And Christ, man, think of every time you work up a sweat. . . ."

"Sure," I nodded, "sure, it's always been blown up." I made a mental note that someday I'd throw the book at Ellis.

He finished his sandwich and started wiping his fat face like he was erasing a blackboard. "What's your interest? Mine's family sedans, the old family workhorse. Fords, Chevys, Plymouths—got a case of all the models from '50 on up, one-eighteenth scale. How about you?"

I didn't answer him, just stared out the window and worked with a toothpick for a long time until he began to get a little nervous. Then I let it drop. "I'm out here to buy a car," I said.

His face went blank, as if somebody had just pulled down a shade. "Damned expensive hobby," he said, ignoring it. "Should've taken up photography instead."

"It's for a friend of mine," I said. "Money's no object."

The waitress came around with the check and Ellis initialed it. "Damned expensive," he repeated vaguely.

"I couldn't make a connection back home," I said. "Friends suggested I try out here."

He was watching me now. "How would you get it back east?"

"Break it down," I said. "Ship it east as crates of machine parts."

"What makes you think there's anything for sale out here?"

I shrugged. "Lots of mountains, lots of forests, lots of empty space, lots of hiding places. Cars were big out here, there must have been a number that were never turned in."

"You're a stalking horse for somebody big, aren't you!"

"What do you think?" I said. "And what difference does it make anyway? Money's money."

If it's true that the pupil of the eye expands when it sees something that it likes, it's also true that it contracts when it doesn't—and right then his were in the cold buckshot stage.

"All right," he finally said. "Cash on the barrelhead and remember, when you have that much money changing hands, it can get dangerous." He deliberately leaned across the table so that his coat flapped open slightly. The small gun and holster were almost lost against the big man's girth. He sat back and spun the lazy Susan with a fat forefinger, spearing an olive as it slid past. "You guys run true to form," he continued quietly. "Most guys from back east come out to buy—I guess we've got a reputation." He hesitated. "We also try and take all the danger out of it."

He stood up and slapped me on the back as I pushed to my feet.

It was the old Jack Ellis again, he of the instant smile and the sparkling teeth.

"That is, we try and take the danger out of it for *us*," he added pleasantly.

It was late afternoon and the rush hour had started. It wasn't as heavy as usual—businesses had been letting out all day—but it was bad enough. I slipped on a mask and started walking toward the warehouse section of town, just outside the business district. The buses were too crowded and it would be impossible to get an electricab that time of day. Besides, traffic was practically standing still in the steamy murk. Headlights were vague yellow dots in the gathering darkness and occasionally I had to shine my pocket flash on a street sign to determine my location.

I had checked in with Monte who said the hospitals were filling up fast with bronchitis victims; I didn't ask about the city morgue. The venal bastards at Air Shed Number Three were even getting worried; they had promised Monte that if it didn't clear by morning, he could issue his alert and close down the city. I told him I had uncovered what looked like a car ring but he sounded only faintly interested. He had bigger things on his mind; the ball was in my court and what I was going to do with it was strictly up to me.

A few more blocks and the crowds thinned. Then I was alone on the street with the warehouses hulking up in the gloom around me, ancient monsters of discolored brick and concrete layered with years of soot and grime. I found the address I wanted, leaned against the buzzer by the loading dock door, and waited. There was a long pause, then faint steps echoed inside and the door slid open. Ellis stood in the yellow dock light, the smile stretching across his thick face like a rubber band. "Right on time," he whispered. "Come on in, Jim, meet the boys."

I followed him down a short passageway, trying not to brush up against the filthy whitewashed walls. Then we were up against a steel door with a peephole. Ellis knocked three times, the peephole opened, and he said, "Joe sent me." I started to panic. *For God's sake, why the act?* Then the door opened and it was as if somebody had kicked me in the stomach. What lay beyond was a huge garage with at least half a dozen ancient cars on the tool-strewn floor. Three mechanics in coveralls were working under the overhead lights; two more were waiting inside the door. They were bigger than Ellis and I was suddenly very glad I had brought along the Mark II.

"Jeff, Ray, meet Mr. Morrison." I held out my hand. They nodded at me, no smiles. "C'mon," Ellis said, "I'll show you the set-up." I tagged after him and he started pointing out the wonders of his domain. "Completely equipped garage—my old man would've been proud of me. Overhead hoist for pulling motors, complete lathe set-up . . . a lot of parts we have to machine ourselves, can't get the originals anymore and of course the last of the junkers was melted down a long time ago." He stopped by a workbench with a large rack full of tools gleaming behind it. "One of the great things about being in the antique business—you hit all the country auctions and you'd be surprised at what you can pick up. Complete sets of torque wrenches, metric socket sets, spanner wrenches, feeler gauges, you name it."

I looked over the bench—he was obviously proud of the assortment of tools—then suddenly felt the small of my back grow cold. It was phony, I thought, the whole thing was phony. But I couldn't put my finger on just why.

Ellis walked over to one of the automobiles on the floor and patted a fender affectionately. Then he unbuttoned his coat so that the pistol showed, hooked his thumbs in his vest, leaned against the car behind him and smiled. Someplace he had even found a broom-straw to chew on.

"So what can we do for you, Jim? Limited stock, sky-high prices, but never a dissatisfied customer!" He poked an elbow against the car behind him. "Take a look at this '73 Chevy Biscayne, probably the only one of its kind in this condition in the whole damned country. Ten thou and you can have it—and that's only because I like you." He sauntered over to a monster in blue and silver with grillwork that looked like a set of kitchen knives. "Or maybe you'd like a '76 Caddy convertible, all genuine simulated-leather upholstery, one of the last of the breed." He didn't add why but I already knew—in heavy traffic the high levels of monoxide could be fatal to a driver in an open car.

"Yours," Ellis was saying about another model, "for a flat fifteen" —he paused and shot me a friendly glance—"oh hell, for you, Jim, make it twelve and a half and take it from me, it's a bargain. Comes with the original upholstery and tires and there's less than ten thousand miles on it—the former owner was a little old lady in Pasadena who only drove it to weddings."

He chuckled at that, looking at me expectantly. I didn't get it. "Maybe you'd just like to look around. Be my guest, go right ahead." His eyes were bright and he looked very pleased with himself; it bothered me.

"Yeah," I said absently, "I think that's what I'd like to do." There was a wall phone by an older model and I drifted over to it.

"That's an early Knudsen two-seater," Ellis said. "Popular make for the psychedelic set, that paint job is the way they really came. . . ."

I ran my hand lightly down the windshield, then turned to face the cheerful Ellis. "You're under arrest," I said. "You and everybody else here."

His face suddenly looked like shrimp in molded gelatin. One of the mechanics behind him moved and I had the Mark II out winging a rocket past his shoulder. No noise, no recoil, just a sudden shower of sparks by the barrel and in the far end of the garage a fifty-gallon oil drum went *karrump* and there was a hole in it you could have stuck your head through.

The mechanic went white. *"Jesus Christ, Jack, you brought in some kind of nut!"* Ellis himself was pale and shaking, which surprised me; I thought he'd be tougher than that.

"Against the bench," I said coldly, waving the pistol. "Hands in front of your crotch and don't move them." The mechanics were obviously scared stiff and Ellis was having difficulty keeping control. I took down the phone and called in.

After I hung up, Ellis mumbled, "What's the charge?"

"Charges," I corrected. "Sections three, four and five of the Air Control laws. Maintenance, sale and use of internal combustion engines."

Ellis stared at me blankly. "You don't know?" he asked faintly. "Know what?"

"I don't handle internal combustion engines." He licked his lips. "I really don't, it's too risky, it's . . . it's against the law."

The workbench, I suddenly thought. The goddamned workbench. I knew something was wrong then, I should have cooled it.

"You can check me," Ellis offered weakly. "Lift a hood, look for yourself."

He talked like his face was made of panes of glass sliding against one another. I waved him forward. *"You* check it, Ellis, you open one up." Ellis nodded like a dipping duck, waddled over to one of the cars, jiggled something inside, then raised the hood and stepped back.

I took one glance and my stomach slowly started to knot up. I was no motor buff but I damned well knew the difference between a gasoline engine and water boiler. Which explained the workbench—the tools had been window dressing. Most of them were brand new because most of them had obviously never been used. There had been nothing to use them on.

"The engines are steam," Ellis said, almost apologetically. "I've got a license to do restoration work and drop in steam engines. They don't allow them in cities but it's different on farms and country estates and in some small towns." He looked at me. "The license cost me a goddamned fortune."

It was a real handicap being a city boy, I thought. "Then why the act? Why the gun?"

"This?" he asked stupidly. He reached inside his coat and dropped the pistol on the floor; it made a light thudding sound and bounced, a pot metal toy. "The danger, it's the sense of danger, it's part of the sales pitch." He wanted to be angry now but he had been frightened too badly and couldn't quite make it. "The customers pay a lot of dough, they want a little drama. That's why—you know—the peephole and everything." He took a deep breath and when he exhaled it came out as a giggle, an incongruous sound from the big man. I found myself hoping he didn't have a heart condition. "I'm well known," he said defensively. "I take ads. . . ."

"The club," I said. "It's illegal."

Even if it was weak, his smile was genuine and then the score became crystal clear. The club was like a speakeasy during the Depression, with half the judges and politicians in town belonging to it. Why not? Somebody older wouldn't have my bias. . . . Pearson's address book had been all last names and initials but I had never connected any of them to anybody prominent; I hadn't been around enough to know what connection to make.

I waved Ellis back to the workbench and stared glumly at the group. The mechanic I had frightened with the Mark II had a spreading stain across the front of his pants and I felt sorry for him momentarily.

Then I started to feel sorry for myself. Monte should have given me a longer briefing, or maybe assigned another Investigator to go with me, but he had been too sick and too wrapped up with the politics of it all. So I had gone off half-cocked and come up with nothing but a potential lawsuit for Air Central that would probably amount to a million dollars by the time Ellis got through with me.

It was a black day inside as well as out.

I holed up in a bar during the middle part of the evening, which was probably the smartest thing I could have done. Despite their masks, people on the street had started to retch and vomit and I could feel my own nausea grow with every step. I saw one man try and strike a match to read a street sign; it wouldn't stay lit, there simply wasn't enough oxygen in the air. The ambulance sirens were a steady wail now and I knew it was going to be a tough night for heart cases. They'd be going like flies before morning, I thought. . . .

Another customer slammed through the door, wheezing and coughing and taking huge gulps of the machine-pure air of the bar. I ordered another drink and tried to shut out the sound; it was too reminiscent of Monte hacking and coughing behind his desk at work.

And come morning, Monte might be out of a job, I thought. I for certain would be; I had loused up in a way that would cost the department money—the unforgivable sin in the eyes of the politicians.

I downed half my drink and started mentally reviewing the events of the day, giving myself a passing score only on figuring out that Pearson had had a stash. I hadn't known about Ellis' operation, which in one sense wasn't surprising. Nobody was going to drive something that looked like an old gasoline-burner around a city—the flatlanders would stone him to death.

But somebody still had a car, I thought. Somebody who was rich and immune from prosecution and a real nut about cars in the first place. . . . But it kept sliding away from me. Really rich men were too much in the public eye, ditto politicians. They'd be washed up politically if anybody ever found out. If nothing else, some poor bastard like the one at the end of the bar trying to flush out his lungs would assassinate him.

Somebody with money, but not too much. Somebody who was a car nut—they'd have to be to take the risks. And somebody for whom those risks were absolutely minimal. . . .

And then the lightbulb flashed on above my head, just like in the old cartoons. I wasn't dead certain I was right but I was willing to stake my life on it—and it was possible I might end up doing just that.

I slipped on a mask and almost ran out of the bar. Once outside, I sympathized with the guy who had just come in and who had given me a horrified look as I plunged out into the darkness.

It was smothering now, though the temperature had dropped a little so my shirt didn't cling to me in dirty, damp folds. Buses were being led through the streets; headlights died out completely within a few feet. The worst thing was that they left tracks in what looked like a damp, grayish ash that covered the street. Most of the people I bumped into—mere shadows in the night—had soaked their masks in water, trying to make them more effective. There were lights still on in the lower floors of most of the office buildings and I figured some people hadn't tried to make it home at all; the air was probably purer among the filing cabinets than in their own apartments. Two floors up, the buildings were completely hidden in the smoky darkness.

It took a good hour of walking before the sidewalks started to slant up and I knew I was getting out toward the foothills . . . I thanked God the business district was closer to the mountains than the ocean. My legs ached and my chest hurt and I was tired and depressed but at least I wasn't coughing anymore.

The buildings started to thin out and the streets finally became completely deserted. Usually the cops would pick you up if they caught you walking on the streets of Forest Hills late at night, but that night I doubted they were even around. They were probably too busy ferrying cases of cardiac arrest to St. Francis. . . .

The Sniffer was located on the top of a small, ancient building off on a side street. When I saw it I suddenly found my breath hard to catch again—a block down, the street abruptly turned into a canyon and wound up and out of sight. I glanced back at the building, just faintly visible through the grayed-down moonlight. The windows were boarded up and there was a For Rent sign on them. I walked over and flashed my light on the sign. It was old and peeling and had obviously been there for years; apparently nobody had ever wanted to rent the first floor. Ever? Maybe somebody had, I thought, but had decided to leave it boarded up. I ran my hand down the boards and suddenly paused at a knothole; I could feel heavy plate glass through it. I knelt and flashed my light at the hole and looked at a dim reflection of myself staring back. The glass had been painted black on the inside so it acted like a black marble mirror.

I stepped back and something about the building struck me. The boarded-up windows, I thought, the huge, oversized windows. . . . And the oversized, boarded-up doors. I flashed the light again at the concrete facing just above the doors. The words were there all right, blackened by time but still readable, cut into the concrete itself by order of the proud owner a handful of decades before. But you could still noodle them out: *RICHARD SIEBEN LINCOLN-MERCURY*.

Jackpot, I thought triumphantly. I glanced around—there was nobody else on the street—and listened. Not a sound, except for the faint murmur of traffic still moving in the city far away. A hot muggy night in the core city, I thought, but this night the parks and the fire escapes would be empty and five million people would be tossing and turning in their cramped little bedrooms; it'd be suicide to try and sleep outdoors.

24

In Forest Hills it was cooler—and quieter. I glued my ear to the boards over the window and thought I could hear the faint shuffle of somebody walking around and, once, the faint clink of metal against metal. I waited a moment, then slipped down to the side door that had "Air Central" on it in neat black lettering. All Investigators had master keys and I went inside. Nobody was upstairs; the lights were out and the only sound was the soft swish of the Sniffer's scribing pens against the paper roll. There was a stairway in the back and I walked silently down it. The door at the bottom was open and I stepped through it into a short hallway. Something, maybe the smell of the air, told me it had been used recently. I closed the door after me and stood for a second in the darkness. There was no sound from the door beyond. I tried the knob and it moved silently in my grasp.

I cracked the door open and peered through the slit—nothing—then eased it open all the way and stepped out onto the showroom floor. There was a green-shaded lightbulb hanging from the ceiling, swaying slightly in some minor breeze so the shadows chased each other around the far corners of the room. Walled off at the end were two small offices where salesmen had probably wheeled and dealed long ago. There wasn't much else, other than a few tools scattered around the floor in the circle of light.

And directly in the center, of course, the car.

I caught my breath. There was no connection between it and Jack Ellis' renovated family sedans. It crouched there on the floor, a mechanical beast that was almost alive. Sleek curving fenders that blended into a louvered hood with a chromed steel bumper curving flat around the front to give it an oddly sharklike appearance. The headlamps were set deep into the fenders, the lamp wells outlined with chrome. The hood flowed into a windshield and that into a top which sloped smoothly down in back and tucked in neatly just after the rear wheels. The wheels themselves had wire spokes that gleamed wickedly in the light, and through a side window I could make out a neat array of meters and rocker switches, and finally bucket seats covered with what I instinctively knew was genuine black leather.

Sleek beast, powerful beast, I thought. I was unaware of walking up to it and running my hand lightly over a fender until a voice behind me said, "It's beautiful, isn't it?"

I turned like an actor in a slow-motion film. "Yeah, Dave," I said, "it's beautiful." Dave Ice of Air Central. In charge of all the Sniffers.

He must have been standing in one of the salesman's offices; it was the only way I could have missed him. He walked up and stood on the other side of the car and ran his left hand over the hood with the same affectionate motion a woman might use in stroking her cat. In his right hand he held a small Mark II pointed directly at my chest.

"How'd you figure it was me?" he asked casually.

"I thought at first it might be Monte," I said. "Then I figured you were the real nut about machinery."

His eyes were bright, too bright. "Tell me," he asked curiously, "would you have turned in Monte?"

"Of course," I said simply. I didn't add that it would have been damned difficult; that I hadn't even been able to think about that part of it.

"So might've I, so might've I," he murmured. "When I was your age."

"For a while the money angle threw me," I said.

He smiled faintly. "It's a family heirloom. My father bought it when he was young, he couldn't bring himself to turn it in." He cocked his head. "Could you?" I looked at him uneasily and didn't answer and he said casually, "Go ahead, Jimmy, you were telling me how you cracked the case."

I flushed. "It had to be somebody who knew—who was absolutely sure—that he wasn't going to get caught. The Sniffers are pretty efficient, it would have been impossible to prevent their detecting the car—the best thing would be to censor the data from them. And Monte and you were the only ones who could have done that."

Another faint smile. "You're right."

"You slipped up a few nights ago," I said.

He shrugged. "Anybody could've. I was sick, I didn't get to the office in time to doctor the record."

"It gave the game away," I said. "Why only once? The Sniffer should have detected it far more often than just once."

He didn't say anything and for a long moment both of us were lost in admiration of the car.

Then finally, proudly: "It's the real McCoy, Jim. Six cylinder in-line engine, 4.2 liters displacement, nine-to-one compression ratio, twin overhead cams and twin Zenith-Stromberg carbs. . . ." He broke off. "You don't know what I'm talking about, do you?"

"No," I confessed, "I'm afraid not."

"Want to see the motor?"

I nodded and he stepped forward, waved me back with the Mark II, and opened the hood. To really appreciate it, of course, you had to have a thing for machinery. It was clean and polished and squatted there under the hood like a beautiful mechanical pet—so huge I wondered how the hood could close at all.

And then I realized with a shock that I hadn't been reacting like I should have, that I hadn't reacted like I should have ever since the movie at the club. . . .

"You can sit in it if you want to," Dave said softly. "Just don't touch anything." His voice was soft. "Everything works on it, Jim, everything works just dandy. It's oiled and greased and the tank is full and the battery is charged and if you wanted to, you could drive it right off the showroom floor."

I hesitated. "People in the neighborhood—"

"—mind their own business," he said. "They have a different attitude, and besides, it's usually late at night and I'm out in the hills in seconds. Go ahead, get in." Then his voice hardened into command: "Get in!"

I stalled a second longer, then opened the door and slid into the seat. The movie was real now, I was holding the wheel and could sense the gearshift at my right and in my mind's eye I could feel the wind and hear the scream of the motor. . . .

There was something hard pressing against the side of my head. I froze. Dave was holding the pistol just behind my ear and in the side mirror I could see his finger tense on the trigger and pull back a millimeter. *Dear God.* . . .

He relaxed. "You'll have to get out," he said apologetically. "It would be appropriate, but a mess just the same."

I got out. My legs were shaking and I had to lean against the car. "It's a risky thing to own a car," I chattered. "Feeling runs pretty high against cars. . . ."

He nodded. "It's too bad."

"You worked for Air Central for years," I said. "How could you do it, and own this, too?"

"You're thinking about the air," he said carefully. "But Jim"—his voice was patient—"machines don't foul the air, men do. They foul the air, the lakes, and the land itself. And there's no way to stop it." I started to protest and he held up a hand. "Oh sure, there's always a time when you care—like you do now. But time . . . you know, time wears you down, it really does, no matter how eager you are. You devote your life to a cause and then you find yourself suddenly growing fat and bald and you discover nobody gives a damn about your cause. They're paying you your cushy salary to buy off their own consciences. So long as there's a buck to be made, things won't change much. It's enough to drive you——" He broke off. "You don't *really* think that anybody gives a damn about anybody else, do you?" He stood there looking faintly amused, a pudgy little man whom I should've been able to take with one arm tied behind my back. But he was ten times as dangerous as Ellis had ever imagined himself to be. "Only suckers care, Jim. I. . . ."

I dropped to the floor then, rolling fast to hit the shadows beyond the circle of light. His Mark II sprayed sparks and something burned past my shirt collar and squealed along the concrete floor. I sprawled flat and jerked my own pistol out. The first shot went low and there was the sharp sound of scored metal and I cursed briefly to myself—I must have brushed the car. Then there was silence and I scrabbled further back into the darkness. I wanted to pot the light but the bulb was still swaying back and forth and chances were I'd miss and waste the shot. Then there was the sound of running and I jumped to my feet and saw Dave heading for the door I had come in by. He seemed oddly defenseless—he was chubby and slow and knock-kneed and ran like a woman.

"Dave!" I screamed. "Dave! STOP!"

It was an accident, there was no way to help it. I aimed low and to the side, to knock him off his feet, and at the same time he decided to do what I had done and sprawl flat in the shadows. If he had stayed on his feet, the small rocket would have brushed him at knee level. As it was, it smashed his chest.

He crumpled and I ran up and caught him before he could hit the floor. He twisted slightly in my arms so he was staring at the car as he died. I broke into tears. I couldn't help that, either. I would remember the things Dave had done for me long after I had forgotten that one night he had tried to kill me. A threat to kill is unreal—actual blood and shredded flesh has its own reality.

I let him down gently and walked slowly over to the phone in the corner. Monte should still be in his office, I thought. I dialed and said, "The Director, please," and waited for the voice-actuated relay to connect me. "Monte, Jim Morrison here. I'm over at——" I paused. "I'm sorry, I thought it was Monte——" And then I shut up and let the voice at the other end of the line tell me that Monte had died with the window open and the night air filling his lungs with urban vomit. "I'm sorry," I said faintly, "I'm sorry, I'm very sorry," but the voice went on and I suddenly realized that I was listening to a recording and that there was nobody in the office at all. Then, as the voice continued, I knew why.

I let the receiver fall to the floor and the record started in again, as if expecting condolences from the concrete.

28

I should call the cops, I thought. I should——

But I didn't. Instead, I called Wanda. It would take an hour or more for her to collect the foodstuffs in the apartment and to catch an electricab but we could be out of the city before morning came.

And that was pretty funny because morning was never coming. The recording had said dryly that the tagged radioactive chimney exhausts had arrived, that the dragon's breath had circled the globe and the winds blowing in were as dirty as the air already over the city. Oh, it wouldn't happen right away, but it wouldn't be very long, either. . . .

Nobody had given a damn, I thought; not here nor any other place. Dave had been right, dead right. They had finally turned it all into a sewer and the last of those who cared had coughed his lungs out trying for a breath of fresh air that had never come, too weak to close a window.

I walked back to the car sitting in the circle of light and ran a finger down the scored fender where the small rocket had scraped the paint. Dave would never have forgiven me, I thought. Then I opened the door and got in and settled slowly back into the seat. I fondled the shift and ran my eyes over the instrument panel, the speedometer and the tach and the fuel and the oil gauges and the small clock. . . . The keys dangled from the button at the end of the hand brake. It was a beautiful piece of machinery, I thought again. I had never really loved a piece of machinery . . . until now.

I ran my hands around the wheel, then located the starter switch on the steering column. I jabbed in the key and closed my eyes and listened to the scream of the motor and felt its power shake the car and wash over me and thunder through the room. The movie at the club had been my only lesson but in its own way it had been thorough and it would be enough. I switched off the motor and waited.

When Wanda got there we would take off for the high ground. For the mountains and the pines and that last clear lake and that final glimpse of blue sky before it all turned brown and we gave up in final surrender to this climate of which we're so obviously proud. . . .

END

The Sumerian Oath

A Polytropic Paramyth

by Philip José Farmer

This story is subtitled "A Polytropic Paramyth," which perhaps means it is a many-valued almost-myth. Then again it perhaps does not. What it does mean though is that it certainly is a chunk of very good, tongue-in-cheek fun by one of our foremost modern myth-makers.

Caught in the Frozen Foods & Ice Cream aisle, with an assassin coming down from each end, Goodbody leaped upon the top of the grocery cart. With the grace and the flair of Doctor Blood (as played by Errol Flynn), Goodbody dived over the top of Ice Cream Cones & Chocolate Syrups. At the same time, the push of his departing feet sent the cart down the aisle into the nearest assassin.

Though Goodbody soared with great aplomb and considerable beauty, he knocked over tall boxes of ice cream cones and fell down on the other side into the Home Hardware & Fix-It-Urself Supplies. The cataract of Goodbody and wrenches, pliers, screwdrivers, boxes of nails, double sockets, and picture wire startled women customers and caused one to faint into Pet Foods & Bird Cages.

Goodbody dived under a railing and then galloped along the front of the store towards the Liquor Department. A shout caused him to look behind. The fools had actually pulled out their scalpels; they were indeed desperate. It was possible, however, that they did not mean to kill him inside the supermarket. They might be herding him into the parking lot, where others would net him.

He yanked over a pocketbook stand as he went by, whirling it so that *The Valley of The Dolls, The Arrangement, Couples,* and *Purple Sex Thing from the Fleshpot Planet* flew out like the hyperactive fingers of desperately hungry and desperately typing pornographers.

The nearest pursuer, waving his scalpel, found that its tip was embedded in *So You Want To Be a Brain Surgeon?*

How appropriate and how terrible, he thought as he fled through the door. He was the author of that best seller, the royalties of which he could not spend because he might find the AMA agents waiting to pick *him* up if *he* picked up the checks.

In the parking lot, almost as bright as day, a car leaped at him. He soared again, performing three entrechats to gain altitude (reminding him of the days when he had entered the operating amphitheater to the applause of famous surgeons and slack-jawed first-year students). He landed between a Chevy and a Caddy and was off. Tires screamed; doors slammed; feet pounded; voices growled.

"Doctor Goodbody! Halt! We mean no harm! This is for your own good! You're sick, man, sick!"

Cornered in the angle formed by two high walls, he turned to face them. Never let it be said that he would whimper, any more than Doctor Kildare, young god, would have whimpered, even if confronted with a large uncollectable bill.

Six came at him with glittering scalpels. He jerked out his own blade, speedy as Doctor Ehrlich's Magic Bullet. He would go down fighting; they would not get off lightly when they crossed steel with a man whose genius with the cutting edge was surpassed only by that of Doc Savage, now retired.

Herr Doktor Grossfleisch, huge as Laird Cregar when he played the medical student in *The Lodger,* floated forward and cast a hypodermic syringe, .1 caliber. The speed and accuracy with which it traveled would have delighted even crusty (but kindly) old Doctor Gillespie, especially as played by Lionel Barrymore. Goodbody responded with a magnificent parry that sent the syringe soaring over the wall, higher than the legendary intern who drank the embalming fluid.

Two eminent doctors, holding straitjackets before them with one hand and suturing needles with the other, like Roman *retiarii,* advanced. He slashed at them with such speed that five of them cried out with involuntary admiration. They hated themselves afterwards for it and would, of course, be reprimanded by the AMA.

Grossfleisch cursed a forbidden curse, for which he would have to pay heavily, though not bloodily. Again he cast a huge syringe with a giant caliber tip, and it sailed over the shoulder of the doctor on Goodbody's left just as Goodbody made a thrust that would have caused Doctor Zorba to go pale with envy. But the needle penetrated

31

Goodbody's extended right arm, and all became as black as the inside of the cabinet of Doctor Caligari.

"Shall we operate, Doctor Cyclops?"

The bright lamp showed six heads in consultation over him. Cyclops' shaven head and thick glasses were not among them. Goodbody had dreamed the words. Coming up from the depths of the dark subconscious, where the only light was the flickering silver of the projector beam on the flickering silver screen, he had brought up with him ancient cherished horrors.

Doctor Grossfleisch, author of *Sponge Counting Techniques* and *Extraordinary Cases of Involved and Involuted Intussusception of the Small Bowel I Have Known,* bent over him. The eyes were as empty and cold as the reflector on the head of a laryngologist. Yet this was the man who had sponsored him, the man who had taught him so much. This was the man who originated the justly famous *When in doubt, cut.*

Doctor Grossfleisch held an ice pick in his goblin-shaped hand.

"Schweinhund! First ve do to you der frontal lobotomy! Den der dissection mitout anesthesia alive yet!"

The ice pick descended towards his eyeball. A door exploded open. A scalpel streaked by Grossfleisch's zeppelin hip and stuck in the operating table, vibrating against Goodbody's strapped arm.

"Halt!"

The six heads turned, and Grossfleisch said, "Ah! Doctor Leibfremd, world-famous healer and distinguished author of *Der Misunderstood Martyrs: Burke und Hare!* Vhat gifs for zuch a dramatic entrance?"

"Doctor Goodbody must be kept in good health! He is the only man with the genius to perform a brain operation on our glorious leader, Doctor Inderhaus!"

Goodbody's skin turned cold, and he felt like fainting.

"Zo, our glorious leader has deep tumors of der cuneus and der lingual areas of der brain? Und Goodbody only has der chenius to cut? Mein Gott, how can ve trust him?"

"We stand behind him," Doctor Leibfremd said, "ready to thrust to the ganglia if he makes one false move!"

Goodbody sneered as if he were correcting an intern. "Why should I do this for you when you'll dissect me alive later?"

"Not so!" Leibfremd cried. "Despite your great crimes, we will let you live if you operate successfully on Doctor Inderhaus! Of course, you will be kept a prisoner, but in Grossfleisch's sanatorium, where, need I remind you, the patients live like kings, or, even better, Beverly Hills Physicians!"

"You would allow me to live?"

"You will die a natural death! You will not be touched by a doctor!" Grossfleisch said. "And you will get a professional courtesy discount, too! Ten percent off your bill!"

"Thank you," Goodbody said humbly. But he was thinking of ways to escape even then. The world must know the ghastly truth.

The day of the great operation, the amphitheater was filled with doctors from all over the world. The life of their glorious leader, Doctor Inderhaus, was at stake, and only the condemned criminal, the Judas, the Benedict Arnold, the Mudd, the Quisling of the medical profession, could save him.

The patient, head shaven, was wheeled in. He shook hands with himself as his colleagues cheered wildly. Tears dripped down his cheeks at this exhibition of love and respect, not unmixed with awe. Then he saw his surgeon approaching, and the benignity of Hyde changed to the hideous face of Jekyll.

Goodbody slipped on his mask and gloves. Grossfleisch held a scalpel to his back, and a man, who looked like Doctor Casey after a hard night with the head nurse, aimed a laser at Goodbody.

"Stand back! Give me room!" Goodbody said. He was icy cold, calm as the surface of a goldfish bowl, his long delicate fingers, which could have been a concert pianist's if he had gone wrong, flexed as if they were snakes smelling blood. A hush fell. Though the audience hated him to a man, despised and loathed him, and longed to spit on him (with no sterilization before or after), they could not help admiring him.

The hours ticked by. Scalpels cut. The scalp was rolled back. Drills growled; saws whined. The top of the skull came out. The keen blades began slicing into the gray wrinkled mass.

"Ach!" Grossfleisch said involuntarily as the forebrain came up like a drawbridge. "Mein Gott! Zuch daringk!"

There was a communal "Ah!" as Goodbody held up the great jellyfish-shaped tumor in his fist. Despite themselves, the doctors gave him a standing ovation that lasted ten minutes.

It was sad, he thought, that the greatest triumph of a series of blazing triumphs, the apex of his career, was also his black defeat, the nadir. And then the patient was wheeled out, and the surgeon was seized, stripped, and strapped. Grossfleisch and Ueberpreis, well-known proctologist and author of the notorious article *Did Doctor Watson Poison His Three Wives?* approached the operating table.

They were smiling with an utterly evil coldness and abhorrently sadistic pleasure, like Doctor Mabuses.

The audience leaned forward. They had always felt that both the patient and doctor were better off without employing anesthesia. The physician could determine the patient's reactions much more accurately and quickly if his responses were not dulled.

"Doctor X, I presume?" Goodbody said as he awoke.

"What!" said the nurse, Mrs. Fell.

"A nightmare. I thought my arms and legs had been cut off. Oh!"

"You'll get used to that," the nurse said. "Anytime you need anything, just press that plate with your nose. Don't be bashful. Doctor Grossfleisch said I was to wait on you hand and foot. I mean. . . ."

"I'm not only a basket case but a crazy basket case," he said. "I'm sure that I've been certified insane, haven't I?"

"Well," Mrs. Fell said, "who knows what insane means! One man's looniness is another man's religion. I mean, one man's schizophrenia is another man's manic-depressiveness. Well, you know what I mean!"

It was no use telling her his story, but he had to.

"Don't just dismiss what I'm about to tell you as the ravings of a maniac. Think about it for a long time; look around you. See if what I say doesn't make sense, even if it seems a topsy-turvy sense."

He had one advantage. She was a nurse, and all nurses, by the time they were graduated, loathed doctors. She would be ready to believe the worst about them.

"Every medical doctor takes the oath of Hippocrates. But, before he swears in public, he takes a private, a most arcane, oath. And that oath is much more ancient than that of Hippocrates, who, after all, died in 377 B.C., comparatively recently.

"The first witch doctor of the Old Stone Age may have given that oath to the second witch doctor. Who knows? But it is recorded, in a place where you will never see it, that the first doctor of the civilized world, the first doctor of the most ancient city-state, that of Sumer, predecessor even of old Egypt, swore in the second doctor.

"The Sumerian oath—scratch my nose, will you, my dear?—required that a medical doctor must never, under any circumstances, reveal anything at all about the true nature of doctors or of the true origin of diseases."

Mrs. Fell listened with only a few interruptions. Then she said, "Doctor Goodbody! Are you seriously trying to tell me that diseases would not exist if it were not for doctors? That doctors manufacture diseases and spread them around? That if it weren't for doctors, we'd

34

all be one hundred percent healthy? That they pick and choose laymen to infect and to cure so they can get good reputations and make money and dampen everybody's suspicions by . . . by . . . that's ridiculous!"

The sweat tickled his nose, but he ignored it. "Yes, Mrs. Fell, that's true! And, rarely, but it does happen, a doctor can't take being guilty of mass murder any more, and he breaks down and tries to tell the truth! And then he's hauled off, declared insane by his colleagues, or dies during an operation, or gets sick and dies, or just disappears!"

"And why weren't you killed?"

"I told you! I saved our glorious leader, the Grand Exalted Iatrogenic Sumerian. They promised me my life, and we don't lie to each other, just to laymen! But they made sure I couldn't escape, and they didn't cut my tongue out because they're sadistic! They get a charge out of me telling my story here, because who's going to believe me, a patient in a puzzle factory? Yes, Mrs. Fell, don't look so shocked! A booby hatch, a nut house! I'm a loony, right? Isn't that what you believe?"

She patted the top of his head. "There, there! I believe you! I'll see what I can do. Only. . . ."

"Yes?"

"My husband is a doctor, and if I thought for one moment that he was in a secret organization . . . !"

"Don't ask him!" Goodbody said. "Don't say a word to any doctor! Do you want to come down with cancer or infectious hepatitis or have a coronary thrombosis? Or catch a brand new disease? They invent a new one now and then, just to relieve the boredom, you know!"

It was no use. Mrs. Fell was just going along with him to soothe him.

And that night he was carried into the depths beneath the huge old house, where torches flickered and cold gray stones sweat and little drums beat and shrill goat horns blew and doctors with painted faces and red robes and black feathers and rattling gourds and thrumming bullroarers administered the Sumerian oath to the graduating class, 1970, of Johns Hopkins. And they led each young initiate before him and pointed out what would happen if he betrayed his profession.

Now + n
Now − n

by Robert Silverberg

It has long been suspected that telepathic powers operate outside of serial time as we know it; dreams that describe future events are one example. Robert Silverberg examines the possibilities of controlled use of these powers in this story set in a detailed and glittering future that, unlike much science fiction, we would all enjoy living in.

All had been so simple, so elegant, so profitable for ourselves. And then we met the lovely Selene and nearly were undone. She came into our lives during our regular transmission hour on Wednesday, October 7, 1987, between 6 and 7 P.M. Central European Time. The money-making hour. I was in satisfactory contact with myself and also with myself. (Now − n) was due on the line first, and then I would hear from (now + n).

I was primed for some kind of trouble. I knew trouble was coming, because on Monday, while I was receiving messages from the me of Wednesday, there came an inexplicable and unexplained break in communications. As a result I did not get data from (now + n) concerning the prices of the stocks in our carryover portfolio from last week, and I was unable to take action. Two days have passed, and I am the me of Wednesday who failed to send the news to the me of Monday, and I have no idea what will happen to interrupt contact. Least of all do I anticipate Selene.

In such dealings as ours no distractions are needed, sexual, otherwise. We must concentrate wholly. At any time there is steady low-level contact among ourselves; we feel one another's reassuring presence. But transmission of data from self to self requires close attention.

I tell you my method. Then maybe you understand my trouble.

My business is investments. I do all my work at this same hour. At this hour it is midday in New York; the Big Board is still open. I can put through quick calls to my brokers when my time comes to buy or sell.

My office at the moment is the cocktail lounge known as the Celestial Room in the Henry VIII Hotel, south of the Thames. My office may be anywhere. All I need is a telephone. The Celestial Room is aptly named. The room orbits endlessly on a silent oiled tract. Twittering sculptures in the so-called galactic mode drift through the air, scattering cascades of polychromed light upon those who sip drinks. Beyond the great picture windows of this supreme room lies the foggy darkness of the London evening, which I ignore. It is all the same to me, wherever I am: London, Nairobi, Karachi, Istanbul, Pittsburgh. I look only for an adequately comfortable environment, air that is safe to admit to one's lungs, service in the style I demand, and a telephone line. The individual characteristics of an individual place do not move me. I am like the ten planets of our solar family: a perpetual traveler, but not a sightseer.

Myself who is (now $- n$) is ready to receive transmission from myself who is (now). "Go ahead, (now $+ n$)," he tells me. (To him I am [now $+ n$]. To myself I am [now]. Everything is relative. N is exactly forty-eight hours these days.)

"Here we go, (now $- n$)," I say to him.

I summon my strength by sipping at my drink. Chateau d'Yquem '79 in a sleek Czech goblet. Sickly-sweet stuff; the waiter was aghast when I ordered it *before dinner. Horreur! Quel aperitif!* But the wine makes transmission easier. It greases the conduit, somehow. I am ready.

My table is a single elegant block of glittering irradiated crystal, iridescent, cunningly emitting shifting moire patterns. On the table, unfolded, lies today's European edition of the *Herald-Tribune*. I lean forward. I take from my breast pocket a sheet of paper, the printout listing the securities I bought on Monday afternoon. Now I allow my eyes to roam the close-packed type of the market quotations in my newspaper. I linger for a long moment on the heading, so there will be no mistake: "Closing New York Prices, Tuesday, October 6." To me they are yesterday's prices. To (now $- n$) they are tomorrow's prices. (Now $- n$) acknowledges that he is receiving a sharp image.

I am about to transmit these prices to the me of Monday. You follow the machination, now?

I scan and I select.

I search only for the stocks that move five percent or more in a single day. Whether they move up or down is immaterial; motion is the only criterion, and we go short or long as the case demands. We need fast action because our maximum survey span is only ninety-six hours at present, counting the relay from (now + n) back to (now − n) by way of (now). We cannot afford to wait for leisurely capital gains to mature; we must cut our risks by going for the quick, violent swings, seizing our profits as they emerge. The swings have to be violent. Otherwise brokerage costs will eat up our gross.

I have no difficulty choosing the stocks whose prices I will transmit to Monday's me. They are the stocks on the broker's printout, the ones we have already bought; obviously (now − n) would not have bought them unless Wednesday's me had told him about them, and now that I am Wednesday's me, I must follow through. So I send:

Arizona Agrochemical, 79¼, +6¾
Canadian Transmutation, 116, +4¼
Commonwealth Dispersals, 12, −1¾
Eastern Electric Energy, 41, +2
Great Lakes Bionics, 66, +3½

And so on through *Western Offshore Corp.,* 99, − 8. Now I have transmitted to (now − n) a list of Tuesday's top twenty high-percentage swingers. From his vantage point in Monday, (now − n) will begin to place orders, taking positions in all twenty stocks on Monday afternoon. I know that he has been successful, because the printout from my broker gives confirmations of all twenty purchases at what now are highly favorable prices.

(Now − n) then signs off for a while and (now + n) comes on. He is transmitting from Friday, October 9. He gives me Thursday's closing prices on the same twenty stocks, from Arizona Agrochemical to Western Offshore. He already knows which of the twenty I will have chosen to sell today, but he pays me the compliment of not telling me; he merely gives me the prices. He signs off, and, in my role as (now), I make my decisions. I sell Canadian Transmutation, Great Lakes Bionics, and five others; I cover our short sale on Commonwealth Dispersals. The rest of the positions I leave undisturbed for the time being, since they will sell at better prices tomorrow, according to the word from (now + n). I can handle those when I am Friday's me.

Today's sequence is over.

In any given sequence—and we have been running about three a week—we commit no more than five or six million dollars. We wish to stay inconspicuous. Our pre-tax profit runs at about nine percent a week. Despite our network of tax havens in Ghana, Fiji, Grand Cayman, Liechtenstein, and Bolivia, through which our profits are funneled, we can bring down to net only about five percent a week on our entire capital. This keeps all three of us in a decent style and compounds prettily. Starting with five thousand dollars six years ago at the age of twenty-five, I have become one of the world's wealthiest men, with no other advantages than intelligence, persistence, and extrasensory access to tomorrow's stock prices.

It is time to deal with the next sequence. I must transmit to (now $-n$) the Tuesday prices of the stocks in the portfolio carried over from last week, so that he can make his decisions on what to sell. I know what he has sold, but it would spoil his sport to tip my hand. We treat ourselves fairly. After I have finished sending (now $-n$) those prices, (now $+n$) will come on line again and will transmit to me an entirely new list of stocks in which I must take positions before Thursday morning's New York opening. He will be able to realize profits in those on Friday. Thus we go from day to day, playing our shifting roles.

But this was the day on which Selene intersected our lives.

I had emptied my glass. I looked up to signal the waiter, and at that moment a slender, dark-haired girl, alone, entered the Celestial Room. She was tall, graceful, glorious. She was expensively clad in a clinging monomolecular wrap that shuttled through a complex program of wavelength-shifts, including a microsecond sweep of total transparency that dazzled the eye while still maintaining a degree of modesty. Her features were a match for her garment: wide-set glossy eyes, delicate nose, firm lips lightly outlined in green. Her skin was extraordinarily pale. I could see no jewelry on her (why gild refined gold, why paint the lily?) but on her lovely left cheekbone I observed a small decorative band of ultra-violet paint, obviously chosen for visibility in the high-spectrum lighting of this unique room.

She conquered me. There was a mingling of traits in her that I found instantly irresistible: she seemed both shy and steel-strong, passionate and vulnerable, confident and ill at ease. She scanned the room, evidently looking for someone, not finding him. Her eyes met mine and lingered.

Somewhere in my cerebrum (now $-n$) said shrilly, as I had said on Monday, "I don't read you, (now $+n$). I don't read you!"

I paid no heed. I rose. I smiled to the girl, and beckoned her toward the empty chair at my table. I swept my *Herald-Tribune* to the floor. At certain times there are more important things than compounding one's capital at five percent a week. She glowed gratefully at me, nodding, accepting my invitation.

When she was about twenty feet from me, I lost all contact with $(now - n)$ and $(now + n)$.

I don't mean simply that there was an interruption in the transmission of words and data among us. I mean that I lost all sense of the presence of my earlier and later selves. That warm, wordless companionship, that ourselvesness, that harmony that I had known constantly since we had established our linkage five years ago, vanished as if switched off. On Monday, when contact with $(now + n)$ broke, I still had communication with $(now - n)$. Now I had no one.

I was terrifyingly alone, even as ordinary men are alone, but more alone than that, for I had known a fellowship beyond the reach of other mortals. The shock of separation was intense.

Then Selene was sitting beside me, and the nearness of her made me forget my new solitude entirely.

She said, "I don't know where he is and I don't care. He's been late once too often. *Finito* for him. Hello, you. I'm Selene Hughes."

"Aram Kevorkian. What do you drink?"

"Chartreuse on the rocks. Green. I knew you were Armenian from halfway across the room."

I am Bulgarian, thirteen generations. It suits me to wear an Armenian name. I did not correct her. The waiter hurried over; I ordered chartreuse for her, a sake martini for self. I trembled like an adolescent. Her beauty was disturbing, overwhelming, astonishing. As we raised glasses I reached out experimentally for $(now - n)$ or $(now + n)$. Silence. Silence. But there was Selene.

I said, "You're not from London."

"I travel a lot. I stay here a while, there a while. Originally Dallas. You must be able to hear the Texas in my voice. Most recent port of call, Lima. For the July skiing. Now London."

"And the next stop?"

"Who knows? What do you do, Aram?"

"I invest."

"For a living?"

"So to speak. I struggle along. Free for dinner?"

"Of course. Shall we eat in the hotel?"

"There's the beastly fog outside," I said.

"Exactly."

Simpatico. Perfectly. I guessed her for twenty-four, twenty-five at most. Perhaps a brief marriage three or four years in the past. A private income, not colossal, but nice. An experienced woman of the world, and yet somehow still retaining a core of innocence, a magical softness of the soul. I loved her instantly. She did not care for a second cocktail. "I'll make dinner reservations," I said, as she went off to the powder room. I watched her walk away. A supple walk, flawless posture, supreme shoulder blades. When she was about twenty feet from me I felt my other selves suddenly return. "What's happening?" (now — *n*) demanded furiously. "Where did you go? Why aren't you sending?"

"I don't know yet."

"Where the hell are the Tuesday prices on last week's carryover stocks?"

"Later," I told him.

"Now. Before you blank out again."

"The prices can wait," I said, and shut him off. To (now + *n*) I said, "All right. What do you know that I ought to know?"

Myself of forty-eight hours hence said, "We have fallen in love."

"I'm aware of that. But what blanked us out?"

"She did. She's psi-suppressant. She absorbs all the transmission energy we put out."

"Impossible! I've never heard of any such thing."

"No?" said (now + *n*). "Brother, this past hour has been the first chance I've had to get through to you since Wednesday, when we got into this mess. It's no coincidence that I've been with her just about one hundred percent of the time since Wednesday evening, except for a few two-minute breaks, and then I couldn't reach you because *you* must have been with her in your time-sequence. And so——"

"How can this be?" I cried. "What'll happen to us if? No. No, you bastard, you're rolling me over. I don't believe you. There's no way that she could be causing it."

"I think I know how she does it," said (now + *n*). "There's a——"

At that moment Selene returned, looking even more radiantly beautiful, and silence descended once more.

We dined well. Chilled Mombasa oysters, salade niçoise, filet of Kobe beef rare, washed down by Richebourg '77. Occasionally I tried to reach myselves. Nothing. I worried a little about how I was going to get the Tuesday prices to (now — *n*) on the carryover stuff, and decided to forget about it. Obviously I hadn't managed to get them to him, since I hadn't received any printout on sales out of that portfolio this evening, and if I hadn't reached him, there was no sense in fretting about reaching him. The wonderful thing about this telepathy

41

across time is the sense of stability it gives you: *whatever has been, must be,* and so forth.

After dinner we went down one level to the casino for our brandies and a bit of gamblerage. "Two thousand pounds' worth," I said to the robot cashier, and put my thumb to his charge-plate, and the chips came skittering out of the slot in his chest. I gave half the stake to Selene. She played high-grav-low-grav, and I played roulette; we shifted from one table to the other according to whim and the run of our luck. In two hours she tripled her stake and I lost all of mine. I never was good at games of chance. I even used to get hurt in the market before the market ceased being a game of chance for me. Naturally, I let her thumb her winnings into her own account, and when she offered to return the original stake I just laughed.

Where next? Too early for bed.

"The swimming pool?" she suggested.

"Fine idea," I said. But the hotel has two, as usual. "Nude pool or suit pool?"

"Who owns a suit?" she asked, and we laughed, and took the drop-shaft to the pool.

There were separate dressing rooms, M and W. No one frets about showing flesh, but shedding clothes still has lingering taboos. I peeled fast and waited for her by the pool. During this interval I felt the familiar presence of another self impinge on me: (now $- n$). He wasn't transmitting, but I knew he was there. I couldn't feel (now $+ n$) at all. Grudgingly I began to admit that Selene must be responsible for my communications problem. Whenever she went more than twenty feet away, I could get through to myselves. How did she do it, though? And could it be stopped? Mao help me, would I have to choose between my livelihood and my new beloved?

The pool was a vast octagon with a trampoline diving-web and a set of underwater psych-lights making rippling patterns of color. Maybe fifty people were swimming and a few dozen more were lounging beside the pool, improving their tans. No one person can possibly stand out in such a mass of flesh, and yet when Selene emerged from the women's dressing room and began the long saunter across the tiles toward me, the heads began to turn by the dozens. Her figure was not notably lush, yet she had the automatic magnetism that only true beauty exercises. She was definitely slender, but everything was in perfect proportion, as though she had been shaped by the hand of Phidias himself. Long legs, long arms, narrow wrists, narrow waist, small high breasts, miraculously outcurving hips. The

42

Primavera of Botticelli. The *Leda* of Leonardo. She carried herself with ultimate grace. My heart thundered.

Between her breasts she wore some sort of amulet: a disk of red metal in which geometrical symbols were engraved. I hadn't noticed it when she was clothed.

"My good-luck piece," she explained. "I'm never without it." And she sprinted laughing to the trampoline, and bounded, and hovered, and soared, and cut magnificently through the surface of the water. I followed her in. We raced from angle to angle of the pool, testing each other, searching for limits and not finding them. We dived and met far below, and locked hands, and bobbed happily upward. Then we lay under the warm quartz lamps. Then we tried the sauna. Then we dressed.

We went to her room.

She kept the amulet on even when we made love. I felt it cold against my chest as I embraced her.

But what of the making of money? What of the compounding of capital? What of my sweaty little secret, the joker in the Wall Street pack, the messages from beyond by which I milked the market of millions? On Thursday no contact with my other selves was scheduled, but I could not have made it even if it had been. It was amply clear: Selene blanked my psi field. The critical range was twenty feet. When we were farther apart than that, I could get through; otherwise, not. How did it happen? How? How? How? An accidental incompatibility of psionic vibrations? A tragic canceling out of my power through proximity to her splendid self? No. No. No. No.

On Thursday we roared through London like a conflagration, doing the galleries, the boutiques, the museums, the sniffer palaces, the pubs, the sparkle houses. I had never been so much in love. For hours at a time I forgot my dilemma. The absence of myself from myself, the separation that had seemed so shattering in its first instant, seemed trivial. What did I need *them* for, when I had *her*?

I needed them for the money making. The money making was a disease that love might alleviate but could not cure. And if I did not resume contact soon, there would be calamities in store.

Late Thursday afternoon, as we came reeling giddily out of a sniffer palace on High Holborn, our nostrils quivering, I felt contact again. (Now + n) broke through briefly, during a moment when I waited for a traffic light and Selene plunged wildly across to the far side of the street.

"——the amulet's what does it," he said. "That's the word I get from——"

Selene rushed back to my side of the street. "Come *on*, silly! Why'd you wait?"

Two hours later, as she lay in my arms, I swept my hand up from her satiny haunch to her silken breast, and caught the plaque of red metal between two fingers. "Love, won't you take this off?" I said innocently. "I hate the feel of a piece of cold slithery metal coming between us when——"

There was terror in her dark eyes. "I couldn't, Aram! I *couldn't!*"

"For me, love?"

"Please. Let me have my little superstition." Her lips found mine. Cleverly she changed the subject. I wondered at her tremor of shock, her frightened refusal.

Later we strolled along the Thames and watched Friday coming to life in fogbound dawn. Today I would have to escape from her for at least an hour, I knew. The laws of time dictated it. For on Wednesday, between 6 and 7 P.M. Central European Time, I had accepted a transmission from myself of (now + n), speaking out of Friday, and Friday had come, and I was that very same (now + n), who must reach out at the proper time toward his counterpart at (now − n) on Wednesday. What would happen if I failed to make my rendezvous with time in time, I did not know. Nor wanted to discover. The universe, I suspected, would continue regardless. But my own sanity—my grasp on that universe—might not.

It was a narrowness. All glorious Friday I had to plot how to separate myself from radiant Selene during the cocktail hour, when she would certainly want to be with me. But in the end it was simplicity. I told the concierge, "At seven minutes after six send a message to me in the Celestial Room. I am wanted on urgent business, must come instantly to computer room for intercontinental data patch, person-to-person. So?" Concierge replied, "We can give you the patch right at your table in the Celestial Room." I shook head firmly. "Do it as I say. Please." I put thumb to gratuity account of concierge and signaled an account-transfer of five pounds. Concierge smiled.

Seven minutes after six, message-robot scuttles into Celestial Room, comes homing in on table where I sit with Selene. "Intercontinental data patch, Mr. Kevorkian," says robot. "Wanted immediately. Computer room." I turn to Selene. "Forgive me, love. Desolated, but must go. Urgent business. Just a few minutes."

She grasps my arm fondly. "Darling, no! Let the call wait. It's our *anniversary* now. Forty-eight hours since we met!"

Gently I pull arm free. I extend arm, show jeweled timepiece. "Not yet, not yet! We didn't meet until half past six Wednesday. I'll be back in time to celebrate." I kiss tip of supreme nose. "Don't smile at strangers while I'm gone," I say, and rush off with robot.

I do not go to computer room. I hurriedly buy a Friday *Herald-Tribune* in lobby and lock myself in men's washroom cubicle. Contact now is made on schedule with (now − *n*), living in Wednesday, all innocent of what will befall him that miraculous evening. I read stock prices, twenty securities, from Arizona Agrochemical to Western Offshore Corp. I sign off and study my watch. (Now − *n*) is currently closing out seven long positions and the short sale on Commonwealth Dispersals. During the interval I seek to make contact with (now + *n*) ahead of me on Sunday evening. No response. Nothing.

Presently I lose contact with (now − *n*). As expected; for this is the moment when the me of Wednesday has for the first time come within Selene's psi-suppressant field. I wait patiently. In a while (Selene − *n*) goes to powder room. Contact returns.

(Now − *n*) says to me, "All right. What do you know that I ought to know?"

"We have fallen in love," I say.

Rest of conversation follows as per. What has been, must be. I debate slipping in the tidbit I have received from (now + *n*) concerning the alleged powers of Selene's amulet. Should I say it quickly, before contact breaks? Impossible. It was not said to me. The conversation proceeds until at the proper moment I am able to say, "I think I know how she does it. There's a——"

Wall of silence descends. (Selene − *n*) has returned to the table of (now − *n*). Therefore I (now) will return to the table of Selene (now). I rush back to the Celestial Room. Selene, looking glum, sits alone, sipping drink. She brightens as I approach.

"See?" I cry. "Back just in time. Happy anniversary, darling. Happy, happy, happy, happy!"

When we woke Saturday morning we decided to share the same room thereafter. Selene showered while I went downstairs to arrange the transfer. I could have arranged everything by telephone without getting out of bed, but I chose to go in person to the desk, leaving Selene behind. You understand why.

In the lobby I received a transmission from (now + *n*), speaking out of Monday, October 12. "It's definitely the amulet," he said. "I can't tell you how it works, but it's some kind of mechanical psi-suppressant device. God knows why she wears it, but if I could only manage to have her lose it we'd be all right. It's the amulet. Pass it on."

I was reminded, by this, of the flash of contact I had received on Thursday outside the sniffer palace on High Holborn. I realized that I had another message to send, a rendezvous to keep with him who has become $(now - n)$.

Late Saturday afternoon, I made contact with $(now - n)$ once more, only momentarily. Again I resorted to a ruse in order to fulfill the necessary unfolding of destiny. Selene and I stood in the hallway, waiting for a dropshaft. There were other people. The dropshaft gate raised open and Selene went in, followed by others. With an excess of chivalry I let all the others enter before me, and "accidentally" missed the closing of the gate. The dropshaft descended, with Selene. I remained alone in the hall. My timing was good; after a moment I felt the inner warmth that told me of proximity to the mind of $(now - n)$.

"——the amulet's what does it," I said. "That's the word I get from——"

Aloneness intervened.

During the week beginning Monday, October 12, I received no advance information on the fluctuations of the stock market at all. Not in five years had I been so deprived of data. My linkings with $(now - n)$ and $(now + n)$ were fleeting and unsatisfactory. We exchanged a sentence here, a blurt of hasty words there, no more. Of course, there were moments every day when I was apart from the fair Selene long enough to get a message out. Though we were utterly consumed by our passion for one another, nevertheless I did get opportunities to elude the twenty-foot radius of her psi-suppressant field. The trouble was that my opportunities to send did not always coincide with the opportunities of $(now - n)$ or $(now + n)$ to receive. We remained linked in a 48-hour spacing, and to alter that spacing would require extensive discipline and infinitely careful coordination, which none of ourselves were able to provide in such a time. So any contact with myselves had to depend on a coincidence of apartnesses from Selene.

I regretted this keenly. Yet there was Selene to comfort me. We reveled all day and reveled all night. When fatigue overcame us we grabbed a two-hour deepsleep wire and caught up with ourselves, and then we started over. I plumbed the limits of ecstasy. I believe it was like that for her.

Though lacking my unique advantage, I also played the market that week. Partly it was compulsion: my plungings had become obsessive. Partly, too, it was at Selene's urgings. "Don't you neglect your work for me," she purred. "I don't want to stand in the way of making *money.*"

Money, I was discovering, fascinated her nearly as intensely as it did me. Another evidence of compatibility. She knew a good deal about the market herself, and looked on, an excited spectator, as I each day shuffled my portfolio.

The market was closed Monday: Columbus Day. Tuesday, queasily operating in the dark, I sold Arizona Agrochemical, Consolidated Luna, Eastern Electric Energy, and Western Offshore, reinvesting the proceeds in large blocks of Meccano Leasing and Holoscan Dynamics. Wednesday's *Tribune,* to my chagrin, brought me the news that Consolidated Luna had received the Copernicus franchise and had risen nine and three-quarters points in the final hour of Tuesday's trading. Meccano Leasing, though, had been rebuffed in the Robomation takeover bid and was off four and one-half since I had bought it. I got through to my broker in a hurry and sold Meccano, which was down even further that morning. My loss was $125,000—plus $250,000 more that I had dropped by selling Consolidated Luna too soon. After the market closed on Wednesday, the directors of Meccano Leasing unexpectedly declared a five-for-two split and a special dividend in the form of a one-for-ten distribution of cumulative participating high-depreciation warrants. Meccano regained its entire Tuesday-Wednesday loss and tacked on 5 points beyond.

I concealed the details of this from Selene. She saw only the glamor of my speculations: the telephone calls, the quick computations, the movements of hundreds of thousands of dollars. I hid the hideous botch from her, knowing it might damage my prestige.

On Thursday, feeling battered and looking for the safety of a utility, I picked up ten thousand Southwest Power and Fusion at thirty-eight, only hours before the explosion of SPF's magnetohydrodynamic generating station in Las Cruces, which destroyed half a county and neatly peeled $90,000 off the value of my investment when the stock finally traded, after a delayed opening, on Friday. I sold. Later came news that SPF's insurance would cover everything. SPF recovered, whereas Holoscan Dynamics plummeted eleven and one-half points, costing me $140,000 more. I had not known that Holoscan's insurance subsidiary was the chief underwriter for SPF's disaster coverage. All told that week I shed more than $500,000. My brokers were stunned. I had a reputation for infallibility among them. Most of them had become wealthy simply by duplicating my own transactions for their own accounts.

"Sweetheart, what *happened?*" they asked me.

My losses the following week came to $1,250,000. Still no news from (now + n). My brokers felt I needed a vacation. Even Selene knew I was losing heavily, by now. Curiously, my run of bad luck seemed to intensify her passion for me. Perhaps it made me look tragic and byronic to be getting hit so hard.

We spent wild days and wilder nights. I lived in throbbing haze of sensuality. Wherever we went we were the center of all attention. We had that burnished sheen that only great lovers have. We radiated a glow of delight all up and down the spectrum.

I was losing millions.

The more I lost, the more reckless my plunges became, and the deeper my losses became.

I was in real danger of being wiped out, if this went on.

I had to get away from her.

Monday, October 26. Selene has taken the deepsleep wire and in the next two hours will flush away the fatigues of three riotous days and nights without rest. I have only pretended to take the wire. When she goes under, I rise. I dress. I pack. I scrawl a note for her. *"Business trip. Back soon. Love, love, love, love."* I catch noon rocket for Istanbul.

Minarets, mosques, Byzantine temples. Shunning the sleep wire, I spend the next day and a half in bed in ordinary repose. I wake and it is forty-eight hours since parting from Selene. Desolation! Bitter solitude! But I feel (now + n) invading my mind.

"Take this down," he says brusquely. "Buy 5000 FSP, 800 CCG, 150 LC, 200 T, 1000 TXN, 100 BVI. Go short 200 BA, 500 UCM, 200 LOC. Clear? Read back to me."

I read back. Then I phone in my orders. I hardly care what the ticker symbols stand for. If (now + n) says to do, I do.

An hour and a half later the switchboard tells me, "A Miss Hughes to see you, sir."

She has traced me! *Calamitas calamitatium!* "Tell her I'm not here," I say. I flee to the roofport. By copter I get away. Commercial jet shortly brings me to Tel Aviv. I take a room at the Hilton and give

48

absolute instructions am not to be disturbed. Meals only to room, also *Herald-Trib* every day, otherwise no interruptions.

I study the market action. On Friday I am able to reach (now $- n$). "Take this down," I say brusquely. "Buy 5000 FSP, 800 CCG, 150 LC, 200 T——"

Then I call brokers. I close out Wednesday's longs and cover Wednesday's shorts. My profit is over a million. I am recouping. But I miss her terribly.

I spend agonizing weekend of loneliness in hotel room.

Monday. Comes voice of (now $+ n$) out of Wednesday, with new instructions. I obey. At lunchtime, under lid of my barley soup, floats note from her. "Darling, why are you running away from me? I love you to the ninth power. S."

I get out of hotel disguised as bellhop and take El Al jet to Cairo. Tense, jittery, I join tourist group sightseeing Pyramids, much out of character. Tour is conducted in Hebrew; serves me right. I lock self in hotel. *Herald-Tribune* available. On Wednesday I send instructions to me of Monday, (now $- n$). I await instructions from me of Friday (now $+ n$). Instead I get muddled transmissions, noise, confusions. What is wrong? Where to flee now? Brasilia, McMurdo Sound, Anchorage, Irkutsk, Maograd? She will find me. She has her resources. There are few secrets to one who has the will to surmount them. How does she find me?

She finds me.

Note comes: "I am at Abu Simbel to wait for you. Meet me there on Friday afternoon or I throw myself from Rameses' leftmost head at sundown. Love. Desperate. S."

I am defeated. She will bankrupt me, but I must have her.

On Friday I go to Abu Simbel.

She stood atop the monument, luscious in windswept white cotton.

"I knew you'd come," she said.

"What else could I do?"

We kissed. Her suppleness inflamed me. The sun blazed toward a descent into the western desert.

"Why have you been running away from me?" she asked. "What did I do wrong? Why did you stop loving me?"

"I never stopped loving you," I said.

"Then—*why?*"

"I will tell you," I said, "a secret I have shared with no human being other than myselves."

Words tumbled out. I told all. The discovery of my gift, the early chaos of sensory bombardment from other times, the bafflement of living one hour ahead of time and one hour behind time as well as in the present. The months of discipline needed to develop my gift. The fierce struggle to extend the range of extrasensory perception to five hours, ten, twenty-four, forty-eight. The joy of playing the market and never losing. The intricate systems of speculation; the self-imposed limits to keep me from ending up with all the assets in the world; the pleasures of immense wealth. The loneliness, too. And the supremacy of the night when I met her.

Then I said, "When I'm with you, it doesn't work. I can't communicate with myselves. I lost millions in the last couple of weeks, playing the market the regular way. You were breaking me."

"The amulet," she said. "It does it. It absorbs psionic energy. It suppresses the psi field."

"I thought it was that. But who ever heard of such a thing? Where did you get it, Selene? Why do you wear it?"

"I got it far, far from here," said Selene. "I wear it to protect myself."

"Against *what?*"

"Against my own gift. My terrible gift, my nightmare gift, my curse of a gift. But if I must choose between my amulet and my love, it is no choice. I love you, Aram, I love you, I love you!"

She seized the metal disk, ripped it from the chain around her neck, hurled it over the brink of the monument. It fluttered through the twilight sky and was gone.

I felt $(now - n)$ and $(now + n)$ return.

Selene vanished.

For an hour I stood alone atop Abu Simbel, motionless, baffled, stunned. Suddenly Selene was back. She clutched my arm and whispered, "Quick! Let's go to the hotel!"

"Where have you been?"

"Next Tuesday," she said. "I oscillate in time."

"What?"

"The amulet damped my oscillations. It anchored me to the time-line in the present. I got in 2459 A.D. Someone I knew there, someone who cared very deeply for me. It was his parting gift, and he gave it knowing we could never meet again. But now——"

She vanished. Gone eighteen minutes.

"I was back in last Tuesday," she said, returning. "I phoned myself and said I should follow you to Istanbul, and then to Tel Aviv, and then to Egypt. You see how I found you?"

50

We hurried to her hotel overlooking the Nile. We made love, and an instant before the climax I found myself alone in bed. (Now + *n*) spoke to me and said, "She's been here with me. She should be on her way back to you." Selene returned. "I went to——"

"——this coming Sunday," I said. "I know. Can't you control the oscillations at all?"

"No. I'm swinging free. When the momentum really builds up, I cover centuries. It's torture, Aram. Life has no sequence, no structure. Hold me tight!"

In a frenzy we finished what we could not finish before. We lay clasped close exhausted. "What will we do?" I cried. "I can't let you oscillate like this!"

"You must. I can't let you sacrifice your livelihood!"

"But——"

She was gone.

I rose and dressed and hurried back to Abu Simbel. In the hours before dawn I searched the sands beside the Nile, crawling, sifting, probing. As the sun's rays crested the mountain I found the amulet. I rushed to the hotel. Selene reappeared.

"Put it on," I commanded.

"I won't. I can't deprive you of——"

"Put it on."

She disappeared. (Now + *n*) said, "Never fear. All will work out wondrous well."

Selene came back. "I was in the Friday after next," she said. "I had an idea that will save everything."

"No ideas. Put the amulet on."

She shook her head. "I brought you a present," she said, and handed me a copy of the *Herald-Tribune,* dated the Friday after next. Oscillation seized her. She went and came and handed me November 19's newspaper. Her eyes were bright with excitement. She vanished. She brought me the *Herald-Tribune* of November 8. Of December 4. Of November 11. Of January 18, 1988. Of December 11. Of March 5, 1988. Of December 22. Of June 16, 1997. Of December 14. Of September 8, 1990. "Enough!" I said. "Enough!" She continued to swing through time. The stack of papers grew. "I love you," she gasped, and handed me a transparent cube one inch high. *"The Wall Street Journal,* May 19, 2206," she explained. "I couldn't get the machine that reads it. Sorry." She was gone. She brought me more *Herald-Tribunes,* many dates, 1988-2002. Then a whole microreel. At last she sank down, dazed, exhausted, and said, "Give me the amulet. It must be within twelve inches of my body to neutralize my field." I slipped the disk into her palm. "Kiss me," Selene murmured.

And so. She wears her amulet; we are inseparable; I have no contact with my other selves. In handling my investments I merely consult my file of newspapers, which I have reduced to minicap size and carry in the bezel of a ring I wear. For safety's sake Selene carries a duplicate.

We are very happy. We are very wealthy.

Is only one dilemma. Neither of us uses the special gift with which we were born. Evolution would not have produced such things in us if they were not to be used. What risks do we run by thwarting evolution's design?

I bitterly miss the use of my power, which her amulet negates. Even the company of supreme Selene does not wholly compensate for the loss of the harmoniousness that was

$$(now - n)$$
$$(now)$$
$$(now + n)$$

I could, of course, simply arrange to be away from Selene for an hour here, an hour there, and reopen that contact. I could even have continued playing the market that way, setting aside a transmission hour every forty-eight hours outside of amulet range. But it is the *continuous* contact that I miss. The always presence of my other selves. If I have that contact, Selene is condemned to oscillate, or else we must part.

I wish also to find some way that her gift will be not terror but joy for her.

Is maybe a solution. Can extrasensory gifts be induced by proximity? Can Selene's oscillation pass to me? I struggle to acquire it. We work together to give me her gift. Just today I felt myself move, perhaps a microsecond into the future, then a microsecond into the past. Selene said I definitely seemed to blur.

Who knows? Will success be ours?

I think yes. I think love will triumph. I think I will learn the secret, and we will coordinate our vanishings, Selene and I, and we will oscillate as one, we will swing together through time, we will soar, we will speed hand in hand across the millennia. She can discard her amulet once I am able to go with her on her journeys.

Pray for us, $(now + n)$, my brother, my other self, and one day soon perhaps I will come to you and shake you by the hand.

Two Odysseys Into the Center

by Barry N. Malzberg

Barry Malzberg is a tall and brooding conscience for us all. He has certain doubts about the meaning and motives of the space race that he presents here in "The Conquest of Mars"—the first of this pair of odysseys. Then, not satisfied with rattling this science fiction holy of holies, he turns around in "Some Notes Towards a Useable Past" and shakes up dear old science fiction itself in a most delightful and acid way.

THE CONQUEST OF MARS

I

Descending with the other man in the landing crate, Blake risks one last appalled look at the space beneath him and then gasps to himself the admission that he can no longer restrain. The scientists have made a terrible mistake. Mars does not exist. They are heading toward nothing.

II

The other man is named Williams. He is four years younger than Blake and did almost as well in all of the selection tests, thus guaranteeing him the role of second in the landing party. Blake has always liked him and they have, up to a point, gotten along fine. But this is all moot. Williams seems to have disappeared, or in any event he is no longer huddled shoulder-to-shoulder with Blake in the craft. Instead there is a grotesque creature with a rather dour expression on what Blake takes to be the face, although strictly speaking the creature does not have a face. "Excuse me," the creature says, "I didn't mean to unsettle you."

"What is this?" Blake says. "What is this?" It occurs to him that this dialogue like all the rest is being picked up by transceivers in the

53

landing craft, and undoubtedly his words are being heard by thousands of employees at the main base—to say nothing of the possibility of other millions digging it through the media. But still, this is disconcerting; they will have to see his point. "What are you doing? Who are you?"

"I'll make this quick and reasonable," the creature says. Its speech is slightly accented; not exactly Russian but one of those exotic satellites. Above all it is precise. "I am a representative of the Martian people. We have been observing you for many centuries as you prepared yourselves for this expedition and, quite frankly, we want no part of you. You are a dangerous race: aggressive and self-destructive and our civilization, although it is a bit on the decadent side, is pleasing to us more or less as it is. We have therefore arranged to move our planet away from your line of descent until such time as you give up this foolishness and return. We have very great scientific resources although we are primarily an artistic culture. You will turn around please, and go back to your ship."

"That's impossible," Blake says. He has scored higher than any other man in the history of the program in tests simulating all possible catastrophes and he finds it easy to be as reasonable as the alien. "We're committed to the line of descent."

"No, you are not. Surely your devices have prevent mechanisms which will reverse the descent. Please use them."

"This is ridiculous," Blake says. "Where is Williams? How do I know that you haven't killed him?" He does not even consider the possibility of hallucination or breakdown, realizing that he is too highly qualified by the program for any kind of psychic difficulty. "I want to know where he is."

"Williams is a hostage," the creature says blandly. "He is being held safely until such time as you reverse descent and return to your ship. He will then be given back to you in perfect condition. He is in complete stasis; he does not even realize that he has been abducted. I assure you that we will not hesitate to kill him, however, if you do not cooperate."

"This is ridiculous. I demand you release him."

"Of course it's ridiculous. You people are invading our territory. You never gave a moment's thought to the possibility that Mars was inhabited and that we might not want you."

"There was never any evidence——"

"You are such an arrogant people," the creature says sadly, "so convinced of your own acumen. I am getting very bored with this discussion, which is rapidly approaching uselessness. You have five minutes to reverse the descent; if you do not, we will kill the hostage. Also, we will kill you. Also, we will kill the creature in your mother ship. Additionally, we shall commence plans to kill everyone on your planet. The stakes are a bit too high," it says, "don't you think?" and vanishes or at least appears to vanish. Perhaps it is still there, lurking behind a wall, observing. In any event, Blake finds himself alone in the capsule.

III

Blake decides to think the thing through. As the result of rigorous mental and physical training he can approach any situation logically, even illogical ones. It is a pity that he must do this alone, but his one attempt to make contact with the transmitter is unsuccessful and he accepts at once the fact that the Martians have cut him off. This is reasonable.

"Let me see," Blake mutters. He always found it best, particularly as his responsibilities in the program increased, to talk out his thoughts for the sake of objectivity. "If I send the craft back to the ship they'll release Williams and allow us to return to Earth, and surely we won't get into any trouble because I'm sure that the base heard every word of this on the transmitters. On the other hand, if I insist on going ahead with the landing they'll kill Williams, kill me, kill MacGregor up there in the ship and arrange to kill everyone else on Earth. Four and a half billion people. But I don't have any assurances that they won't do it anyway. But then again on the other hand I can hardly go on with the landing because there's nothing to . . . well . . . land *on*. That's a point to be considered. But I have to consider that maybe they shut off the transmitters so *nobody* knows what's going on in here, in which case if I turn around we'll return home in disgrace and I might even get jailed. That's a point to think about. But you have to think that there's about ten billion dollars tied up in this program, which is ten years behind schedule anyway, and it's going to look very bad if I don't even *try* to make a Mars landing and anyway the whole thing may be a bluff. They may have no powers at all, even if they did make Mars vanish and take Williams away and put some kind of monster in his place. Yes, I'll take that into account too, when I make the decision."

There seems nothing more to say. All the variables have been charted in; now Blake, as commander of the mission, must make his choice. According to his chronometer he has two minutes left. He decides to take both of them. He closes his eyes and leans his head heavily upon his chest, an old childish habit the project psychiatrists were not interested in disabusing him of since it served a symbolic need. He thinks.

IV

In the action-adventure science fiction stories which he read as a boy, long before he became interested in the program, Blake remembers that human beings were often threatened by aliens with one kind of terrible fate or another . . . but always were able to get out of it because of some kind of cleverness, some aspect of the situation that the aliens, in their stupidity, had missed. The humans were cunning crafty beings, usually outnumbered, always with the odds against them, but they had won because essentially they were better and smarter than the aliens and that was all that counted.

Unfortunately this recollection cannot help him much now; the alien seems to have covered all the elements of the situation and if there is something that Blake has missed he cannot seem to bring it to mind. True, the alien's speech has been a little distorted and rambling, and toward the end its hostility had given a clue that it might for some reason or another be frightened . . . but in a minute and half or less (one minute now, Blake sees on his chronometer) it would not be easy to spot the alien's weak point and turn it against him.

Still, you had to have hope. The heroes in the action-adventure pulp stories always had that, even in the last seconds, and one way or the other, something had come to them at the last instant. The important thing was to keep on thinking and fighting all the way through. Blake squeezes his eyes even more tightly shut, balls his hands into fists, and concentrates. Something will happen. In the pulp stories it always did. Besides that, the program had never, in all of their training, programmed in even the possibility of something as embarrassing as this. He has faith in the program. It will not fail him now.

V

"Well?" the creature says, returning, settling easily in the space near Blake, "have you made your decision? Will you reverse?"

"You can't fool me," Blake says quietly. He checks his chronometer. "I have thirty seconds left." He opens his eyes, measuring the alien to see if there is any change in its aspect, but there is not. The hell with it. He closes his eyes again.

"That's quite true," the creature admits, "but we have to have a little warning as well. Right now we're scheduled to kill Williams, you and the man in the ship in, uh, twelve seconds. We have to have a little room for reversal. You now have eight seconds."

"All right," Blake says, his head between his knees. "That's all right, I've made my decision. I believe you're bluffing. Anyway, there's no way that you could go ahead and do it; if you do we'll send another ship with nuclears and blow up Mars. See? I've got a bigger threat, topping yours, and that's the secret."

"I'm sorry," the creature says. It pokes Blake so insistently in his ribs that at last he must open his eyes and confront it. Indeed there does seem to be genuine sorrow painted on the horrid, random features. "We're a gentle race. I regret this. I really do. But there must be an end to this, you see."

It goes away again and one second later, or maybe it is two or three (Blake is not counting), something dreadful happens inside him and there is a feeling of implosion; then he is descending even more rapidly than the ship itself and quite shortly there is nothing whatsoever.

Blake's last feeling is rage. That the Martians would make threats is understandable (they must protect their own options), but that they would have the *gall*——

VI

When he comes to he is in another kind of small room and two old scientists who he all at once remembers (along with everything else) are looking at him, and they are beaming and nodding and smiling and touching one another, and at last one says to the other (and Blake knows that he will remember this as long as he lives; he is that proud), "He'll do, he'll do, he'll do; he's your Captain, do you understand that? This is the kind of man we *need* to send to Mars."

SOME NOTES TOWARD A USEABLE PAST

FIRST NOTE: The universe is large, bigger than hell that is to say; and man is small, a bare specter in the endless, ravening reaches of the cosmos. But there is pride in man and dignity too, an acceptance of that essential *humanity* which is the core of his *individuality* and which also foreshadows the roots of his destiny. In all those bleak uncharted wastes reaching, perhaps, to the very lip of heaven itself, the unspeakable womb of our origin, men can voyage out and out (and out and out) until one is reminded of those splendid words of the prophet: *Hemeni o mahatov menachem heil* (in matter is form; in structure is content). So it is spoken and as the eyes of men reach toward the stars their hearts are truly in finite qualification with the older, the better, the more meaningful parts of themselves.

SECOND NOTE: They touched down on the planet at 1400 hours, making three large dents in the earth. The landing was a difficult one because—well, because the spaceship was out of commission and it was a *forced* landing. Smith and Jones, the two highly individuated cosmic scouts, came out cautiously into the cool strange air of the twilight and Smith tapped his helmet, inhaling the pure sweetness of an earth-type atmosphere.

"Wow, Jones," he exclaimed reverently, "it's the real thing: just like home. Crack your helmet."

And that is exactly what Jones did on the spot and he found the air fine but somehow disturbing because it all seemed *too* good, too peaceful, like in WEIRD TALES it was too much like a dream and his ferocious, barbarian, cunning earth-type impulses warned him and so he told Smith to watch out for the possibility of dangerous natives but Smith laughed and said that Jones was merely being the most corrupt kind of earthman: he could not apprehend the possibility of pure beauty. *Now that is too bad,* Smith thought and said, "Look, this is an oasis, we have found a true oasis Jones and everybody reveres us for what we have found or will as soon as we report the good tidings back to earth. Consider what we have! An earth-type planet, only the sixteenth ever discovered in this region of the Crab Legs Galaxy located in the diurnal west of the star cluster of the Diomedes turning left for direct exposition at the intergalactic directional point of origin."

"That's true," said Jones, "but how will we ever back out of here? Our ship is wrecked and we are stranded on this earth-type planet."

"You tell me. You're the technological part of this team, I'm only the poet."

"Well, then," Jones said, "being at least a man of practical nature I'll try to make some kind of repair," and they shook hands on it but before they could really get going on the repair and the consequently triumphant return to earth they were discovered and eaten alive by the strange monsters of Willingston 7 who thought that *they* were the only true inhabitants of the universe and who were too primitive to have yet evolved interstellar travel or the intricacies of an earth-type conscience. I forgot to say that they were killed with trans-fixed matter displacements. So Willingston 7 remains untapped to this day which is too bad as earthmen seek in the lonely wastes but then again the basic conflict as established between these two will certainly live as long as the ages can praise solid characterization and a solid, well-plotted story line.

THIRD NOTE:
THE TECH ROOM RATINGS FOR JULY

⅛ *Starmen Run,* by P. F. Glade   2.245
2 *The Violent Monster* by G. F. Pay   2.371
3 *The Chessmen of Socrates* by G. P. Plade   3.4
4 *Moon Yarn* (IV) by Glade Paf   3.6193
5 *Pathetic Fallacy* by Paf G. Pade   3.6194

A tight one this month! But those yarns all came in around where they should be! Incidentally, *Moon Yarn* will be having a sequel just as soon as "Tech" Paf finishes up at the factory and can give the new yarn his fullest attention! I think you'll like this one; it's about metal, chromium, tensors, ultrasonic punishment and the Hieronymous Chain and there isn't a woman in it!

FOURTH NOTE: The time machine took Martin back to the twelfth century A.D. where he slew his father's great-ancestor to say nothing of uprooting the earth on which Carthage would have stood, then came back to his own time, 2012 A.D., expecting not to be there but he was. "Oh ho!" Martin screamed, "time is not continuous but an alternate series of parallel conceptions which diverge at the moment of consequentiality to produce a series of parallel lives. Therefore, none of us is truly of anything but himself." And was much gladdened by this insight but, nothing if not energetic, went back to 44 B.C. and encountered the Emperor Nero in his private gardens, fucking a slave chastely under filaments of garments which concealed their genitals to say nothing of the (female) slave's large, ponderous, delicious breasts. "What the hell are *you* doing here?" Nero queried in familiar fashion and taking note of Menachem's peculiar garb and the peculiar aspect of the time machine in the doughty traveler's left hand, added, "It's 44 B.C.; we don't want any twenty-first-century interlopers and besides, time's an individual, not a constant and I never heard of this before, therefore it never happened." Nero vaulted from the slave, making sure that her body was still covered, and moved toward Martin menacingly with a sword in his right hand; Martin turned on the power of his time machine in an attempt to make a hasty exit but found that something had happened to the solidifier-condensing coils which, instead of passing smoothly through the dimensional trap, quasi-lasered through an infinitesimal warp and contrived to explode negatively through the carborundum. This meant that he was trapped and had to fight the menacing Roman potentate! Seizing his own weapon from a rear pants-pocket—it was a German luger he had captured during the invasion of Normandy sixty-eight years ago when he had been a very young man—he pulled the trigger and blew a neat hole in the tyrant's chest which resulted in the depraved idiot falling through himself and deep into the twenty-first century where he rose to a position of power and ascendancy and even became an important producer in the realie-feelies. Martin, meanwhile, stayed in Rome with the slave—her name was Roxanne and he discovered to his delight that she had no nipples—and took over the chores and duties of the Emperor Nero. No one knew the difference because Martin was a just and wise despot who had a career in violin-adjustment somewhere in his past so when the time came for him to fulfill the myth he did it very nicely although for the first time. Time, therefore, proved to be a closed cycle: he and Nero had merely swapped roles. This proved that the universe was totally orderly and that there is no madness in it.

Of course.

FIFTH NOTE: In the bleakest reaches of the universe, on the tenth-rate abandoned planet of a forgotten star, a grave is laid. The grave has a headstone which says HERE WAS A MAN. The only other symbols on this planet are a collection of pulp magazines and several still photographs of naked women in questionable poses, all of this circled around the grave itself and hammered in with knives. The story behind this is very unique and very interesting, involving events which occurred in the ninety-third century, long after Man had spread out to the seedling stars far from Mother Earth. The name of this man who lies in the grave is not really important since he is all men but anyway it is Sam Ross and he will never be dead, never dead so long as a life itself exists and a condition of destiny. What he did was to journey to the various planets in the huge solar system, singing and playing his guitar for sustenance, a wanderer of the interstellar pathways. His only comfort was his deck of pornographic playing cards which he kept in his guitar case and he would sit in the cafes of the various planets, looking at them one by one and thinking his harmless psychopath's thoughts until one night, the interstellar police team came in to patrol the bar and arrested him on charges of gross and comic indecency.

His attempts to resist the arrest resulted in a bullet in his spine which first paralyzed and then lingeringly killed him. He spent his last days in the Deneb XVLL asylum, surrounded by nuns, drinking huge carafes of space cocktails which were held for him, and looking over his cards which were suspended by a wire above his bed. When he died—they all happened to be Catholic but held nothing against a libertarian stranger—they agreed that it was tragic and that his death was more than a simple, muted anonymity of extinction because he had been at all times extremely courteous to them.

What they did in commemoration, then, was to look for a deserted planet for him and there he was buried just the way that he would have always wanted—with a headstone saying those words I told you about earlier, with the cards around him and also some pulp magazines since the occupants of this culture read a great deal of cheap escape literature. Later on his story became a ballad and was popularized. So Ross lies today, sentimentalized, a culture hero, no one knowing or understanding that he was a simple, perverse planetary scout. And if they understood this they would not care. This is part of the eternal wonder of the universe as man forages out to discover in the womb of time the nascence of his individuality in the motherhood of possibility.

SIXTH NOTE: Smith journeyed to an alternate time-track. It was called earth-prime or Llanavogel and he became an adventure amidst the fairies, elves, gremlins, and magicians of that wonderful plane. He was on a search for the Holy Grail which would take him back to his own life but you would hardly know that he cared from all the marvelous experiences he had and all the things he learned while fighting his enemy Jom, a bearded giant who lived on a mountain top with eighteen imprisoned virgins and made things very difficult for the fairies and gremlins before Smith showed them the way. He was seven feet tall in Llanavogel with large feet and a knack for pouring out ballads in a tenor voice which made the elves in particular tremble and dream wistfully of an alternate earth in which they too might have the comforts, the necessities and the security of an orderly existence for a change: a civil service job.

SEVENTH NOTE:
Dear Tech Room: I liked all the yarns and it was awful close but probably that one about the Emperor Nero was the most satisfying because of the sense of wonder. Where is that sense of wonder? We don't seem to have it any more and things just aren't quite the same. I liked the one about the fairies too. What can I say? I loved them all. At least someone is out there trying to make me happy. My address is right here under my signature and I'd like other fen to gafia and correspond with me; I have a lot of old magazines and new ideas

(ha, ha!) and Ghod knows if there are any "Tek" fen out there I'd like to talk to them about "Tek" or chess. So, won't someone please come on and get in touch with me; here I am, right where I always always been, please write me, I'd like to hear from any of you others, just please write to me, someone please write because if I don't hear from someone else in my predicament I swear I'm crazy to write but

EIGHTH NOTE: So and so lived in this year and the society was oriented at that time to such and such and so and so wasn't happy with such and such so he decided to do this and that which put him in revolt against such and such but eventually after a long struggle of this and that so and so happened and they took paperback rights.

Darkness

by André Carneiro,
translated by Leo L. Barrow

André Carneiro is a determinedly handsome man; a poet, film maker, novelist, photographer and critic—who also writes a very good short story in his spare time. His Introdução ao Estudo da "Science-Fiction," *published by a state commission of literature in São Paulo, is the best introduction to the study of science fiction yet written, though unhappily it is not yet translated into English.* "Darkness" *is not only a good story, but it provides a fascinating peep into the totally different world of Brazilian science fiction.*

Waldas accepted the reality of the phenomenon a little later than the others. Only on the second day, when everybody was commenting on the growing darkness and the dimming of the lights did he admit it was true. An old lady was shouting that the world was coming to an end. People gathered in little groups, most of them offering metaphysical explanations, mixed with the scientific commentaries from the papers. He went to work as usual. Even the boss, always distant, was at the window, talking intimately. Most of the employees didn't show up. The huge room full of desks, mostly unmanned, defined the degree of importance of the event.

Those people who always watched the weather were the first to notice. The sunlight seemed a little weaker, houses and objects were surrounded by growing shadows. At first they thought it was an optical illusion, but that night even the electric lights were weaker. Women noticed that liquids didn't reach the boiling point and food remained hard and uncooked. Authoritative opinions were cited, opinions heard on the radio. They were vague and contradictory. Nervous people were provoking panic and the train and bus stations were filled with those leaving town. No one knew where they were going. The news programs said that the phenomenon was universal, but Waldas doubted this.

The latest telegrams, however, were affirmative; the shadow was growing rapidly. Someone struck a match, and the tests began. Everyone made these tests: they would light a lighter or turn on a flashlight in a dark corner, noticing the weaker illumination. Lights didn't brighten the room as before. It couldn't be a universal visual effect. It was possible to run one's fingers through fire without burning them. Many were frightened, but Waldas wasn't one of them. He went home at four o'clock; the lights were on. They gave off very little light— seemed like reddish balls, danger signals. At the lunch counter where he always ate, he got them to serve him cold sandwiches. There was only the owner and one waitress, who left afterwards, walking slowly through the shadows.

Waldas got to his apartment without difficulty. He was used to coming home late without turning on the hall lights. The elevator wasn't working so he walked up the stairs to the third floor. His radio emitted only strange sounds, perhaps voices, perhaps static. Opening the window, he confronted the thousands of reddish glows, lights of the huge buildings whose silhouettes stood out dimly against the starless sky. He went to the refrigerator and drank a glass of milk; the motor wasn't working. The same thing would happen to the water pump. He put the plug in the bath tub and filled it. Locating his flashlight, he went through his small apartment, anxious to find his belongings with the weak light. He left the cans of powdered milk, cereal, some crackers and a box of chocolates on the kitchen table and closed the window, turned out the lights and lay down on the bed. A cold shiver ran through his body as he realized the reality of the danger.

He slept fitfully, dreamed confused and disagreeable dreams. A child was crying in the next apartment, asking its mother to turn on the lights. He woke up startled. With the flashlight pressed against his watch, he saw that it was eight o'clock in the morning. He opened the windows. The darkness was almost complete. You could see the sun in the east, red and round, as if it were behind a thick smoked glass. In the street dim shapes of people passed by like silhouettes. With great difficulty Waldas managed to wash his face; he went to the kitchen and ate rice crispies with powdered milk. Force of habit made him think about his job. He realized that he didn't have any place to go, and he remembered the terror he felt as a child when they locked him in a closet. There wasn't enough air, and the darkness oppressed him. He went to the window and took a deep breath. The red disk of the sun hung in the dark background of the sky. Waldas couldn't coordinate his thoughts; the darkness kept making him feel like running for help. He clenched his fists, repeated to himself, "I have to keep calm, defend my life until everything returns to normal."

He had a married sister who lived three blocks away.

The need to communicate with someone made him decide to go there, to help her family in any way he could. In the darkness of the hallway, he used the wall as a guide. On one side of the hall, a man's anxious voice asked, "Who is it out there?"

"It's me, Waldas from apartment 312," he answered.

He knew who it was, a graying man who had a wife and two children.

"Please," the man asked, "tell my wife that the darkness is going to end; she has been crying since yesterday and the kids are scared." Waldas approached slowly. The woman must be standing next to her husband, sobbing quietly. He tried to smile even though they couldn't see him.

"Don't worry, ma'am, it's pretty dark but you can still see the sun out there. There is no danger; it won't last long."

"Do you hear," the man seconded, "it's only the darkness, no one is going to suffer, you need to stay calm for the children's sake." By the sounds Waldas sensed that they were all clinging to one another. He remained silent for a few moments and then started to go away. "I have to go now, if you need anything. . . ." The man said goodbye, encouraging his wife. "No, thank you very much. This won't last long."

On the steps he couldn't see a thing. He heard bits of conversation coming from the doors of the different apartment buildings. The lack of light made people speak more loudly, or their voices sounded more clearly against the general silence.

He reached the street. The sun was high, but it hardly gave off any light, perhaps less than that of the waning moon. From time to time men went by, alone or in groups. They spoke in loud voices, some still joked when they stumbled in the depressions in the street. Waldas started to walk slowly, mentally visualizing the road to his sister's house. The reddish outline that silhouetted the buildings was diminishing. With his arms extended he could hardly see his fingers. He walked slowly, amazed by those who passed him hurriedly. The whining of a small dog came from some balcony. There was crying in the distance, confused shouts, people calling. Someone was walking and praying.

Waldas kept close to the wall so they wouldn't run into him. He must have been halfway there. He stopped to catch his breath. His chest was heaving, searching for air; his muscles tense and tired. His only point of reference was a blotch of disappearing sun. For a moment he imagined that the others could see more than he. But now shouts and cries were rising everywhere. Waldas turned around. The pulsating red disk had disappeared. The blackness was absolute. Without the silhouette of the building, he felt lost. It was impossible to continue. He would try to return to the apartment. Feeling the wall, identifying some doors and shop windows, he started back, his feet dragging on the pavement. He was sweating and trembling, all his senses concentrating on the way back.

Turning the corner, he heard the unintelligible words of a man coming in his direction. Perhaps drunk, and shouting loudly, he forcibly grabbed Waldas who, trying to pry himself loose, pleaded for calmness. The man shouted all the louder, meaningless things. Desperate, Waldas grabbed him by the throat, pushed him backwards. The man fell and began to moan. His hands extended in front of him in defense, Waldas walked on a bit. Behind him the drunk was crying and moaning in pain. A loose window was rattling, and sounds previously muffled by the noise of radios and cars were coming from the houses and apartments. In the darkness, his hands groping, recognizing different landmarks and doors of iron bars, walls of residences and their big gates, he fell on the first steps of the stairway. Someone shouted:

"Who is it out there?"

"It's me, Waldas, from the third floor."

"Were you outside? Can you see anything?"

"No, you can't see a thing anywhere."

There was a silence, and he slowly went on up the stairs. Moving carefully he opened the door and lay down on the bed.

It was a short and anxious respite. He couldn't relax his muscles, couldn't think calmly. He dragged himself out to the kitchen, managed to open his watch with a knife. He felt the hands. It was 11 o'clock, or noon, more or less. He dissolved powdered milk in a cup of water and drank it. There was a knocking on his door; his heart beat more rapidly. It was his neighbor, asking for some water for the children. Waldas told him about the full bathtub, and went with him to get his wife and children. His prudence had paid off. They held hands and the human chain slid along the hall, the kids calmer, even his wife who, no longer crying, kept repeating, "Thank you, thank you very much." Waldas took them to the kitchen, made them sit down, the children clinging to their mother. He felt the cupboard, broke a glass, then found an aluminum pan which he filled from the bathtub and took to the table. He surrendered cups of water to the fingers that groped for them. He couldn't keep them level without seeing and the water spilled onto his hands. As they drank, he wondered if he should offer them something to eat. The boy thanked him and said that he was hungry. Waldas picked up the big can of powdered milk and began to prepare it carefully. While he made the slow gestures of opening the can, counting the spoonfuls and mixing them with water, he spoke in a loud voice. They encouraged him, telling him to be careful and praising his ability. Waldas took more than an hour to make and ration out the milk and the effort, the certainty that he was being useful, did him good.

One of the boys laughed at something funny. For the first time since the darkness had set in, Waldas felt optimistic, that everything would turn out all right. They spent an endless time after that in his apartment, trying to talk. They would lean on the window sill, searching for some distant light, seeing it at times, all enthused, only to discover the deceit that they wouldn't admit. Waldas had become the leader of that family; he fed them and led them through the small world of four rooms which he knew with his eyes closed. They left at nine or ten that night, holding hands, Waldas accompanied them, helped put the children to bed. In the streets desperate fathers were shouting, asking for food. Waldas had closed the windows so he couldn't hear them. What he had would be enough to feed the five of them for one or two more days. Waldas stayed with them, next to the children's room. They lay there talking, their words like links of presence and company. They finally went to sleep, heads under their pillows like shipwrecked sailors clinging to logs, listening to pleas for help that they couldn't possibly answer. They slept, dreaming about the breaking of a new day, a blue sky, the sun flooding their rooms, their eyes, hungry from fasting, avidly feeding on the colors. It wasn't that way.

The hands of Waldas' watch indicated it was more or less eight o'clock. The others began to stir and holding hands they filed back to his kitchen where they ate their frugal meal of cereal and milk. The children bumped into the furniture, got lost in the small living room; their mother scolded them anxiously. Once settled in the armchairs they didn't know what to do with themselves.

They went back over the causes of the phenomenon, inventing reasons and hypotheses that transcended science. Waldas commented imprudently that the situation could continue forever. The woman began to cry; it was difficult to calm her. The kids asked questions which were impossible to answer. Suddenly Waldas felt anxious to do something; he got up, was going out to investigate. They protested; it would be dangerous and useless. He had to reassure them that he wouldn't go more than sixty feet from the building, just to the corner, that he wouldn't cross the street, etc.

Outside, he leaned against the wall, listening. A cold wind whistled through the wires, dragged pieces of paper along with a soft noise. There was howling in the distance, becoming more intense from time to time, and voices, many unintelligible voices. He stood still, tense and waiting, and then walked a few yards. Only his ears could capture the pulsations of the city drowned in darkness. With his eyes opened or closed it was the same black well, without beginning or end. It was terrible to remain there, quietly waiting for nothing.

The ghosts of his youth surrounded Waldas, and he returned to his building almost running, scratching his hands along the wall, stumbling on the stairs, while frightened voices shouted: "Who is it out there? Who is out there?" He answered, out of breath, taking the stairs two at a time until he reached his friends who were bumping into each other trying to find him, afraid that he had been hurt, asking him what had happened. He laughed, confessing that he had become frightened.

Enclosed for the rest of the day they worked and talked a lot, describing what they were doing. The chain of words which linked them together eventually broke. None of them could know, but they all raised their heads at the same time, listening, breathing heavily, waiting for a miracle which wasn't materializing.

Rationed and divided, the box of chocolates had come to an end. There was still cereal and powdered milk. If the light didn't return soon it would be cruel to predict the consequences. The hours passed. Lying down again, eyes closed, fighting to go to sleep, they waited for the morning with its beams of light on the window. But they woke as before, their eyes useless, the flames extinguished, the stoves cold and their food running out. Waldas divided the last of the cereal and milk. They became uneasy. The building had ten floors; Waldas thought he ought to go to the top floor to look into the distance.

He went out and started up. Questions came from the apartments. "Who is out there? Who is it going up the stairs?" On the sixth floor one voice assured him, "You can go up there if you like, but you are wasting your time. I was just there with two others. You can't see a thing, anywhere." Waldas ventured, "My food has run out, I have a couple and two children with me. Could you help me?" The voices answered, "Our supply will only last until tomorrow. We can't do a thing. . . ." Waldas decided to go back down. Could he tell his friends the truth?

"I didn't go all the way up. I found someone who had been there a short time ago. He said you could see something, very distant, he couldn't explain what it was." The couple and their children were filled with hope when he suggested the only idea that might work. He would go out again, and break into a grocery store about a hundred yards away.

Armed with a crowbar from his toolbox, he was leaving his shelter to steal food. It was frightening to think what he might encounter. The darkness had erased all distinctions. Waldas walked next to the wall, his mind reconstructing the details of this stretch, his hands investigating every indentation. Inch by inch his fingers followed the outline of the building until they came to the corrugated iron door. He couldn't be wrong.

It was the only commercial establishment on the block. He bent over to find the lock. His hands didn't encounter resistance. The door was only half closed. He stooped over and entered without making a sound. The shelves on the right would have food and sweets. He collided with the counter, cursed and remained motionless, muscles tensed, waiting. He climbed over the counter and began to reach out with his hand; it touched the board and he started running it along the shelf. There was nothing; of course, they sold it before the total darkness. He raised his arm, searching more rapidly. Nothing, not a single object. He started climbing without worrying about the noise, his fingers dry from the accumulated dust. He climbed down carelessly, his body bent forward, his hands moving frantically in every direction, foolishly getting scratched and cut against the wall as if they were competing for cans and merchandise that didn't exist. Many times Waldas returned to the same point where he had begun his search. There was nothing, not in any corner. He stopped, still anxious to begin again but knowing that it wouldn't do any good. For those with no reserve food it was obvious that the grocery stores had been the only solution.

Waldas sat down on an empty box and tears filled his eyes. What could he do? Return with his failure, renew the search in other more distant stores, whose exact locations he didn't know?

He took up the crowbar again and with short careful steps he started back home in search of his invisible friends. Suddenly he stopped, his hands searching for a familiar landmark. Step by step he advanced a few more yards, discovering doors and walls until he came to an unknown corner. He had to go back to the store and start again from there. He went back the way he had come, scratching his fingers in the darkness, feeling for a corrugated door which wasn't appearing. He was lost. He sat down on the sidewalk, his temples throbbing. He struggled up like a drowning man and shouted, "Please, I'm lost, I need to know the name of this street." He repeated it time after time, each time more loudly, but no one answered him. The more silence he felt around him, the more he implored, asking them to help him for pity's sake. And why should they? He himself, from his own window, had heard the cries of the lost asking for help, their desperate voices causing one to fear the madness of an assault. Waldas started off without any direction, shouting for help, explaining that four persons depended on him. No longer feeling the walls, he walked hurriedly in circles, like a drunk, begging for information and food. "I'm Waldas, I live at number 215, please help me."

There were noises in the darkness; impossible for them not to hear him. He cried and pleaded without the least shame, the black pall reducing him to a helpless child. The darkness stifled him, entering through his pores, changing his thoughts. Waldas stopped pleading. He bellowed curses at his fellowmen, calling them evil names, asking them why they didn't answer. His helplessness turned into hate and he grasped the crowbar, ready to obtain food by violence. He came across others begging for food like himself. Waldas advanced, brandishing his crowbar, until he collided with someone, grabbing him and holding him tightly. The man shouted and Waldas, without letting him go, demanded that he tell him where they were and how they could get some food. The other seemed old and broke into fearful sobs. Waldas relaxed the pressure, released him. He threw the weapon into the street, and sat down on the sidewalk listening to the small sounds, the wind rattling windows in the abandoned apartments. Different noises emerged from several directions, deep, rasping and sharp sounds, from animals, men perhaps, trapped or famished. A light rhythmic beating of footsteps was approaching. He yelled for help and remained listening. A man's voice, some distance away, answered him. "Wait, I'll come and help you."

The man carried a heavy sack and was panting from the effort. He asked Waldas to help him by holding one end, he would go in front. Waldas sensed something inexplicable. He could hardly follow the man as he turned the corners with assurance. A doubt passed through his mind. Perhaps his companion could see a little, the light was coming back for the others. He asked him, "You walk with such assurance, you can't by any chance see a little?" The man took a while to answer. "No, I can see absolutely nothing. I am completely blind."

Waldas stammered, "Before this . . . too?" "Yes, blind from birth, we are going to the Institute for the Blind, where I live."

Vasco, the blind man, told him that they had helped lost persons and had taken in a few; but their stock of food was small and they couldn't take anybody else in. The darkness continued without any sign of ending. Thousands of people might die from starvation and nothing could be done. Waldas felt like a child that adults had saved from danger. At the Institute they gave him a glass of milk and some toast. In his memory, however, the image of his friends was growing, their hearts jumping at every sound, going hungry, waiting for his return. He spoke to Vasco. They deliberated. The apartment building was large, all the others living there also deserved help, something quite impracticable. Waldas remembered the children; he asked them to show him the way or he would go alone. He got up to leave, stumbled over something, falling. Vasco remembered that there was a bathtub full of water, and water was one thing they needed. They brought two big plastic containers and Vasco led Waldas to the street. They tied a little cord around both their waists.

Vasco, who knew the neighborhood, walked as fast as possible, choosing the best route, calling out the name of the streets, changing course when they heard suspicious sounds or mad ravings. Vasco stopped and said softly, "It must be here." Waldas advanced a few steps, recognized the door latch. Vasco whispered for him to take off his shoes; they would go in without making any noise. After tying their shoes to the cord, they entered with Waldas in front, going up the stairs two at a time. They bumped into things along the way and heard unintelligible voices from behind the doors.

Reaching the third floor they went to his neighbor's apartment, knocked softly and then more loudly. No one answered. They went to Waldas' apartment. "It's me, Waldas, let me in." His neighbor uttered an exclamation like someone who didn't believe it and opened the door, extending his arm for his friend to grasp. "It's me all right, how is everybody? I brought a friend who saved me and knows the way."

In the bathroom they filled the two plastic containers with water and Vasco tied them to the backs of the two men with strips of cloth. He also helped to identify some useful things they could take. They took off their shoes and in single file, holding hands, started for the stairs. They went hurriedly; they would inevitably be heard. On the main floor, next to the door, a voice inquired: "Who are you?" No one answered and Vasco pulled them all out into the street. In single file they gained distance; it would be difficult to follow them.

It took more time to return because of the children, and the stops they made to listen to nearby noises. They arrived at the Institute exhausted, with the temporary feeling of relief of soldiers after winning a battle.

Vasco served them oatmeal and milk and went to talk to his companions about what they would do to survive if the darkness continued. Another blind man fixed them a place to sleep, which came easily since they hadn't slept for a long time. Hours later Vasco came to awaken them, saying that they had decided to leave the Institute and take refuge on the Model Farm that the Institute owned a few miles outside the city. Their supplies here wouldn't last long and there was no way to replenish them without danger.

Although the way was longer, they planned to follow the railroad tracks which ran a few blocks from the Institute.

The meeting room was a big place; the murmur of voices forming a steady bubbling. Vasco must have been older or had some authority over the others. He told them that a completely realistic appraisal of their situation was indispensable if they hoped to survive. He spoke to his blind companions first, affirming that the darkness which afflicted the others was nothing new to them. They had taken eleven persons into the Institute. With the twelve blind people who already lived there they were twenty-three in all. The food that could be eaten would last them only six or seven days. It would be risky to wait and hope that everything would return to normal in that time, to say nothing of the chance of being assaulted or robbed by lost and hungry people. Normally there were ten people on the Model Farm. They raised several crops, had food in stock for commerce, and had a great quantity of drinking water; with careful use and rationing, this could guarantee their existence for a long time. Cooperation and obedience to all decisions were imperative. They would leave the Asylum in silence, without answering any call.

The blind men finished distributing the full sacks, suitcases, and boxes for the trip. Waldas, standing still and useless, thought about how many times he had passed these men with their dark glasses, their white canes, their heads fixed, always facing forward. True, he always gave them a brief thought of pity. Ah, if they had only known then how one day they would become the magic protectors, capable of saving other beings, beings made of flesh, muscles, thoughts, and with useless eyes, the same as theirs.

Like mountain climbers, they formed four groups linked by a cord. The most doubtful part would be getting through all the streets until they came to the railroad tracks. They asked for complete silence. The anonymous cries that they heard in the darkness were transformed into small obstacles that had to be avoided. The column, loaded with food, steered clear of those who begged for a piece of bread to sustain their lives. The wind brought all sorts of cries as the file of ship-wrecked persons slipped through the darkness in this strangest of flights, with blind men at the helm. When their shoes touched the endless steel of the railroad tracks, the tension eased. Their progress became painful; they had to measure their steps to avoid stumbling on the crossties. Time passed; to Waldas it seemed like many hours. Suddenly they stopped. There was a train or some box cars ahead of them. Vasco went to investigate, alone. A whisper passed from mouth to mouth made them renew their journey. They had to go around the box cars. The sound was coming from one of them. They went by the cars with their hearts pounding, their ears almost touching the wooden doors. A man or an animal, locked in, dying. . . . Everything was being left behind, their tired feet moved on an endless belt. In this nightmarish tunnel, Waldas felt like a condemned man wearing his hood of death. The darkness brought all life—the concentration of all his senses—to his shoes which were trudging along over the crushed rocks, between the parallel limits of the tracks.

Waldas was surprised when the cord tied to his waist pulled him into a dirt road. Without knowing how, he realized that they were in the country. How did the blind men find the exact spot? Perhaps through their sense of smell, the perfume of the trees like ripe limes. He breathed deeply. He knew that odor; it came from eucalyptus trees. He could imagine them in straight lines, on each side of the road. The column stopped; they had arrived at their unseen destination. For the time being the urgent fight to keep from dying of hunger had ended.

The blind men brought them a cold soup that seemed to contain oatmeal and honey. Vasco directed the difficult maneuver to keep them from colliding. They had shelter and food. And the others who remained in the city, the sick in the hospitals, the small children . . . ? No one could or wanted to know.

While Waldas had been moving about in his own neighborhood and apartment he remembered the form of the buildings, the furniture and objects. In his new surroundings, his inexperienced fingers touching here and there could not give him any base for an idea about their relationships.

There were carrots, tomatoes and greens in the gardens, some ripe fruit in the orchard. They should distribute equal rations, a little more for the children. There was speculation as to whether the green vegetables would wilt after so many days without sunshine. The man in charge of the small hen house told how he had fed the hens every day since the sun stopped shining, but they hadn't laid since then.

With the tension of immediate danger relaxed, Waldas felt the reactions that the darkness provoked. His words no longer followed a direct line to the eyes of the person he was addressing; there was no lifting of the eyebrows nor nodding of the head to give emphasis to his arguments. To speak without seeing anyone always raised the doubt as to whether the other was paying attention. In the muscles of his face, now more inert, he sensed the lack of expression which characterizes blind persons. Conversations lost their naturalness and when they didn't respond immediately it seemed like they hadn't listened.

Waldas was learning. If he had discovered a hole or irregularity the day before, his hands would now recognize the already touched surface. But when his hands and feet groped over a new way, only sounds could guide him, or he had to call for help from the experienced sons of darkness.

They were in their sixth day without light. The temperature had dropped but that was normal for this time of year. Therefore, the sun must be warming the atmosphere, one way or another. The phenomenon could not have been of a cosmic order. Someone quoted prophecies from the Bible, the end of the world. Another suggested a mysterious invasion by another planet. Vasco said that, even without consulting his watch, he could still perceive a subtle difference between night and day. Waldas figured that it was just a habit, the organism was accustomed to the successive periods of work and rest. From time to time someone would climb a ladder placed outside, next to the door and turn his head in all four directions. Sometimes they would shout enthusiastically as they perceived vague spots of light. Everyone would get all excited, walking towards the door with their arms extended, some of them in the wrong direction, running into walls and asking, "Where are you? Did you see something? What was it? What was it?" This was repeated so often that the excitement when "someone glimpsed something" wore off. After many tests and discussions, the darkness remained complete.

The rescued persons showed a perceptible note of bitterness in the things they said. When they tried happy phrases, the shadows eliminated the smile from their lips, the vivacity from their eyes. The blind men had a different inflection in their voices. In Vasco you could sense more clearly the manner of one who acts with assurance and moves with ease. Those same men with white canes and dark glasses who used to ask humbly which bus was coming, or who drew away slowly before the pitying eyes of the passersby, now were rapid, efficient, miraculous with their manual ability. They answered questions and led their charges by the arm with the solicitude and satisfaction of the borrowed charity they used to receive. They were patient and tolerant of errors and misconceptions. Their private misfortune had become everyone's. There was little time for relaxation, but after the last meal the blind people sang, accompanied by two guitars. Waldas noted a natural enthusiasm and even a happiness that the situation did not call for.

Waldas noticed that the children got along better than the adults. His neighbor's two sons were afraid at first, but the constant proximity of their companions encouraged them to go out on explorations which became difficult to control. They were scolded and even paddled, something which provoked the intervention of conciliatory voices.

Finally, much to Waldas' surprise, they achieved a routine for the trips to the bathroom, washing up and bathing at the edge of the river, the important hours for the meals which were becoming more and more insipid—wilted greens, cucumbers, tomatoes, papaya, oatmeal, milk, honey, not always identifiable by their sense of taste. No catastrophe, no human event would have been more extraordinary or more dangerous than this one. If the blackness which enveloped them brought physical discomfort and problems, it was nothing compared to the thoughts that the impenetrable wall distilled into their minds. Might it be the end of the world that people had predicted since time immemorial? They had to put aside this sinister prospect and keep on taking care of the common essential things such as feeding and clothing the body. Many prayed aloud, asking for a miracle.

Without sight to distract one's mind, it was difficult to endure the idle moments. Dedication to work was exaggerated. Would the world return to normal or would they all die slowly? This constituted a crushing dilemma, weightier than the darkness suffocating them. Vasco seemed worried about the future, but much less so than Waldas. Placed in the same experience, they found it impossible to approach it from the same point of view.

They were already in their sixteenth day when Vasco called Waldas aside. He told him that even the reserves of oatmeal, powdered milk, and canned goods that they had saved were almost gone. And their nervous condition was becoming aggravated; it wouldn't be prudent to warn the others. Arguments came up over the least thing and were prolonged without reason. Most of them were on the edge of nervous collapse.

During the early hours of the eighteenth day they were awakened by shouts of joy and animation. One of the refugees who hadn't been able to go to sleep had felt a difference in the atmosphere. He climbed the ladder outside the house.

There was a pale red ball on the horizon.

Everyone came out at once, pushing and falling, and remained there in a contagious euphoria waiting for the light to increase. Vasco asked if they really did see something, if it wasn't just another false alarm. Someone remembered to strike a match and after a few attempts the flame appeared. It was fragile and without heat, but visible to the eyes of those who looked upon it as a rare miracle.

The light increased slowly, in the way that it had disappeared.

This was a perfect day with unexpected and total joys that worked like some powerful stimulant. Their hearts seemed warmed, full of good will. Their eyes were reborn like innocent and blameless children. They wanted their meals outside and Vasco agreed since the normal days seemed about to return. The sun took its expected course across the sky. At four o'clock in the afternoon you could already distinguish a person's shadow at a distance of four yards. After the sun went down, the complete darkness returned. They built a fire in the yard, but the flames were weak and translucent and consumed very little of the wood. It went out frequently and the refugees would light it again with pieces of paper and blow on it, conserving the pallid fountain of light and warmth, symbol of future life. At midnight it was difficult to convince them that they should go to bed. Only the children slept. Those who had matches struck one from time to time and chuckled to themselves as if they had found the philosopher's stone of happiness.

At four thirty in the morning they were up and outside. No dawn in the history of the world was ever awaited like this one. It wasn't the beauty of the colors, the poetry of the horizon coming into view amid the clouds, the mountains, the trees and the butterflies. As in the age of fire when man shielded his fire and worshiped it, the divinity of light was awaited by the refugees as a condemned man awaits the official with the commutation of his sentence. The sun was brighter; unaccustomed eyes were closed; the blind men extended the palms of their hands towards the rays, turned them over to feel the heat on both sides. Different faces came forth, with voices you could recognize, and they laughed and embraced each other. Their loneliness and their differences disappeared in that boundless dawn. The blind people were kissed and hugged, carried in triumph. Men cried, and this made their eyes, unaccustomed to the light, turn even redder. About noon the flames became normal and for the first time in three weeks they had a hot cooked meal. Little work was done for the rest of the day. Flooded with light, they absorbed the scenes about them, walking through the places where they had dragged themselves in the darkness.

And the city? What had happened to the people there? This was a terribly sobering thought and those who had relatives ceased to smile. How many had died or suffered extreme hardships? Waldas suggested that he should investigate the situation the next day. Others volunteered, and it was decided that three should go.

Waldas spent a bad night. The impact of all those days was beginning to have its effect. His hands trembled, he was afraid, of what he didn't know. Return to the city, renew his life . . . go to the office, his friends, women . . . . The values he had once held remained subverted and buried in the darkness. It was a different man who was tossing and squirming in an improvised bed without being able to sleep. A square of light coming from a small lamp in the hallway was flickering through the transom, a sign that all was well. His memory brought him rapid fragments, a dog howling, a man moaning on the sidewalk, his hand brandishing the crowbar, Vasco leading him through the streets, his boss talking in front of the window. . . . Bits of his childhood were mixed in as sleep slowly took over. He tossed and turned, his brow wrinkled in a struggle with his dreams.

The three refugees left as the sun was coming up, walking along the road that would lead them to the railroad tracks. One of them was middle aged, married and without children. His wife had stayed behind in the country house. The other must have been the same age as Waldas. His brothers and sisters lived in another part of the city. He had been saved by a blind man and had not been able to return to his home.

They went around a curve and the city came into view. After the first bridges, the tracks began to cross streets. Waldas and his companions went down one of them. The first two blocks seemed very calm, with a few persons moving about, perhaps a bit more slowly. On the next corner they saw a group of people carrying a dead man, covered with a rough cloth, to a truck. The people were crying. A brown army truck went by, its loudspeaker announcing an official government bulletin. Martial law had been declared. Anyone invading another's property would be shot. The government had requisitioned all food supplies and was distributing them to the needy. Any vehicle could be commandeered if necessary. It advised that the police be immediately notified of any buildings with bad odors so that they could investigate the existence of corpses. The dead would be buried in common graves.

Waldas didn't want to return to his own apartment building. He remembered the voices calling through the half opened doors and he, in his stocking feet, slipping away, leaving them to their fate. He would have to telephone the authorities if there was a bad odor. He had already seen enough; he didn't want to stay there. His young companion had talked to an officer and had decided to look for his family immediately. Waldas asked if the telephones were working and learned that some of the automatic circuits were. He dialed his brother-in-law's number and after a short while there was an answer. They were very weak but alive. There had been four deaths in the apartment house. Waldas told them briefly how he had been saved and asked if they needed anything. No, they didn't, there was some food, and they were a lot better off than most.

Everyone was talking to strangers, telling all kinds of stories. The children and the sick were the ones who had suffered most. They told of cases of death in heartbreaking circumstances. The public services were reorganizing, with the help of the army, to take care of those in need, bury the dead and get everything going again. Waldas and his middle-aged companion didn't want to hear any more. They felt weak, weak with a certain mental fatigue from hearing and seeing incredible things in which the absurd wasn't just a theory but what really had happened, defying all logic and scientific laws.

The two men were returning along the still empty tracks, walking slowly under a pleasantly clouded sky. A gentle breeze rustled the leaves of the green trees and birds flitted among their branches. How had they been able to survive in the darkness? Waldas thought about all this as his aching legs carried him along. His scientific certainties were no longer valid. At that very moment men still shaken by the phenomenon were working electronic computers making precise measurements and observations, religious men in their temples explaining the will of God, politicians dictating decrees, mothers mourning the dead that had remained in the darkness.

Two exhausted men walked along the ties. They brought news, perhaps better than could be expected. Mankind had resisted. By eating anything resembling food, by drinking any kind of liquid, people had lived for three weeks in the world of the blind. Waldas and his companion were returning sad and weakened, but with the secret and muffled joy of being alive. More important than rational speculations was the mysterious miracle of blood running through one's veins, the pleasure of loving, doing things, moving one's muscles and smiling. Seen from a distance the two were smaller than the straight tracks that enclosed them. Their bodies were returning to their daily routine, subject to the forces and uncontrollable elements in existence since the beginning of time. But, as their eager eyes took in every color, shade, and movement, they gave little thought to the mysterious magnitude of their universe, and even less to the plight of their brothers, their saviours, who still walked in darkness.

There were planets, solar systems and galaxies. They were only two men, bounded by two impassive rails, returning home with their problems.

On the Wheel

by Damon Knight

When not editing the Orbit *series of anthologies and founding the Science Fiction Writers of America, Damon Knight is a wickedly precise short story writer. It is a pleasure to welcome him to* Nova *with a story that could just as well be titled "One Man's Meat."*

From his perch in the foretop of the *Vlakengros,* Akim could see almost straight down into the cargo well of the old tub, where half a dozen trogs were still scrambling about. Nearby stood his father and the shipmaster, Hizoor Niarefh. Akim could see the tops of their turbaned heads and the bright shafts of their lances. The trogs, black and foreshortened, were like clumsy insects. Akim blew out his breath impatiently and lifted his eyes to the horizon. Westward, above the low hills of the mainland, the sun lay behind veils of purple and gold. A faint offshore breeze roughened the water. To the east, above the ocean, one of the moons had already risen. It was the end of his watch; another day was gone, wasted. Nothing ever happened on the *Vlakengros.*

At last there was a stirring, a distant shout. The trogs were climbing over the rail into their catamarans. Akim waited, twitching with impatience, until a figure stepped leisurely toward the foot of the mast and began to climb.

It was his brother Ogo, who had pimples and never smiled. "Pig," said Akim. He swung himself down the side of the lookout without waiting for Ogo to climb in; his toes caught the rope ladder and he started down. Ogo's dark head appeared above him. "Squid!" Akim shook his fist and kept on descending.

The deck trembled faintly under his feet as he crossed toward the forecastle; the auxiliaries were on, they were under way. Smells of cooking came from the galley. Akim ran down the companionway, snatched a meat pie from the table and was out again, followed by the curses of the cooks. Eating as he went, he reached his cubby and shut the door behind him. He tossed his fire lance into the rack, pulled off turban and robe, and sank down in his chair before the viewer. Now, at last!

He remembered exactly where he had left off, but he thumbed the rewind, listened to the tape squeal for a few moments, then punched "play." The screen lighted. There he was, Edward Robinson, opening the door at the end of the long hall. Still chewing, Akim settled lower into his chair, careful not to move his eyes a millimeter from the screen. The room was large but divided by frosted glass partitions into a jungle of smaller spaces. Behind one of these partitions, looking out through a hole in it, sat a girl with pink and white skin. Over her glossy brown hair she wore a telephone headset. Somewhere in the labyrinth behind her, close and yet invisible, a voice was raised in anger. She looked at Robinson with weary indifference. "Yes, can I help you?"

He advanced, straightening his thin shoulders, and took a folded paper out of his pocket. He unfolded it and laid it on the counter. "Central Employment sent me."

"All right, fill this out." She handed him a card. Along the wall to his right were straight chairs in which three young men sat. One was biting his pencil and scowling. Robinson sat down and began filling out his card. Name. Address. Sex. Age. Race (crossed out by a heavy black line). Education. Previous Employment (list your last three jobs, with dates, duties performed, and reason for leaving). Robinson made up the education, the dates, the reasons, and one of the jobs. While he was doing this, one of the other young men was called. He walked down the corridor between the glass partitions and disappeared. Robinson finished his card and gave it to the girl behind the partition, who was filing her nails. A typewriter clattered somewhere. The second young man was called. Robinson looked around, saw a copy of *Time* on the table beside him, and picked it up. He read an article about dynamic Eric Woolmason who at the age of forty-one was forging a new empire in Pacific Northwest public utilities. The third young man stood up suddenly and crumpled his card. His face was pink. He glanced sidelong at Robinson, then walked out. The girl at the window looked after him with a faint one-sided smile. "Well, goodbye," she murmured.

Robinson began to read the ads in the back of the magazine. He did not think about the coming interview, but his heart was thumping and his palms were moist. At last the girl's voice said, "Mr. Robinson." He stood up. She pointed with her pencil. "Straight down. End of the hall."

"All hands! All hands!" He sat up with a jerk, his heart racing. The room was dark except for the tiny lighted screen. The bellowing voice went on, "All hands to stations! All hands!"

Akim staggered out of the chair, painfully confused. He got into his robe somehow, snatched up the fire lance. Where was his turban? In the screen, a tiny Robinson was walking between the rows of frost-white partitions. He hit the "off" button angrily and lurched out of the room.

Abovedecks, searchlights and the jets of fire lances were wavering across the windy darkness. Something heavy fell to the deck and lay snapping and squealing. A half-naked sailor ran up and hit it with an axe. Akim kept on going. He could see that the foretop was crowded already—three lances were spitting up there. There was another shriek from the sky, a pause, then a splash near the bow. He ran to the quarterdeck rail and found a place between his brother Emmuz and his uncle's cousin Hudny. A searchlight in the bow probed the sky like a skeletal finger. Something appeared in it and was gone. The beam swung, caught it again. Half a dozen lance flames spitted it. It fell, trailing oily smoke. There were more shrieks, splashes. Back toward the waist, there was a flurry of running feet, curses, shouts. Something was thrashing, tangled in the foremast shrouds. A voice screamed, "Don't shoot, you fool! Up the mast and chop it!"

Something came whistling through the darkness under the search-beam. Akim crouched, raised his lance, fired. The flame illuminated a ferocious tusked head, a pink hairless body, leathery wings. There was a shriek and a stench, and the thing plopped down beyond him like a sack of wet meal. Someone hit it with an axe.

The noise died away. The searchlights continued to swing across the darkness. After a time, one of them picked up another bright shape, but it was far away, swinging wide around the ship, and the lance-flames missed it.

"Any more?" came a bellow from the deck.

"No, your worship," answered a voice from the foretop.

"All right then, secure."

Akim lingered glumly to watch the deckhands gather up the bodies and throw them over the side. Pigs were the only excitement in these latitudes; in the old days, it was said, ships had fought them for days with musket and cutlass. But now, not ten minutes since the first

82

alarm, it was all over. A few sailors were swabbing the blood away with sea water, the rest were drifting back belowdecks.

Yawning, Akim went back to his cubby. He was tired, but too restless to go to bed. He wondered whether he was hungry and thought of going to the galley again, but it did not seem worth the effort. With a sigh, he sat in front of the viewer and switched it on.

There was Robinson, walking stiffly into a large area filled with desks cluttered with papers and typewriters. A heavy dark-haired man with black-rimmed glasses stood waiting. His white shirtsleeves were rolled to the elbow. "Robinson? I'm Mr. Beverly." At other desks, a few men glanced up, all pale, unsmiling. Beverly gave Robinson a brief, moist handshake and motioned to a chair. Robinson sat down and tried not to look self-conscious. Glancing at the card in his hand, Beverly said, "Not much experience in this line. Do you think you can handle it?"

Robinson said, "Yes, I think—well, I think I can handle it." He crossed his legs, then uncrossed them.

Beverly nodded, pursing his lips. He reached for a magazine on the desk, pushed it an inch closer. "You're familiar with this publication?"

The cover had a picture of a woman in a tramp's costume smoking a cigar, and a headline, "SMOKES TEN STOGIES A DAY." "Yes, I've seen it," Robinson answered. He tried to think of something else to say. "It's, uh, the kind of thing you read in barbershops, isn't it?"

Beverly nodded again, slowly. His expression did not change. Robinson crossed his legs. "Your job," Beverly said, "would involve choosing pictures for the magazine from photos like these." He pointed to the next desk; it was covered with disorderly heaps of photographs. "Do you think you could do that?"

Robinson stared at the topmost picture, which showed a young woman in what appeared to be a circus costume. He could see the powder caked on her dimpled face, and the beads of mascara on her eyelashes. "Yes, sure. I mean, I think I could handle it."

"Uh-huh. Okay Robinson, thanks for coming in. We'll let you know. Go out that way, if you don't mind." He gave Robinson another handshake and turned away.

Robinson walked to the elevator. He knew he was not going to get the job, and even if he did get it, he would hate it. In the street, he turned west and walked against a tide of blank-eyed, gum-chewing faces. A taxi went over a manhole cover, clink-clank. Steam was rising from an excavation at the corner. The world was like a puzzle with half the pieces missing. What was the point of all these drab buildings, this dirty sky?

In his room, he made some hash and eggs and ate it, reading the *Daily News* and listening to the radio. Then he poured a cup of instant coffee and took it to the easy chair in the corner. On the table beside him lay a paperback book. The cover showed a half-naked red-skinned young man whose smooth muscles bulged as he struck with a scimitar at a monstrous flying boar. A maiden in metal breastplates cowered behind him, and there was ship's rigging in the background. Robinson found his place, bent the book's spine to flatten it, and began to read.

Sometime during the night (he read), the young crewman awoke with a start. He had fallen asleep in his chair, and his legs were cramped, his neck stiff. He got up and walked back and forth the few steps the cubby allowed, but it was not enough, and he went out into the passage. The ship was silent and dark. On an impulse, he climbed the companionway and emerged under a spectral sky. The deck was awash with moonlight. Up in the foretop, there was a wink of red as the lookout lighted his pipe. That would be Rilloj, his second cousin, a heavy, black-browed man who had the same ox-like face as his father, and his uncle Zanid, and all the rest. On the whole ship there was not one of them he could talk to, not one who understood his yearnings.

Hugging himself for warmth, he walked over to the lee rail. A few stars shone above the dim horizon. Up there, somewhere, unreachable and unknown, there must be worlds of mystery, worlds where a man could *live*. Gigantic cities thronged with people, exotic machines, ancient wisdom. . . .

And he was Akim, seventeen years old, a crewman on the *Vlaken-gros*. As he turned, he felt a queer loss of balance for an instant; the world seemed to split, and he had a glimpse of a ragged crack with grayness showing through it. Then it was gone, but it had frightened him. What could cause such a thing?

Back in his cubby, he sat down heavily in front of the screen. He would be sorry for it in a few hours, when the watch turned him out, but after all, what else was there? He turned on the machine. There was Robinson, reading in his chair. A cigarette beside him in the ashtray had burned to a long gray ash. The alarm clock read two-thirty. It was the gray turning point of the night, when the eyes are dry and the blood flows thin. Robinson yawned, read another line without interest, then shut the book and tossed it aside. He began to realize how tired he really was. He shut off the viewer, pulled his bunk down out of the wall, stripped off his robe. He got up and headed for the bathroom, unbuttoning his shirt as he went. He brushed his teeth, wound the alarm clock (but did not set it), undressed and got in between the rumpled sheets. He went to the head, made sure his door was secure, then rolled into the bunk. As he lay there between sleep and waking, the events of the day got all mixed up somehow with the story he had been viewing. Tomorrow they would be at their next port of call, and he would pick up his unemployment check. Maybe he would get a job. The ship was rolling gently. Under the edge of the blind, the neons winked red-blue, red-green, red-blue. Good night, good night. Sleep tight, don't let the seapigs bite.

Miss Omega Raven

by Naomi Mitchison

Mrs. Mitchison mailed this story from Africa, from Botswana, where she had gone to take care of some business for her tribe. She had to hurry back to Scotland for some more business, this time with the Highland Council. One can only admire her energy—as well as her talent that gave us "Mary and Joe" in Nova 1, *and now this deeply understanding story of a completely different type of mutation.*

The others were always quick, always first. Was it because of what they did to us when we were young, when they took us out of our nests before our feathers were more than quills and fed us this other food and made us sleep and put the little wires on to our heads so that we could look back and forward? We became different. And yet I think I became the most different of all. We knew what was ahead and how to get it. We knew, not deep inside where there is no choice like knowing in our necks and wings the moves of the mating flight when all is Now. No, not that. We knew with the parts of ourselves that choose. Thinking, they called it, remembering, looking ahead. I was the latest hatched, damp and flabby, my beak making squeals, the pieces of shell still stuck to me. I had not seen my mother. I opened eyes and saw him, the God-man with the special food. He became her. I had to follow him to do what he did, to become him. How else? Yet because of that I was more changed. But they took us a long way in the dark in a box and made us fly. By then our wings were grown. We felt a need but did not know what it was.

When we flew we were in a different place with open stretches of rocks and trees, but no built walls. But inside we knew it. We knew the ways in which we were going to live. The food. And there were the mates. Oh beautiful, with the deep part which has no choice, I knew this was my need. I must get one. I must get the most beautiful, the best, shining dark of feathers, bright of eye. We must dance together in the air. That was what wings were for. We forgot the humans who had reared us; we forgot to look forward and back. But perhaps I did not quite forget. Perhaps that was what went wrong.

I did not at once leap into the air, crooning and bubbling, to chase the top bird, the raven of ravens, Alpha Corax. My feathered tufts were slow to come to the erect and welcoming sign which should draw him, yes, to lay his neck over mine. Others did it, my hated sisters, jumping with touched beaks, ruffling, courting, crooning. And the mates responded, answering with the same love notes, the same stiffening and relaxing, so that feathers ruffled and beaks snapped. It was clear already who was top, who could peck whom, though it had scarcely yet become clear to us female fledglings. [Even during the courting dance when air became buoyant and welcoming, inviting to enormous heights of glory from which one could dive flashingly, the wind booming one's feathers or even when the mate, turning on his back, invited with his beating spread wings but warned with beak and claws.] One after another the couples began to take flight. But I—I? Surely I could not be the one left out! But I was. For me and for one other, no mate. There had been two more of us than of them. Or perhaps two of them had died in the rearing. She, the other unmated, was even more hateful than the wives. Each of them had taken the rank of her husband and would keep it for life. We ravens settle each with her own mate for always.

This way each took orders and gave orders, each pecked in punishment and was herself pecked; it was the same with the husbands. Only the most beautiful, the bravest, the top raven Alpha Corax, gave orders. Nobody pecked him. He led the flock to roost or to hunt. He watched and warned for enemies and sometimes attacked. His beak was sharpest.

But I was lowest of the low. She—the other unmated—pecked me and I had to accept this, jumping away from food, not pecking back. All that was in the deep part of me. I could not escape being how I was. There was no choice. But also I was angry and that anger was in the other part of me driving me to plan. That part of me thought of a future in which I would not be pecked. I knew I was becoming ugly. My feathers were draggled. I was thin, for I always got the worst share, either of flesh or eggs or the rarer grain and nuts. No wonder I was a pecked on with nobody to peck. Had God-man made me this? If he had not made me something other I could not have questioned what I was.

So things went on. The beautiful one watched and led us to food; so did his wife. She saw with his eyes. She too led the flight in which I was last. And I knew two opposite things: in the deep part of me—that this was how it was but, in the outside, the changed and choosing part—that this was not for always and one day there would be a choice and a plan. But the choice did not come. The mates made their nests, beautiful, enviable, with heathers and grasses and earth and small sticks, lined deliciously with worked, soft grasses and feathers, ready for eggs. Once I tried to sit on a nest but how I was driven out, with what pain and anger! I tried to join in flights, I tried to croon and preen to each of the males but I aroused nothing in any of them, since they had only one image in their constant minds. They also had been in the hands of the God-men but now they had forgotten. I being alone, could not forget.

Then came the chipping of the eggs, the young, the tremendous drive and bustle of feeding. I was looked on, knowing what it was I missed; it was I driven from the dead lamb that was feasting us. It was I who saw the God-men circling us, with what intent I did not know, yet believed it was not evil. It was not they who had left me hungry. They spoke to one another or so I supposed. I also saw that they took some of the nestlings while they fed others with their own kind of food. The mothers were disturbed briefly but none of us could feel that the God-men were enemies. They were only high beyond us, beyond the top of the Alphas; they could give orders. They could peck us to the bone and any of us must submit, but because they had also fed us they did not do that; they did not need to. The one on whom my nestling eyes had first opened was there. He looked at my thin and draggled body; he had brought pieces of food, not their own kind, but good raw meat. He gave me some and I tried to gulp it quickly before the other unmated could see and drive me off. Yet she came, and her black beak drove at me; feathers flew. The deep, inside part of me was making me cower and accept. But the one I had not forgotten, the God-man had shown himself; it was meat he had given. He sent the knowledge of choice back into me. In a moment she was the pecked on. I made her feathers fly! It was impossible and it had happened.

Once pecked, she accepted. That was the first lesson. For both of us. I hated her. I could not stop pecking. Even when the God-man picked me up so that she could run and then flap away. Through the wriggle of my held wings and the straining of my body I felt his hands thinking about me. My beak wanted to peck, my claws to scratch; the beak pointed yet unable to peck him. He was my mother; the one I had opened eyes on. He held me but it came to me that I also held him.

88

Then there was a feast again. A cow had given birth. She moved away with the calf, leaving what else had come out of her red and wet in the grass. That was for us. But now I had one to peck and drive off if she came near me and the one who before had pecked her could not at once change to pecking me. The old pattern had been made. Yet because she too had been with the God-men and had been partly changed by them, so that she had choice, she began to know that I had taken the place of the other and also she was afraid in case I did not accept it. Sometimes her pecking was not hard. But I did not attack at once, not when she was with her nest and her mate.

The leaves of the great nest trees had spread and become green to live the leaves' life. Then they browned and drooped and loosened and the leaf flocks swirled briefly in air and then dropped and were still and useless. The young birds began to fly. But from every nest the God-men climbing quietly had taken one. I was watching, the mothers not always. They and their mates swirled and clattered and called uselessly, and yet they all knew, in the parts of their minds that looked forward and back, that the God-men had the right and this way was best for all.

And now cold days began and we all scattered again, though the pairs kept partly together. There was less food in winter and less light—time to find it. And I began to peck back at the next above me. Her mate looked on uncertainly but it was not he I wanted. I did not want any mate; it was the wrong season. I wanted only to be top. By the next season I could take this one's place, but it was not enough. What then?

The God-man came. My own. Was he top God-man or was it possible that all were top? They did not seem to hurt one another. But perhaps they did in some way hidden from ravens; who could tell? No use asking even if one knew what or how to ask. What is asking? So it went. But one day the God-man was gone and with him in a box went the wife of Alpha Corax, the top raven. Where had she gone? We did not know what to think, only that all were perturbed. She, with him, had led the foraging parties of the ravens. He was used to her being with him. He called; she was not there. He made the croonings and the mating cries; she did not answer. But all of us felt something in the deep part that wanted to answer, even before the season of mating. There was movement and small noises. Feathers rose and a posturing walk began. And then my own God-man looked at me and he too made a mating cry and he lifted his arms flapping. He was me. He had taken me from the egg and changed me so that I could hatch

89

out of the old patterns. And then suddenly it was I who was answering Alpha Corax; it was I who was with him, who had taken top place. I was the same as my God-man, my top God.

Now it was I who would have Alpha Corax, the top bird, the most beautiful, the raven of ravens. At mating time we would dance together in the air and then we would build our nest. But today, now, he knew and acknowledged me. I was Alpha today. I could peck the one below me and not one of them could peck me. I would become beautiful and glossy; my feathers would always lie smooth; I would bite and swallow all the bloodiest bits of the food. I would have the best nest, safe, not out in the edges.

All this happened. It happened to me. Now I am mated forever with Alpha Corax. Yes, at first there were those that rebelled, that had it in the bottom of their minds that I was still the pecked one, Omega Raven. Yes, some of them tried to peck me. But how I pecked them back, scattering feathers and blood! For I remembered the other food and the little wires that made me more than myself. I remembered God-man who made me into top pecker, breaker of custom. My God-man, top God. God-man and I.

The Poet in the Hologram in the Middle of Prime Time

by Ed Bryant

The author of this story showed that he had the makings of a writer when he turned his back on the establishment—and a hard-earned M.A.—and went to work in a stirrup buckle factory so he could labor away at his fiction. He also attended the first Clarion Workshop in Fantasy and Science Fiction which certainly bodes well for that course. Now, with a keen modern eye, he looks carefully at the world of commercial entertainment and some of the jollies it may have in store for us.

COMPUTER LINK:

    MEDIUM SHOT—THE POET SEATED IN HIS CHAIR
    EFFECTS: NORMAL SCALE—H-FIGURES DISTORT $\pm 2\%$
    AIR DISPERSAL: GRAVEYARD EARTH, RAINSOAKED
    INSERT 100 MICROGRAMS ETK-10 IN PROP WINE

FADE IN:

Entrapment. Fearing, Ransom downed the last of the wine

> *ruby flowing, richer than blood it drains*

He smiled ruefully. It was a bad line: the choice of words was trite, the metaphor was a cliché. But, he suspected, it was more than typical of his work these days. Ransom flipped the wine bottle over his right shoulder. The empty decanter, unbreakable, bounced across the carpet

> *decry the permanence of plastic;*
> *outliving even our rock tombs.*

The man in the chair grimaced and belched. Better. He looked at the device on the coffee table and grinned widely.

91

The device was genuine. So was the bouquet of blue flowers in the vase beside it. Most of the rest of the room was fake: the table was ersatz walnut, the dark-grained paneling on the walls was imitation.

Ransom stood and stared out the window, down a hundred levels at the sprawl of Greater Ellay. He wasn't really looking out a window, of course. His rooms were interred deep within the labyrinthian apartment block. The window was an electronic screen. Once, besides offering a view of the external world, it could pick up more than eighty television channels. Back when TV was *the* entertainment medium.

The window, not being a window, could not be opened. If it really were a window, it still would stay permanently shut. On Ransom's level of the urban stack, no one could breathe the polluted sky; shovel it, maybe, but not inhale. Air was piped into Ransom's apartment—first filtered, cleansed, sterilized; then oxygenated, ionized, humidified properly, heated, certified carcinogen-free, and consigned to the alveoli of Ransom's lungs.

Ransom frowned at the slight undulation of his surroundings.

Too much wine, he thought. *Too much for efficiency and not enough for courage.* He crossed to the coffee table, realizing he was weaving. *But sufficient for action.*

He looked down at his contraband toy; then his chin raised and he wrinkled his nose. His nostrils enclosed the slightest scent, a smell undefined, yet disturbingly suggestive. Dark. Moist. Cool. Slightly sweet with decay.

Twenty years old, the memory was. Black veils, black clothes, so starkly contrasted with the white marble of the face. Ransom's father's face, waxy and dead. It had rained that morning and the burying ground was still spongy with moisture. That was when graves could still be dug. Before the premium on vacant land resurrected every inhabitant of the cemetery and sent his remains to the crematorium. Even now the dust of Ransom's father's remains was probably in the process of precipitating out of the air sighing into Ransom's living room.

The poet sniffed, and sniffed again

    at the corpse-smell of my own funeral

He picked up the bomb from the coffee table. Childishly amazed at how much leashed destruction could be held in the palm of his hand, Ransom again grinned.

The two watchers, offstage. Consumer Participation Evaluators, they were officially termed. Amelia Marchin, for her own peculiar reasons, called them "neilsons." This was reputed to be some sort of in-joke, but then Amelia possessed a marvelously esoteric knowledge of her field.

The two CPE's watched the stick-figure bumbling through illusion after illusion.

"This is definitely too melodramatic," said the taller one, making a cryptic notation subvocally on his recorder.

"I disagree," said the second CPE, the shorter of the pair. "On the contrary, I feel that this performance is the highest form of art. There is a great deal to be said on behalf of spontaneity."

"So where does the spontaneity leave off?" asked the first CPE. "And where does the external manipulation of the director begin?"

"I don't have the slightest idea. The line of distinction is marvelously subtle." He poured himself a glass of amber liquid. "Have a drink?" he invited.

The first CPE proffered his glass. The two watchers settled back comfortably to watch the show.

DISSOLVE TO:

STILL SHOT OF

The poet bleeding.

> *"Iron and sapphire caverns of frost*
> *Coat the chrome cylinders of mind."*

The two lines lie inert on the white paper desert for more than an hour while Ransom grapples with the poem. The night is unending repetition of coffee hot and cold, recorded music and silence, turning the thermostat up and down, remembering and staring at vistas far beyond the walls of the room, sitting quiet, stalking, pacing, tensing and relaxing. On the wall, the clock's hands lag heavily.

> *"Below, the volcano slumbers*
> *Unseen, yet sensed with bleak desire."*

Ransom never works harder than when he forges his songs. And there is nothing he loves more. Not Melissa, not food, drink, nor any other pleasure. For they are all here in his poetry.

> *"Dim awareness vaguely suspects*
> *Vanished dreams; the promise of fire."*

Dawn is graying the black scan of Ransom's eastern electronic window. The poet yawns and stretches, feeling the cramp of his muscles relax painfully. He looks down at the manuscript, at the words inked out and changed, some a dozen times or more. He sees the dull gleam of flecked silver peeking out of the slag.

Ransom, satisfied for the moment, fixes a simple breakfast.

DIRECT CUT TO:

STILL SHOT OF

The poet loving. Ransom leans on one elbow on the softness of the bed. Below him, Melissa is faceless in shadow.

Sensing his mood, she asks, "What's wrong?"

"Nothing, Love," lies Ransom. What's wrong is the poet's life; he is dissatisfied with himself, with his actions. And no one is to blame except himself. The realization is unpleasant; it intrudes into the ecstasy of the moment

> *I wish that somehow I*
> *could come*
> *to you*
> *now*
> *and ease this bitter moment*
> *finding solace*
> *between your thighs*

Ransom hates the intrusion of the world into this moment; he forces it back into a mental recess. Melissa is warmly damply ready. He touches her. They joy in the pleasure of just about the last human endeavor not yet supplanted by machines.

DIRECT CUT TO:

STILL SHOT OF

The poet standing high above the world. Years before.

The late afternoon light slants across the mountainside. From his rock promontory jutting high out of the scrub pine, the poet silently watches the forest below. The trees thin out as they advance up the slopes to the clusters of broken boulders thrusting at the sky. Far below him, a road coils among trees and rocks. A campfire lifts a thin smoke-trail into the crisp November air. The winding trail is nudged Ransom's way by the wind and he can smell the slightly acrid tang of wood-smoke. A mottling of clouds scuds southward; their ever-shifting shadows crisscross the valley floor.

Ransom, young and alone, stands on his rock. This is his first trip here. The first of many to these mountains west of Denver. Snatches of Gerard Hopkins' "The Windhover" leap from his memory as the ragged north wind crowds him.

Ransom feels a sensation of aliveness here—more so than in the Ellay hive. *I'll write about this someday,* he thinks, *before these mountains are gutted for their metals or leveled for freeways. I can't stop their rape, but maybe I can evoke their memory.*

Someday he will.

DIRECT CUT TO:

STILL SHOT OF

The poet whoring.

KATYA

The last time was too much. I can't go on with it.

MARSHALL

You have to; if only for the child.

In a fit of disgust, Ransom sweeps his hand across the desk and the half-finished script scatters to the carpet like dead leaves. The title page lands face up: "Darkness Comes Cheap: an original play for holovision." The poet punches out the combination for three ounces of Scotch, no chaser, on his kitchen console. The glass automatically fills as Ransom retrieves the strewn fruit of his career. He straightens up with a fistful of paper and dumps it back on the desk.

The Scotch is drained in an extended gulp. Then Ransom is back to his work, his staff of life.

To Ransom, the sheets on the desk are rubbish. His love lies on the shelf across the room. A slim volume in a subdued jacket, a book of poems called *Blue Mountains Above Denver*. Beside it in a folder are the beginnings of another book. They have long lain unfinished. They will remain so.

DIRECT CUT TO:

STILL SHOT OF

The poet celebrating.

The bar is old, cheap, dirty. It squats in the tawdry business belt that half-encircles the starport. Ransom often rides the tube here— sometimes to watch the giant silver ships lift away to the space-sea, but mostly to drink and talk with his friends in the bar.

> *"Sometimes I live in the country,*
> *Sometimes I live in the town;*
> *Sometimes I have a great notion*
> *To go to the river and drown."*

English folk songs; Welsh, German, French, American, Russian. Tobacco smoke and cannabis fumes cloy the air. Liquor is plentiful. With an arm around the thin shoulders of his friend Morales and the container of inexpensive vodka gripped in a free hand, Ransom roars out verses, sometimes getting the lyrics right, sometimes not.

The song muddles to a crashing finale with an enthusiastic "And rest in the arms of love."

The glow of the song is transient and Ransom frowns. Morales seeing the expression asks, "My friend, you are unhappy?"

"Ever get the feeling you sold out?"

Morales shrugs. "Selling out is merely good business."

"It's also self-betrayal," says Ransom. He takes a long, thoughtful draught of vodka. "So much for beating the system on its own terms. I fooled myself."

"Hey!" shouts Morales to the bouzuki player in the corner. "We wish another song."

COMPUTER LINK:
MEDIUM SHOT—OFFICE INTERIOR
AIR DISPERSAL JUNGLE WIDE-SPECTRUM BUT SUBDUED
AUDIO EFFECTS: LIMITED RANGE SUBSONICS (TENSION BUILDING)
EFFECTS: H-FIGURES NORMAL SCALE

Amelia Marchin. Director General of UniCom, the most powerful woman in the North American communications industry. One of the most powerful women anywhere. Sleekly beautiful as a panther: hair black and eyes green, lithe, intelligent, ruthless, graceful. Also feral. And today, displeased.

"I'm resigning," the object of her displeasure had told her. "Quitting. Getting out. Now."

"No," said Amelia Marchin. "At one time I would have allowed you to leave UniCom. I would have been regretful, but I would have accepted your resignation. After all, you're one of the top holovision writers in the field. But now, I'm afraid that your termination of any contract with us is out of the question."

Ransom rose to his feet. His face reddened to match the shag of his beard. He bent and slammed a fist down on Amelia's desk. "Like hell it's out of the question! If I want to leave, I'll go. There are still laws against slavery."

Amelia watched him, amused. "Yes. There are, unfortunately." She smiled placatingly. "Now sit down, Ransom. It won't do any good for you to try to intimidate me with bluster."

It wouldn't. Ransom knew that from prior experience. He sat.

"You know," said Amelia, "you're a real anomaly. You write and adapt some of UniCom's highest rated shows, yet you don't own a holovision set yourself."

"Holovision stinks," said Ransom. "I write your scripts so I can buy enough food to live on while I write poetry. That's all. I've saved up enough credits so I can live for a while and write. So no more scripts."

"We need you," said Amelia quietly.

Ransom was startled. Statements like that from the Director General were not forthcoming every day. He looked at her inquisitively.

"You have immense talent. You are a genius and an articulate one. That's a remarkable combination in any age, but particularly in this century of ours."

"Thanks for the compliment," said Ransom. "But you're hedging. Why don't you want me to resign?"

She showed her white even teeth in a smile. "UniCom has developed a radical innovation in holovision programming; we need your talent and ability to help make it viable."

Ransom laughed, shockingly loud in the cool, subdued interior of the office. "Give aid and comfort to the enemy? Hell no!"

Amelia arched an eyebrow, inclined her head slightly, and again smiled.

DISSOLVE TO:

COMMERCIAL BREAK

WIDE-ANGLE SHOT—TYPICAL UNICOM APPLIANCE STORE EXTERIOR. CAMERA PANS TO CATCH WELL-DRESSED COUPLE APPROACHING ON SLIDEWALK.

"Come right on in, folks!" The salesman's voice boomed, a distillation of friendliness and cheery enthusiasm. His face was the standard family sales issue: a composite of every man's favorite uncle. The happy salesman waved the couple, who smiled in return, into the store. "Welcome to UniCom's great Twenty-Twenty Sale!"

"Twenty-Twenty Sale?" inquired the woman alertly, her eyes clear and widely blue and abrim with curiosity.

"Right!" said the salesman. "It's the first week of the new year and already we've declared a special sale with tremendous savings for you shoppers at all UniCom outlets in North America."

"Savings?" asked the husband. "That really sounds great!"

"Great is right! But just wait until you see what's even greater—UniCom's new line of holovision sets for 2020!"

"Oh dear," said the wife. "We already have a holovision set." There was regret in her voice at having to disappoint the salesman who looked so much like her favorite uncle.

"Not like this one, you don't!" The salesman pivoted and dramatically indicated a shining black box on a crystal dais. "Friends, you undoubtedly have an old-style holovision—the kind that only gives you three-dimensional pictures and stereo sound."

"Of course," said the husband, puzzled. "It's the best set on the market."

"Not any more! Not now that UniCom has added a whole new dimension to holograms!"

The prospective customers appeared properly astonished and intrigued. "A new dimension?" they asked in concert.

"Brand new! It's now possible for you——" he pointed to the woman. "And you——" he gestured at the man. "To actually participate, to star in your own favorite holovision shows, right in the comfort and convenience of your own home."

The couple looked struck by wonder.

"Imagine——" said the woman.

CAMERA PULLS BACK—PANS TO SALESMAN. CLOSE SHOT—HIS FACE

"That's right, friends! Imagine yourself the star of your own show in your own home! All you need is the fantastic new Twenty-Twenty holovision plan, available only from UniCom. For complete details and a free demonstration, visit your local UniCom Appliance Mart *today!*"

COMPUTER LINK:

SAME AS PREVIOUS SCENE—AMELIA'S OFFICE

DISSOLVE TO:

A capering of miniscule actors. The troupe strutted and fretted across the top of Amelia's desk. The drama was without sound, yet Ransom could whisper the lines to accompany the action. He had written them.

"Consider the popular communication media created by electronics," said Amelia.

Ransom continued to watch the Lilliputian production of "Darkness Comes Cheap."

"First there was radio during the first half of the last century. For all practical purposes, it was a one-dimensional medium—sound. It was largely replaced by two-dimensional television. Then in the seventies and eighties came the three-dimensional moving images of holovision." Her voice had the self-assured inflection of a high priestess reading aloud from the holy book. "Now UniCom is ready to advance the progression further."

Amelia touched a small panel of controls beside her chair and the hologram on the desk expanded to normal human scale and beyond to fill the entire room.

A heroically proportioned couple were silently making love close by Ransom's shoulder. He idly reached out to the holographic girl's hip, his hand disappearing into the intangible flesh.

"Just wonderful," said the poet. "Another step in the progression. What now? Are you going to plug the program right into the viewer's brain?"

"Not yet, Ransom. Maybe next season." Amelia moved a control and the hologram's soundtrack cut in. Over the heavy breathing, she asked, "What's the missing element?"

Ransom shrugged.

"Participation," said Amelia.

Ransom looked apprehensive, shoved back his chair. "I'm getting a premonition. I don't think I want to hear about this."

"On the contrary. You do want to hear. You've got an incredible curiosity—otherwise you wouldn't be so perceptive in your poetry and, occasionally, your scripts." She moved a hand and the H-figures winked out. The woman reached into an aperture in her desk and lifted out a black box. Featureless, it was about twenty centimeters long, Ransom guessed. Perhaps half that wide and deep.

"Participation," Amelia repeated. "It's all right here. This is a direct link between any holovision set and UniCOMP." The entire ten levels beneath Amelia's office was UniCOMP.

"How about that!" said Ransom. "You know how impressive I find your tin macrocephalus."

"Wait, Ransom. You'll be impressed; I promise you that. Listen, now. Imagine yourself home with your 'Darkness Comes Cheap' scheduled on the holovision."

Ransom nodded.

"How would you like to play your protagonist, Marshall? How would you like to actually perform the lead role in your drama— more than that, even to *be* Marshall?"

The poet raised his eyebrows politely.

"You can do it, Ransom!" Excitement welled in Amelia's voice. "This box will do it. UniCOMP directs the whole production. Your lines are cued subliminally. Your subscription to UniCom covers simple props, special effects, even hallucinogenic aids to ensure your responsiveness to UniCOMP's stimuli."

Ransom stared unbelievingly at her.

"Listen, Ransom. You don't even have to follow the script. Feedback circuits let your own initiatives and reactions determine the direction of the action. This is the ultimate in participatory entertainment; it lets everyone's imagination loose, frees everybody's natural talents."

"You're crazy!" said the poet, unmasked horror contorting his face. "You're absolutely mad!"

Amelia registered surprise. "What's the matter? You're a poet and a writer—probably the closest we can come to a Renaissance man. Don't tell me you're shocked at the unveiling of a new artform?"

"This isn't art," said Ransom, his face again reddening, and his voice thick. "It's completely the opposite." His features worked painfully as he sought the right words. "It's perversion. It's destroying art by bringing it down to the ultimate common denominator."

"I didn't realize you were a snob."

"I'm not. It's just that——" Ransom shook his head violently, his eyes screwed shut. "It's just that we've leveled art, so thoroughly vulgarized it through television and holovision. Even before electronics, we did the job with incompetent abridgements and even comic-book versions of great works." He leaned forward, looked at Amelia's impassive panther eyes. "This method of yours will cut the underpinnings from every poet and playwright and author from the early Greeks down to right now. Amelia, can't you see what literature will be like when every person in the world can stamp Shakespeare and Dostoievsky and Joyce to the mold of his own subjective tastes?"

Amelia shrugged. "North America is still a democracy," she said.

Ransom's voice broke hoarsely: "What's worse, this thing you're proposing is all the manipulation of a machine—a sterile, cold, unfeeling machine." His face twisted again. "God help us all if people accept this."

"They will. The process has been thoroughly consumer-tested. The results were favorable for marketing."

Ransom stood back from the desk and looked sick. "You've sold your soul, Amelia."

The woman smiled. "Souls, Ransom? You're in our business too."

"No," whispered Ransom.

"Now then. We're debuting UniCOMP's participatory holovision process in sixty days. We want you to do an original script for our first public offering."

"No." Ransom shook his head.

Amelia's voice hardened. "Ransom, you're going to provide us with our drama."

"No." Ransom backed toward the door. "I won't. I hope nobody will."

"It's what the public wants; it's what they will get." She motioned with her hand and the door glided open behind the poet.

"Come back when you cool off," she said. "But don't wait too long. UniCom doesn't want a last minute, slap-dash job."

"Shit," said Ransom distinctly. The door slid shut.

Alone, Amelia ruffled through the papers on her desk. "Ransom," she whispered, almost a sigh. "If only you were a better poet."

EFFECTS: (OPTICAL) FUZZ H-FIGURES, THEN BRING TO FOCUS.
CLOSE SHOT—INTERCUT CONVERSATION
AIR DISPERSAL: CORDITE

DISSOLVE TO:

Morales. In any culture there is always someone who can procure the forbidden: women, drugs, books, whatever is anathema to the established system of values. That was the role of Morales in Ransom's world.

"I want a bomb," said Ransom.

"So?" said Morales matter-of-factly. "What kind? How big? Do you want to blow up a street cafe? a car? a superson liner? Do you wish lots of pretty fireworks, or just a low-yield, unobtrusive, neutron grenade?"

"I hadn't really thought about that." The poet reflected quietly. "I want a bomb small enough to conceal in my clothing, yet powerful enough to destroy a—oh, most of a three-hundred level building."

Morales whistled in admiration. "You don't ask for much, my friend. But I think I can help you. What you desire has been banned by the World Council for twenty years. I believe it was called a fusion grenade or some-such." He jotted notes on a small pad. "About a ten-kilotonner should do nicely," Morales mumbled. "Let's see, fully shielded from electronic detectors, of course."

Ransom nodded. That sounded like a good idea.

Morales looked up from his notes. "Well, Ransom, that should do it. I won't, of course, ask you specifically what you are going to do with this device. No, it is better that I stay as ignorant as possible in case the Peace Enforcers become involved." He snapped the notepad shut and slipped it into his tunic.

"Um, about the price," said Ransom.

"Ah yes." He silently totaled a figure. "Eleven hundred credits should cover it nicely."

Ransom began making out a transfer chit.

"Plus," said Morales. Ransom raised his head. "A signed first edition of your *Blue Mountains Above Denver*."

"There was only one edition." Ransom smiled. "With pleasure."

DIRECT CUT TO:

A fine pair of Consumer Participation Evaluators, becoming happily inebriated in the course of their duties.

The first CPE yawned. "This is becoming too predictable."

The second shrugged his shoulders. "So is Greek tragedy." He was a short, stout man and it was hard for him to shrug. He managed.

The first CPE, the taller one, touched his teeth to the cold rim of his glass. "Well, I'll take a good Restoration comedy any time."

COMPUTER LINK:

AERIAL SHOT—ZOOM TO CLOSE-UP OF POET ON SLIDEWALK

EFFECTS: H-FIGURES 5% SMALLER THAN SCALE

AUDIO EFFECTS: SUBLIMINAL EXCERPTS FROM SOUSA MARCHES

AIR DISPERSAL: ROSES

DIRECT CUT TO:

Ransom. He strode along with the flow of the slidewalk, doubling his rate of travel. The bomb was a solidly reassuring weight in his belt-pouch. The poet whistled a tune in exhilaration

knowing I'm to die
and death will be well
for the world and me

The slidewalk was a glass bead arch that spanned the hazy gulf between Ransom's apartment block and the transit station. The poet felt a slight giddiness as the transparent tube swept him out into the open void between buildings. Far above him was a dull-slate sky, cloud-streaked with black. Almost at the zenith was a dimmed sun. Below was a checkerboard of the tops of lesser buildings.

The transit depot was congested, as usual. Ransom gently maneuvered through the throngs of commuters until he found the correct level and proper gate for the Burbank tube.

The trip was not spectacular: the hiss of the air being evacuated from the tube, the initial crackle of the propulsion field, the soft glow of artificial illumination as the car traversed the light and darkness of spaces and buildings. Abruptly the car arced out into a vast open space where reared the arrogant thrust of the UniCom Tower.

"Burbank Exit El-three, UniCom," intoned the car's automated conductor.

Ransom disembarked and stood, fists on hips, looking up at the endless tiered levels of UniCom.

The fear came from deep inside him. Not just intellectual apprehension. This was visceral fear—gut-level. Fear and regret. Regret at never seeing another nightfall or sunrise. Regret at never loving another woman. Regret at never writing another poem.

But with the fear was something exalting. Ransom's mercurial mood flickered to elation. There was something melodramatically grand about this confrontation. On one side of the board were ranged UniCom, Amelia Marchin, the UniCOMP holovision process, all the resources of a multibillion credit corporation. *Like one of my scripts,* laughed Ransom inwardly. In opposition was Ransom: bulky, shaggy-bearded, ebullient, with a bomb in his pocket.

It's hardly fair to you, Ransom addressed the tower. *A lone man is always the fiercest of opponents.*

There was no hesitation in his stride as the poet moved toward the entrance to UniCom. It seemed to Ransom that he was stepping almost in time with the half-heard cadence of some distant brass-band march. He drew a deep breath. There were roses in the air. Victory roses

> *better lilies, for the bier of my enemy and for my*
> *coffin too*

"Amelia Marchin," said Ransom to the security guard. "I'm expected."

The guard subvocalized into a throat-mike, received an answer. "Certainly, sir. Take lift eight, please."

Ransom floated up the indicated shaft. One barrier crossed. Morales had assured him that the device was sufficiently shielded to escape any form of detection other than physical search. And the latter was unlikely in the extreme; in this civilized age, *nobody* would carry a bomb with them to a business appointment. Yet a small premonitive worry twinged at Ransom's conscious. Something was *wrong.*

The poet had to transfer to a different lift at the two-hundredth level. Again he spoke the shibboleth "Amelia Marchin" and once more he was motioned upward. Another guard in a blue uniform was waiting for him at level three hundred.

"This way, sir." He turned and Ransom followed. "Please enter, sir." The guard held a door open. Ransom entered. It was dark. The door sighed shut behind him.

The room was completely lightless. Ransom stumbled forward. "Amelia, what the hell are you doing?" Illuminators in the ceiling glowed softly on. The poet looked around. He was in a circular room, about twenty meters in diameter, featureless except for a carved wooden table standing in the center. There was a scrap of paper lying on the table.

Ransom walked to the center of the room, his heels echoing on the tiled floor. On the table was a note, carefully hand-printed. It read:

> Dear Ransom,
>
> Another poet wrote you a message four and a quarter centuries ago. Shakespeare: *As You Like It:* II, 7, lines 139–140.
>
> Best,
> Amelia Marchin

He knew the reference. Melancholy Jacques. "All the world's a stage. . . ." Ransom stood frozen, looped in ice coils of upwelling horror. His hand went to his belt-pouch, fumbled it open, rummaged inside.

A block of wood.

The poet screamed a long animal cry of anguish, of pain, of betrayal: a wail that keened up and up until it flared incandescently, like a bomb.

DISSOLVE TO:

THE CREDITS INTERWOVEN THROUGH A FLICKERING PROCESSIONAL MONTAGE OF FACES

MORALES

Morales looks up from the book of poems. He offers a Latin, shoulder-shrugging sigh. "Life," he says, "is like that."

THE TALLER CPE

The taller Consumer Participation Evaluator raises a glass in toast to his friend. "Life is art."

THE SHORTER CPE

"No," says his companion. "Art is life."

UNICOMP

UniCOMP hums ruminatively. "Art is ultimately undefinable," flashes on the read-out screen.

AMELIA

Amelia Marchin smiles gently as she looks down at the world from her office on the three-hundredth level of the UniCom Tower. "Life," she murmurs, "is only sometimes real."

RANSOM

Ransom says nothing.

FADE OUT:

The Old Folks

by James E. Gunn

James Gunn is a lean, quiet mid-westerner who teaches at the University of Kansas in Lawrence, and is a little tired of people knowing that town only as the one Quantrill raided. He writes a deceptively simple, apparently nostalgic, story about the midwest of legend—that soon proves to have a most sharp sting in its tail.

They had been traveling in the dusty car all day, the last few miles in the heat of the Florida summer. Not far behind were the Sunshine State Parkway, Orange Grove, and Winter Hope, but according to the road map the end of the trip was near.

John almost missed the sign that said, "Sunset Acres, Next Right," but the red Volkswagen slowed and turned and slowed again. Now another sign marked the beginning of the town proper: SUNSET ACRES, Restricted Senior Citizens, Minimum Age—65, Maximum Speed—20.

As the car passed the sign, the whine of the tires announced that the pavement had changed from concrete to brick.

Johnny bounced in the back seat, mingling the squeak of the springs with the music of the tires, and shouted above the engine's protest at second gear, "Mommy—Daddy, are we there yet? Are we there?"

His mother turned to look at him. The wind from the open window whipped her short hair. She smiled. "Soon now," she said. Her voice was excited, too.

They passed through a residential section where the white frame houses with their sharp roofs sat well back from the street, and the velvet lawns reached from red-brick sidewalks to broad porches that spread like skirts around two or three sides of the houses.

At each intersection the streets dipped to channel the rain water and to enforce the speed limit at 20 m.p.h. or slower. The names of the streets were chiseled into the curbs, and the incisions were painted black: Osage, Cottonwood, Antelope, Meadowlark, Prairie. . . .

The Volkswagen hummed along the brick streets, alone. The streets were empty, and so, it seemed, were the houses; the white-curtained windows stared senilely into the Florida sun, and the swings on the porches creaked in the Florida breeze, but the architecture and the town were all Kansas—and the Kansas of fifty years ago, at that.

Then they reached the square, and John pulled the car to a stop alongside the curb. Here was the center of town—a block of green-sward edged with beds of pansies and petunias and geraniums. In the center of the square was a massive, two-story, red-brick building. A square tower reached even taller. The tower had a big clock set into its face. The heavy, black hands pointed at 3:32.

Stone steps marched up the front of the building toward oak doors twice the height of a man. Around the edges of the buildings were iron benches painted white. On the benches the old men sat in the sun, their eyes shut, their hands folded across canes.

From somewhere behind the brick building came the sound of a brass band—the full, rich mixture of trumpet and trombone and sousa-phone, of tuba and tympani and big, bass drum.

Unexpectedly, as they sat in the car looking at the scene out of another era and another land, a tall black shape rolled silently past them. John turned his head quickly to look at it. A thin cab in the middle sloped toward spoked wheels at each end, like the front ends of two cars stuck together. An old woman in a wide-brimmed hat sat upright beside the driver. From her high window she frowned at the little foreign car, and then her vehicle passed down the street.

"That was an old electric!" John said. "I didn't know they were making them again."

From the back seat Johnny said, "When are we going to get to Grammy's?"

"Soon," his mother said. "If you're going to ask the way to Buffalo Street, you'd better ask," she said to John. "It's too hot to sit here in the car."

John opened the door and extracted himself from the damp socket of the bucket seat. He stood for a moment beside the baked metal of the car and looked up each side of the street. The oomp-pah-pah of the band was louder now and the yeasty smell of baking bread dilated his nostrils, but the whole scene struck him as unreal somehow, as if this all were a stage setting and a man could walk behind the buildings and find that the backs were unpainted canvas and raw wood.

"Well?" Sally said.

John shook his head and walked around the front of the car. The first store sold hardware. In the small front window were crowbars and wooden-handled claw hammers and three kegs of blue nails; one of the kegs had a metal scoop stuck into the nails at the top. In one corner of the window was a hand mower, its handle varnished wood, its metal wheels and reel blue, except where the spokes had been touched with red and yellow paint and the curved reel had been sharpened to a silver line.

The interior of the store was dark; John could not tell whether anyone was inside.

Next to it was "Tyler's General Store," and John stepped inside onto sawdust. Before his eyes adjusted from the Sunshine State's proudest asset, he smelled the pungent sawdust. The odor was mingled with others—the vinegar and spice of pickles and the ripeness of cheese and a sweet-sour smell that he could not identify.

Into his returning vision the faces swam first—the pale faces of the old people, framed in white hair, relieved from the anonymity of age only by the way in which bushy eyebrows sprouted or a mustache was trimmed or wrinkles carved the face. Then he saw the rest of the store and the old people. Some of them were sitting in scarred oak chairs with rounded backs near a black, potbellied stove. The room was cool; after a moment John realized that the stove was producing a cold breeze.

One old man with a drooping white mustache was leaning over from the barrel he sat on to cut a slice of cheese from the big wheel on the counter. A tall man with an apron over his shirt and trousers and his shirt sleeves hitched up with rubber bands came from behind the counter, moving his bald head with practiced ease among the dangling sausages.

"Son," he said, "I reckon you lost your way. Made the wrong turn off the highway, I warrant. Heading for Winter Hope or beyond and mistook yourself. You just head back out how you come in and——"

"Is this Sunset Acres?" John said.

The old man with the yellow slice of cheese in his hand said in a thin voice, "Yep. No use thinking you can stay, though. Thirty-five or forty years too soon. That's what!" His sudden laughter came out in a cackle.

The others joined in, like a superannuated Greek chorus, "Can't stay!"

"I'm looking for Buffalo Street," John said. "We're going to visit the Plummers." He paused and then added, "They're my wife's parents."

The storekeeper tucked his thumbs into the straps of his apron. "That's different. Everybody knows the Plummers. Three blocks north of the square. Can't miss it."

"Thank you," John said, nodding, and backed into the sunshine. The interrupted murmur of conversation began again, broken briefly by laughter.

"Three blocks north of the square," he said as he inserted himself back in the car.

He started the motor, shifted into first, and turned the corner. As he passed the general store he thought he saw white faces peering out of the darkness, but they might have been feather pillows hanging in the window.

In front of the town hall an old man jerked in his sleep as the car passed. Another opened his eyes and frowned. A third shook his cane in their general direction. Beyond, a thin woman in a lavender shawl was holding an old man by the shoulder as if to tell him that she was done with the shopping and it was time to go home.

"John, look!" Sally said, pointing out the window beside her.

To their right was an ice-cream parlor. Metal chairs and round tables with thin, wire legs were set in front of the store under a yellow awning. At one of the tables sat an elderly couple. The man sat straight in his chair like an army officer, his hair iron-gray and neatly parted, his eyebrows thick. He was keeping time to the music of the band with the cane in his right hand. His left hand held the hand of a little old woman in a black dress, who gazed at him as she sipped from the soda in front of her.

The music was louder here. Just to the north of the town hall, they could see now, was a bandstand with a conical roof. On the bandstand sat half a dozen old men in uniforms, playing instruments. Another man in uniform stood in front of them, waving a baton. It was a moment before John realized what was wrong with the scene. The music was louder and richer than the half-dozen musicians could have produced.

But it was Johnny who pointed out the tape recorder beside the bandstand, "Just like Daddy's."

It turned out that Buffalo Street was not three blocks north of the square but three blocks south.

The aging process had been kind to Mrs. Henry Plummer. She

110

was a small woman, and the retreating years had left their detritus of fat, but the extra weight seemed no burden on her small bones and the cushioning beneath the skin kept it plump and unwrinkled. Her youthful complexion seemed strangely at odds with her blue-white curls. Her eyes, though, were unmistakably old. They were faded like a blue gingham dress.

They looked at Sally now, John thought, as if to say, "What I have seen you through, my dear, the colic and the boys, the measles and the mumps and the chickenpox and the boys, the frozen fingers and the skinned knees and the boys, the parties and the late hours and the boys. . . . And now you come again to me, bringing this larger, distant boy that I do not like very much, who has taken you from me and treated you with crude familiarity, and you ask me to call him by his first name and consider him one of the family. It's too much."

When she spoke her voice was surprisingly small. "Henry," she said, a little girl in an old body, "don't stand there talking all day. Take in the bags! These children must be starved to death!"

Henry Plummer had grown thinner as his wife had filled out, as if she had grown fat at his expense. Plummer had been a junior executive, long after he had passed in age most of the senior executives, in a firm that manufactured games and toys, but a small inheritance and cautious investments in municipal bonds and life insurance had made possible his comfortable retirement.

He could not shake the habits of a lifetime; his face bore the wry expression of a man who expects the worst and receives it. He said little, and when he spoke it was usually to protest. "Well, I guess I'm not the one holding them up," he said, but he stooped for the bags.

John moved quickly to reach the bags first. "I'll get them, Dad," he said. The word "Dad" came out as if it were fitted with rusty hooks. He had never known what to call Henry Plummer. His own father had died when he was a small child, and his mother had died when he was in college; but he could not find in himself any filial affection for Plummer. He disliked the coyness of "Dad," but it was better than the stiffness of "Mr. Plummer" or the false camaraderie of "Henry."

With Mrs. Plummer the problem had not been so great. John recalled a joke from the book he had edited recently for the paperback publishing firm that employed him. "For the first year I said, 'Hey, you!' and then I called her 'Grandma.' "

He straightened with the scuffed suitcases, looking helplessly at Sally for a moment and then apologetically at Plummer. "I guess you've carried your share of luggage already."

"He's perfectly fit," Mrs. Plummer said.

Sally looked only at Johnny. Sally was small and dark-haired and pretty, and John loved her and her whims—"a whim of iron," they called her firm conviction that she knew the right thing to do at any time, in any situation—but when she was around her mother John saw reflected in her behavior all the traits that he found irritating in the old woman. Sometime, perhaps, she would even be plump like her mother, but now it did not seem likely. She ran after Johnny fourteen hours a day.

She held the hand of her four-year-old, her face flushed, her eyes bright with pride. "I guess you see how he's grown, Mother. Ten pounds since you saw him last Christmas. And three inches taller. Give your grandmother a kiss, Johnny. A big kiss for Grammy. He's been talking all the way from New York about coming to visit Grammy—and Granddad, too, of course. I can't imagine what makes him act so shy now. Usually he isn't. Not even with strangers. Give Grammy a great big kiss."

"Well," Mrs. Plummer said, "you must be starved. Come on in. I've got a ham on the stove, and we'll have sandwiches and coffee. And, Johnny, I've got something for you. A box of chocolates, all your own."

"Oh, Mother!" Sally said. "Not just before lunch. He won't eat a bite."

Johnny jumped up and down. He pulled his hand free from his mother's and ran to Mrs. Plummer. "Candy! Candy!" he shouted. He gave Mrs. Plummer a big, wet kiss.

John stood at the living room window listening to the whisper of the air conditioning and looking out at the Florida evening. He could see Johnny playing in the pile of sand his thoughtful grandparents had had dumped in the back yard. It had been a relief to be alone with his wife, but now the heavy silence of disagreement hung in the air between them. He had wanted to leave, to return to New York, and she would not even consider the possibility.

He had massed all his arguments, all his uneasiness, about this strange, nightmarish town, about how he felt unwanted, about how it disliked them, and Sally had found his words first amusing and then disagreeable. For her Sunset Acres was an arcadia for the aged. Her reaction was strongly influenced by that glimpse of the old couple at the ice cream parlor.

John had always found in her a kind of Walt Disney sentimentality, but it had never disturbed him before. He turned and made one last effort, "Besides, your parents don't even want us here. We've been here only a couple of hours and already they've left us to go to some meeting."

"It's their monthly town hall meeting," Sally said. "They have an obligation to attend. It's part of their self-government or something."

"Oh, hell," John said, turning back to the window. He looked from left to right and back again. "Johnny's gone."

He ran to the back door and fumbled with it for a moment. Then it opened, and he was in the back yard. After the sterile chill of the house, the air outside seemed ripe with warm black earth and green things springing through the soil. The sandpile was empty; there was no place for the boy to hide among the colorful Florida shrubs which hid the back yard of the house behind and had colorful names he could never remember.

John ran around the corner of the house. He reached the porch just as Sally came through the front door.

"There he is," Sally cried out.

"Johnny!" John shouted.

The four-year-old had started across the street. He turned and looked back at them. "Grammy," he said.

John heard him clearly.

The car slipped into the scene like a shadow, silent, unsuspected. John saw it out of the corner of his eye. Later he thought that it must have turned the nearby corner, or perhaps it came out of a driveway. In the moment before the accident, he saw that the old woman in the wide-brimmed hat was driving the car herself. He saw her head turn toward Johnny, and he saw the upright electric turn sharply toward the child.

The front fender hit Johnny and threw him toward the sidewalk. John looked incredulously at the old woman. She smiled at him, and then the car was gone down the street.

"Johnny!" Sally screamed. Already she was in the street, the boy's head cradled in her lap. She hugged him and then pushed him away to look blindly into his face and then hugged him again, rocking him in her arms, crying.

John found himself beside her, kneeling. He pried the boy away from her. Johnny's eyes were closed. His face was pale, but John couldn't find any blood. He lifted the boy's eyelids. The pupils seemed dilated. Johnny did not stir.

"What's the matter with him?" Sally screamed at John. "He's going to die, isn't he?"

"I don't know. Let me think! Let's get him into the house."

113

"You aren't supposed to move people who've been in an accident!"

"We can't leave him here to be run over by someone else."

John picked up his son gently and walked to the house. He lowered the boy onto the quilt in the front bedroom and looked down at him for a moment. The boy was breathing raggedly. He moaned. His hand twitched. "I've got to get a doctor," John said. "Where's the telephone?"

Sally stared at him as if she hadn't heard. John turned away and looked in the living room. An antique apparatus on a wooden frame was attached to one wall. He picked up the receiver and cranked the handle vigorously. "Hello!" he said. "Hello!" No answer.

He returned to the bedroom. Sally was still standing beside the bed. "What a lousy town!" he said. "No telephone service!" Sally looked at him. She blinked.

"I'll have to go to town," John said. "You stay with Johnny. Keep him warm. Put cold compresses on his head." They might not help Johnny, he thought, but they would keep Sally quiet.

She nodded and headed toward the bathroom.

When he got to the car, it refused to start. After a few futile attempts, he gave up, knowing he had flooded the motor. He ran back to the house. Sally looked up at him, calmer now that her hands were busy.

"I'm going to run," he told her. "I might see that woman and be unable to resist the impulse to smash into her."

"Don't talk crazy," Sally said. "It was just an accident."

"It was no accident," John said. "I'll be back with a doctor as soon as I can find one."

John ran down the brick sidewalks until his throat burned and then walked for a few steps before breaking once more into a run. By then the square was in sight. The sun had plunged into the Gulf of Mexico, and the town was filled with silence and shadows. The storefronts were dark. There was no light anywhere in the square.

The first store was a butcher shop. Hams hung in the windows, and plucked chickens, naked and scrawny, dangled by cords around their yellow feet. John thought he smelled sawdust and blood. He remembered Johnny and felt sick.

Next was a clothing store with two wide windows under the name "Emporium." In the windows were stiff, waxen dummies in black suits and high, starched collars; in lace and parasol. Then came a narrow door; on its window were printed the words, "Saunders and Jones, Attorneys at Law." The window framed dark steps.

114

Beside it was a print shop—piles of paper pads in the window, white, yellow, pink, blue; reams of paper in dusty wrappers; faded invitations and personal cards; and behind them the lurking shapes of printing presses and racks of type.

John passed a narrow bookstore with books stacked high in the window and ranged in ranks into the darkness. Then came a restaurant; a light in the back revealed scattered tables with checkered cloths. He pounded at the door, making a shocking racket in the silence of the square, but no one came.

Kittycorner across the street, he saw the place and recognized it by the tall, intricately shaped bottles of colored water in the window and the fancy jar hanging from chains. He ran across the brick street and beat on the door with his fist. There was no response. He kicked it, but the drug store remained silent and dark. Only the echoes answered his summons, and they soon died away.

Next to the drug store was another dark door. The words printed across the window in it said, "Joseph M. Bronson, M.D." And underneath, "Geriatrics Only."

John knocked, sure it was useless, wondering, "Why is the town locked up? Where is everybody?" And then he remembered the meeting. That's where everyone was, at the meeting the Plummers couldn't miss. No one could miss the meeting. Everyone had to be there, apparently, even the telephone operator. But where was it being held?

Of course. Where else would a town meeting be held? In the town hall.

He ran across the street once more and up the wide steps. He pulled open one of the heavy doors and stepped into a hall with tall ceilings. Stairways led up on either side, but light came through a pair of doors ahead. He heard a babble of voices. John walked towards the doors, feeling the slick oak floors under his feet, smelling the public toilet odors of old urine and disinfectant.

He stopped for a moment at the doors to peer between them, hoping to see the Plummers, hoping they were close enough to signal without disturbing the others. The old people would be startled if he burst in among them. There would be confusion and explanations, accusations perhaps. He needed a doctor, not an argument.

The room was filled with wooden folding chairs placed neatly in rows, with a wide aisle in the middle and a narrower one on either side. From the backs of the chairs hung shawls and canes. The room had for John the unreal quality of an etching, perhaps because all the backs of the heads that he saw were silver and gray, here and there accented with tints of blue or green.

At the front of the room was a walnut rostrum on a broad platform. Behind the rostrum stood the old man Sally had pointed out in the ice cream parlor. He stood as straight as he had sat.

The room buzzed as if it had a voice of its own, and the voice rose and fell, faded and returned, the way it does in a dream. One should be able to understand it, one had to understand it, but one couldn't quite make out the words.

The old man banged on the rostrum with a wooden gavel; the gavel had a small silver plate attached to its head. "Everyone will have his chance to be heard," he said. It was like an order. The buzz faded away. "Meanwhile we will speak one at a time, and in a proper manner, first being recognized by the chair.

"Just one moment, Mr. Samuelson.

"For many years the public press has allowed its columns to bleed over the voting age. 'If a boy of eighteen is old enough to die for his country, he is old enough to vote for its legislators,' the sentimentalists have written.

"Nonsense. It takes no intelligence to die. Any idiot can do it. Surviving takes brains. Men of eighteen aren't even old enough to take orders properly, and until a man can take orders he can't give them.

"Mrs. Richards, I have the floor. When I have finished I will recognize each of you in turn."

John started to push through the doors and announce the emergency to the entire group, but something about the stillness of the audience paralyzed his decision. He stood there, his hand on the door, his eyes searching for the Plummers.

"Let me finish," the old man at the rostrum said. "Only when a man has attained true maturity—fifty is the earliest date for the start of this time of life—does he begin to identify the important things in life. At this age, the realization comes to him, if it ever comes, that the individual has the right to protect and preserve the property that he has accumulated by his own hard work, and, in the protection of this right, the state stands between the individual and mob rule in Washington. Upon these eternal values we take our stand: the individual, his property, and state's rights. Else our civilization, and everything in it of value, will perish."

The light faded from his eyes, and the gavel which had been raised in his hand like a saber sank to the rostrum. "Mr. Samuelson."

In the front of the room a man stood up. He was small and bald except for two small tufts of hair above his ears. "I have heard what you said, and I understand what you said because you said it before. It is all very well to talk of the rights of the individual to protect his property, but how can he protect his property when the government taxes and taxes and taxes—state governments as well as Washington? I say, 'Let the government give us four exemptions instead of two.'"

A cracked voice in the back of the room said, "Let them cut out taxes altogether for senior citizens!"

"Yes!"

"No!"

A small, thin woman got up in the middle of the audience. "Four hundred dollars a month for every man and woman over sixty-five!" she said flatly. "Why shouldn't we have it? Didn't we build this country? Let the government give us back a little of what they have taken away. Besides, think of the money it would put into circulation."

"You have not been recognized, Mrs. Richards," the chairman said, "and I declare you out of order and the Townsendites as well. What you are advocating is socialism, more government not less."

"Reds!" someone shouted. "Commies!" said someone else. "That's not true!" said a woman near the door. "It's only fair," shouted an old man, nodding vigorously. Canes and crutches were waved in the air, a hundred Excaliburs and no Arthur. John glanced behind him to see if the way was clear for retreat in case real violence broke out.

"Sally!" he exclaimed, discovering her behind him. "What are you doing here? Where's Johnny?"

"He's in the car. He woke up. He seemed all right. I thought I'd better find you. Then we'd be closer to the doctor. I looked all over. What are you doing here?"

John rubbed his forehead. "I don't know. I was looking for a doctor. Something's going on here. I don't know what it is, but I don't like it."

"What's going on?"

Sally tried to push past him, but John grabbed her arm. "Don't go in there!"

The Chairman's gavel finally brought order out of confusion. "We are senior citizens, not young hoodlums!" he admonished them. "We can disagree without forgetting our dignity and our common interests, Mrs. Johnson."

A woman stood up at the right beside one of the tall windows that now framed the night. She was a stout woman with gray hair pulled back into a bun. "It seems to me, Colonel, that we are getting far from the subject of this meeting—indeed, the subject of all our meetings—and that is what we are going to do about the young people who are taking over everything and pushing us out. As many of you know, I have no prejudices about young people. Some of my best friends are young people, and, although I cannot name my children among them, for they are ingrates, I bear my son and my two daughters no ill will."

She paused for a deep breath. "We must not let the young people get the upper hand. We must find ways of insuring that we get from them the proper respect for our age and our experience. The best way to do this, I believe, is to keep them in suspense about the property—the one thing about us they still value—how much there is and what will become of it. Myself, I pretend that there is at least two or three times as much. When I am visiting one of them, I leave my check book lying carelessly about—the one that has the very large and false balance. And I let them overhear me make an appointment to see a lawyer. What do I have to see a lawyer about, they think, except my will?

"Actually I have written my will once and for all, leaving my property to the Good Samaritan Rest Home for the Aged, and I do not intend to change it. But I worry that some clever young lawyer will find a way to break the will. They're always doing that when you disinherit someone."

"Mrs. Johnson," the Colonel said, "you have a whole town full of friends who will testify that you always have been in full possession of your faculties, if it ever should come to that, God forbid! Mrs. Fredericks?"

"Nasty old woman," Sally muttered. "Where are Mother and Father? I don't see them. I don't think they're here at all."

"Sh-h-h!"

"I'm leaving my money to my cat," said a bent old woman with a hearing aid in her ear. "I'm just sorry I won't get to see their faces."

The Colonel smiled at her as he nodded her back to her seat at the left front. Then he recognized a man sitting in the front row. "Mr. Saunders."

The man who arose was short, straight, and precise. "I would like to remind these ladies of the services of our legal aid department. We have had good luck in constructing unbreakable legal documents. A word of caution, however—the more far-fetched the legatee, though to be sure the more satisfying, the more likely the breaking of the will. There is only one certain way to prevent property from falling into the hands of those who have neither worked for it nor merited it—and that is to spend it.

118

"Personally, I am determined to spend on the good life every cent that I accumulated in a long and—you will pardon my lack of humility —distinguished career at the bar."

"Your personal life is your own concern, Mr. Saunders," the Colonel said, "but I must tell you, sir, that we are aware of how you spend your money and your time away from here. I do not recommend it to others nor do I approve of your presenting it to us as worthy of emulation. Indeed, I think you do our cause damage."

Mr. Saunders had not resumed his seat. He bowed and continued, "Each to his own tastes—I cite an effective method for keeping the younger generation in check. There are other ways of disposing of property irretrievably." He sat down.

John pulled Sally back from the doors. "Go to the car," he said. "Get out of here. Go back to the house and get our bags packed. Quick!"

"Mrs. Plummer?" the Colonel said.

Sally pulled away from John.

The familiar figure stood up at the front of the room. Now John could identify beside her the gray head of Henry Plummer, turned now toward the plump face of his wife.

"We all remember," Mrs. Plummer said calmly, "what a trial children are. What we may forget is that our children have children. I do my best not to let my daughter forget the torments she inflicted upon me when she was a child. We hide these things from them. We conceal the bitterness. They seldom suspect. And we take our revenge, if we are wise, by encouraging their children to be just as great a trial to their parents. We give them candy before meals. We encourage them to talk back to their parents. We build up their infant egos so that they will stand up for their childish rights. When their parents try to punish them, we stand between the child and the punishment. Fellow senior citizens, this is our revenge: that their parents will be as miserable as we were."

"Mother! No!" Sally cried out.

The words and the youthful voice that spoke them rippled the audience like a stone tossed into a pond. Faces turned toward the back of the meeting room, faces with wrinkles and white hair and faded eyes, faces searching, near-sighted, faces disturbed, faces beginning to fear and to hate. Among them was one face John knew well, a face that had dissembled malice and masqueraded malevolence as devotion.

"Do as I told you!" John said violently. "Get out of here!"

For once in her life, Sally did as she was told. She ran down the hall, pushed her way through the big front doors, and was gone. John looked for something with which to bar the doors to the meeting room, but the hall was bare. He was turning back to the doors when he saw the oak cane in the corner. He caught it up and slipped it through the handles. Then he put his shoulder against the doors.

In the meeting room the gathering emotion was beginning to whip thin blood into a simulation of youthful vigor, and treble voices began to deepen as they shouted encouragement at those nearest the doors.

"A spy!"

"Was it a woman?"

"A girl."

"Let me get my hands on her!"

The first wave hit the doors. John was knocked off balance. He pushed himself forward again, and again the surge of bodies against the other side forced him back. He dug in his feet and shoved. A sound of commotion added to the shouting in the meeting room. John heard something—or someone—fall.

The next time he was forced from the doors the cane bent. Again he pushed the doors shut; the cane straightened. At the same moment he felt a sharp pain across his back. He looked back. The Colonel was behind him, breathing hard, the glow of combat in his eyes and the cane in his hand upraised for another blow, like the hand of Abraham over Isaac.

John stepped back. In his hand he found the cane that had been thrust through the door handles. He raised it over his head as the Colonel struck again. The blow fell upon the cane. The Colonel drew back his cane and swung once more, and again his blow was parried, more by accident than skill. Then the doors burst open, and the wild old bodies were upon them.

John caught brief glimpses of flying white hair and ripped lace and spectacles worn awry. Canes and crutches were raised above him. He smelled lavender and bay rum mingled with the sweet-sour odor of sweat. He heard shrill voices, like the voices of children, cry out curses and maledictions, and he felt upon various parts of his body the blows of feeble fists, their bones scarcely padded, doing perhaps more damage to themselves than to him, though it seemed sufficient.

He went down quickly. Rather too quickly, he thought dazedly as he lay upon the floor, curled into a fetal position to avoid the stamping feet and kicks and makeshift clubs.

He kept waiting for it to be over, for consciousness to leave him, but most of the blows missed him, and in the confusion and the milling about, the object of the hatred was lost. John saw a corridor that led between bodies and legs through the doors that opened into the meeting room. He crawled by inches toward the room; eventually he found himself among the chairs. The commotion was behind him.

Cautiously he peered over the top of a fallen chair. He saw what he had overlooked before—a door behind the rostrum. It stood open to the night. That was how the Colonel, with instinctive strategy, had come up behind him, he thought, and he crept toward it and down the narrow steps behind the town hall.

For a moment he stood in the darkness assessing his injuries. He was surprised: they were few, none serious. Perhaps tomorrow he would find bruises enough and a lump here and there and perhaps even a broken rib or two, but now there was only a little pain. He started to run.

He had been running in the darkness for a long time, not certain he was running in the right direction, not sure he knew what the right direction was, when a dark shape coasted up beside him. He dodged instinctively before he recognized the sound of the motor.

"John!" It was a voice he knew. "John?"

The Volkswagen was running without lights. John caught the door handle. The door came open. The car stopped. "Move over," he said, out of breath. Sally climbed over the gear shift, and John slid into the bucket seat. He released the hand brake and pushed hard on the accelerator. The car plunged forward.

Only when they reached the highway did John speak again. "Is Johnny all right?"

"I think so," Sally said. "But he's got to see a doctor."

"We'll find a doctor in Orange Grove."

"A young one."

John wiped his nose on the back of his hand and looked at it. His hand was smeared with blood. "Damn!"

She pressed a tissue into his hand. "Was it bad?"

"Incredible!" He laughed harshly and said it again in a different tone. "Incredible. What a day! And what a night! But it's over. And a lot of other things are over."

Johnny was crying in the back seat.

"What do you mean?" Sally asked. "Hush, Johnny, it's going to be all right."

"Grammy!" Johnny moaned.

"The letters. Presents for people who don't need anything. Worrying about what mother's going to think. . . ."

The car slowed as John looked back toward the peaceful town of

Sunset Acres, sleeping now in the Florida night, and remembered the wide lawns and the broad porches, the brick streets and the slow time, and the old folks. "All over," he said again.

Johnny still was crying.

"Shut up, Johnny!" he said between his teeth and immediately felt guilty.

"John!" Sally said. "We mustn't ever be like that toward our son."

She wasn't referring just to what he had said, John knew. He glanced back toward the small figure huddled in the back seat. It wasn't over, he thought; it was beginning. "It's over," he said again, as if he could convince himself by repetition. Sally was silent. "Why don't you say something?" John asked.

"I keep thinking about how it used to be," she said. "He's my father. She's my mother. How can anything change that? You can't expect me to hate my own father and mother?"

It wasn't over. It would never be over. Even though the children sometimes escaped, the old folks always won: the children grew up, the young people became old folks.

The car speeded up and rushed through the night, the headlights carving a corridor through the darkness, a corridor that kept closing behind them. The corridor still was there, as real in back as it was revealing in front, and it could never be closed.

The Steam-Driven Boy

by John Sladek

Science fiction is beginning to parody itself, which can only be a Very Good Thing. There is nothing like a touch of humor to destroy the pompous and self-inflated. John Sladek, an American now residing in London, is a humorist, and a generally black one at that, with books like **Black Alice** *and* **The Reproductive System.** *He now delivers the final and definitive time-travel story.*

Captain Charles Conn was thinking so hard his feet hurt. It reminded him of his first days on the force, back in '89, when walking a beat gave him headaches.

Three time-patrolmen stood before his desk, treading awkwardly on the edges of their long red cloaks and fingering their helmets nervously. Captain Conn wanted to snarl at them, but what was the point? They already understood his problems perfectly—they were, after all, Conn himself, doubling a shift.

"Okay, Charlie, report."

The first patrolman straightened. "I went back to three separate periods, sir. One when the President was disbanding the House of Representatives, one when he proclaimed himself the Supreme Court, one when he was signing the pro-pollution bill. I gave him the whole business—statistics, pictures, news stories. All he would say was, 'My mind's made up.' "

Chuck and Chas reported similar failures. There was no stopping the President. Not only had he usurped all the powers of federal, state and local government, but he used those powers to deliberately torment the population. It was a crime to eat ice cream, sing, whistle, swear, or kiss. It was a *capital* offense to smile, or to use the words "Russia" or "China." Under the Safe Streets Act it was illegal to walk, loiter or converse in public. And of course Negroes and anyone else "conspicuous" were by definition criminals, and came under the jurisdiction of the Race Reaction Board.

The Natural Food Act had seemed at first almost reasonable, a response to scientists' warnings about depleting the soil and endangering the environment. But the fine print specified that henceforth no fertilizers were to be used but human or canine excrement, and all farm machinery was forbidden. In time the newspapers featured pictures of farmers trudging past their rusting tractors to poke holes in the soil with sharp sticks. And in time, the newspapers had their paper supply curtailed. Famine warnings were ignored until the government had to buy wheat from C****.

"Gentlemen, we've tried everything else. *It's time to think about getting rid of President Ernie Barnes.*"

The men began to murmur among themselves. This was done with efficiency and dispatch, for Patrolman Charlie, knowing that Chuck was going to murmur to him first, withheld his own murmuring until it was his turn. And when Chuck had murmured to Charlie, he fell silent, and let Charlie and Chas get on with their murmuring before he murmured uneasily to Chas.

The captain spoke again. "Getting rid of him in the past would be easier than getting rid of him now, but it's only part of the problem. If we remove him from the past, we have to make sure no one notices the big jagged hole in history we'll leave. Since as time-police we have the only time-bikes around, the evidence is going to make us look bad. Remember the trouble we had getting rid of the pyramids? For months, everyone went around saying, 'What's that funny thing on the back of the dollar?' Remember that?"

"Hey Captain, what is that funny thing—?"

"Shut up. The point is, you can change some of the times some of the time, and, uh, some of the—— Look at it this way: Ernie must have shaken hands with a million people. We rub *him* out, and all these people suddenly get back all the germs they rubbed off *on* him. Suddenly we have an epidemic."

"Yeah, but Captain, *did* he ever shake any hands? He never does any more. Just sits there in the White Fort, all fat and ugly, behind his FBI and CIA and individualized anti-personnel missiles and poison germ gas towers and—and that big, mean dog."

Captain Conn glared the patrolman down, then continued: "My idea is, we kidnap Ernie Barnes from his childhood, back in 1937. And we leave a glass egg."

"A classic?"

"A *glass egg*. Like they used to put under chickens when they took

124

away their children. What I mean is, we substitute an artificial kid for the real one. Wilbur Grafton says he can make a robot replica of Ernie as he looked in 1937."

Wilbur Grafton was a wealthy eccentric and amateur inventor well known to all members of the time-patrol. Their father, James Conn, was one of Wilbur's employees.

"Another thing. Just in case somebody back in 1937 gets suspicious and takes him apart, we'll have the robot built of pre-1937 junk. Steam-driven. No use giving away the secrets of molecular circuitry and peristaltic logic before their time."

The four of them, with a fifth patrolman (Carl), arrived one evening at the mansion of Wilbur Grafton. To the butler who admitted them, each man said "Hello, Dad," to which their unruffled father replied, "Good evening, sir. You'll find Mr. Grafton in the drawing room."

The venerable millionaire, immaculate in evening clothes, welcomed them, then excused himself to prepare the demonstration. James poured generous drinks, and while some of the party admired the authentic 1950's appointments of the room—including a genuine "stereo" phonograph—others watched television. It was almost curfew time, and the channels were massed with Presidential commercials:

"Sleep well, America! Your President is safe! Yes, thanks to I.A.M.—individual antipersonnel missiles—no one can harm our Leader. Think of it: over ten billion eternally vigilant little missiles all around the White Fort, guarding his sleep and yours. And don't forget—there's one with *your* name on it."

Wilbur Grafton returned and at curfew time one of the men asked him to begin the demonstration. He wheezed with delight. His glasses twinkling, he replied: "My good man, the demonstration is already going on." Pressing one of his shirt studs, he added, "And here is— The Steam-Driven Boy!"

His body parted down the middle and swung open in two half-shells, revealing a pudgy youngster in knitted swim trunks and striped T-shirt, who was determinedly working cranks and levers. The boy stopped operating the "Grafton wheeze-laugh" bellows, climbed out of the casing, took two steps, and froze.

"Then where's the real Wilbur Grafton?" asked Chuck.

"Right here, sir." The butler put down a priceless Woolworth's decanter and pulled his own nose, hard. Clanking and creaking, he parted like a mummy case to give up the living Grafton, once more flawlessly attired.

"Must have my little japes," he wheezed, as the real James came in with more drinks. "Now, allow me to re-animate our little friend for you."

He inserted a crank in the boy's ear and gave it several vigorous turns. With a light chuffing sound, and emitting only a hint of vapor, the small automaton came to life. That piggish nose, those wide-spaced eyes, that malicious grin were familiar to all present from Your President Cares posters.

As the white-haired inventor stooped to make some further adjustment at the back of the automaton's fat neck, "Ernie" kicked him authentically in the knee.

"Did you see that precision?" Wilbur gloated, dancing on one leg.

The robot was remarkably realistic, complete to a frayed strip of dirty adhesive tape on one shiny elbow. Charlie made the mistake of squatting down and offering Ernie some candy. Two other patrolmen helped their unfortunate comrade to a sofa, where he was able to get his head back to stop the bleeding. The little machine shrieked with delight until Wilbur managed to shut it off.

"I am confident that his parents will never notice the switch," he said, leading the way to his workshop. "Let me show you the plans."

The robot had organs analogous to those of a living being, as Wilbur Grafton's plans showed. The heart and veins were really an intricate hydraulic system; the liver a tiny distillery to volatilize eaten food and extract oil from it. Part of this oil replenished the veins, part was burned to feed the spleen's miniature steam engine. From this, belts supplied power to the limbs.

Digressing, Wilbur explained how his grandfather, Orville Grafton, had developed a peculiar substance, a plate of it would vary in thickness according to the intensity of light striking it.

"While grandfather could make nothing more useful of this 'graftonite' than bas-relief photographs, I have used it (along with mechanical irises and gelatine lenses) to form the boy's eyes," he said, and pointed to a detail. "When a tiny image has been focused on each graftonite 'retina,' a pantographic scriber traces swiftly over it, translating the image to motions in the brain."

Similar levers conveyed motions from the gramophone ears, and from hundreds of tiny pistons all over the body—the sense of touch.

The hydraulic fluid was a suspension of red particles like blood corpuscles. When it oozed to the surface through pores, these were filtered out—it doubled as perspiration.

The brain contained a number of springs, wound to various tensions. With the clockwork connecting them to various limbs, organs and facial features, these comprised Ernie's "memory."

Grafton let the plans roll shut with a snap and ordered James to charge the glasses with champagne. "Gentlemen, I give you false Ernie Barnes—from his balloon lungs out to his skin of rubberized lawn, fine wig and dentures—an all-American boy, made in the U.S.A.!"

"One thing, though," said the captain. "Won't his parents notice he doesn't—well, *grow?*"

Sighing, the inventor turned his back for a moment, and gripped the edge of his workbench to steady himself. A solemn silence descended upon the group as they saw him take off his glasses and rub his eyes.

"Gentlemen," he said quietly, "I have taken care of everything. In one year's time, this child will appear to be suddenly stricken with influenza. His fever will rise, he will weaken. Finally I see him call his mother's name. She approaches the bedside.

"'Mom,' he says, 'I'm sorry I've been such a wicked kid. Can you find it in your heart to forgive me? For—for I'm going to be an angel from now on.' His eyes flutter shut. His mother bends and kisses the burning forehead. This triggers the final mechanism, and Ernie appears to—to——"

They understood. One by one, the time-patrol put down their glasses and slipped silently from the room. Carl was elected to take the robot back to 1937.

"He was supposed to bring the kid here to headquarters," said Captain Charles Conn. "But he never showed up. And Ernie's still in power. What went wrong?" A worried frown puckered his somewhat bland features as he leafed through the appointment calendar.

"Maybe his timer went wrong," Chas suggested. "Maybe he got off his time-bike at the wrong place. Maybe he had a flat—who knows?"

"He should have been back by now. How long can it take to travel fifty years? Well, no time to figure it out now. According to the calendar, we've all got to double again. I go back to become Charlie. Charlie, you go back to fill in as Chuck. Chuck becomes Chas, and Chas, you take over for Carl." He paused, as the men exchanged badges. "As for Carl—we'll all be finding out what happens to him soon enough. Let's go!"

And, singing the time-patrol song (yes, they felt silly, but such was the President's mandate) in deep bass voices, they climbed on their glittering time-bicycles, set the egg-timers on their handlebars, and sped away.

Carl stepped out from behind a tree in 1937. The kid was kneeling in his sandpile, apparently trying to tie a tin can to a puppy's tail. The gargoyle face looked at Carl with interest.

"GET OUTA MY YARD! GET OUT OR I'LL TELL ON YA! YOU HAFTA PAY ME ONE APPLE OR ELSE I'LL——"

Still straddling the time-bike, Carl slipped forward to that autumn, picked a particularly luscious apple, and bought a can of ether at the drugstore. Clearly it would take both to get this kid.

"I 'spose," said the druggist, "I 'spose ya want me to ask ya why you're wearing a gold football helmet with wings on it and a long red cape. But I won't. Nossir, I seen all kinds. . . ."

In revenge, Carl shoplifted an object at random: a Mark Clubb Private Eye Secret Disguise Kit.

Blending back into his fading-out self, Carl held out both hands to the boy. The right held a shiny apple. The left held an ether-soaked handkerchief.

As Carl shoved off into the gray, windswept corridors of time, with the lumpy kid draped over his handlebars, it occurred to him he needed a better hiding place than Headquarters. The FBI would swoop down on them first, searching for their missing President. A better place would be the mansion of Wilbur Grafton. Or even . . . hmmm.

"An excellent plan!" Wilbur sat by the swimming pool, nursing his injured knee. "We'll smuggle him into the White Fort itself—the one place no one will think of looking for him!"

"One problem is, how to get him in, past all the guards and the——"

Wilbur pushed up his glasses and meditated. "You know the President's dog—that big ugly mongrel that appears with him in the Eat More Horsemeat commercials—Ralphie?"

Compulsively Carl sang: "Ralphie loves it, every bite/Why don't you try horse tonight?"

"I've been working on a replica of that dog. It should be big enough to contain the boy. You dispose of the real dog tonight, after curfew, then we'll disguise the boy and send him in."

When the dog came out of the White Fort to organically fertilize the lawn, Carl was waiting with the replica dog and an ether-soaked rag. Within a few minutes he had consigned the replica to a White Fort guard and dropped Ralphie in the dim, anonymous corridors of time. No one need fear the boy's discovery, for the constraints of the dog-shell were such that he could make only canine sounds and motions.

Carl reported back to the mansion.

"I have a confession to make," said the old inventor. "I am not Wilbur Grafton, only a robot.

"The real Wilbur Grafton invented a rejuvenator. Wishing to try it without attracting attention, he decided to travel into the past—back to 1905, where he would work as an assistant to his grandfather, Orville Grafton."

"Travel back in time? But that takes a time-bike!"

"Precisely. To that end, he agreed to cooperate with the time-patrol. On the night he demonstrated the Steam-Driven Boy, you recall he left the room and returned wearing the James shell? It was I in the shell. The real Wilbur slipped outside, borrowed one of your time-bikes, and went to 1905. He returned the bike on automatic control. I have taken his place ever since."

Carl scratched his head. It seemed to make a kind of sense. "Why are you telling me all this?"

"So that you might benefit by it. Using your disguise kit, you can pose as Wilbur Grafton yourself. I realize a time-patrolman's salary is small—especially when one has to do quintuple shifts for the same money. Meanwhile I have a gloriously full life. You could slip back in time and replace me." The robot handed him an envelope. "Here are instructions for dismantling me—and for making the rejuvenator, should you ever feel the need for it. This is a recorded message. Good-bye."

Why not, Carl thought. Here was the blue swimming pool, the "stereo," the whole magnificent house. James, his father, stood discreetly by, ready to pour champagne. And the upstairs maid was uncommonly pretty. It could be a long, long life, rejuvenated from time to time. . . .

Ernie sprawled in a giant chair, watching himself on television. When a guard brought in the dog, it bit him. He was just about to call the vexecutioner, to teach Ralphie a lesson, when something in the animal's eyes caught his attention.

"So it's *you*, is it?" He laughed. "Or I should say, so it's *me*. Well, don't bite me again, understand? If you do, I'll leave you inside that thing. And make you eat nasty food, while I sing about it on TV."

"Poop," the child was thinking, Ernie knew.

"I can do it, kid. I'm the President, and I can do anything I like.

That's why I'm so fat." He stood up and began to pace the throne room, his stomach preceding him like a front wheel.

"Poopy-poop," thought the boy. "If you can do anything, why don't you make everybody go to bed early, and wash their mouths out if they say——"

"I do, I do. But there's a little problem there. You're too young to understand this—I don't understand it all myself, yet—but 'everybody' is you, and you're me. I'm all the people that ever were and ever will be. All the men, anyway. All the women are the girl who used to be upstairs maid at Wilbur Grafton's."

He began explaining time-travel to little Ernie, knowing the kid wasn't getting half of it, but going on the way big Ernie had explained it all to him: Carl Conn, posing as Wilbur, had grown old. Finally he'd decided it was time to rejuve, and go back in time. Fierce old Ralphie, still lurking in the corridors of time, had attacked him, and there'd been quite an accident. One part of Carl had returned to 1905, to become Orville Grafton. Another part of him got rejuvenated, along with the dog, and had popped out in 1937.

"That Carl-part, my boy, was you. The rejuvenator wiped out some of your memory—except for dreams—and it made you look all different.

"You see, your job and mine, everybody's job, is to weave back and forth in time—" he wove his clumsy hands in the air, "—being people. My next job is to be a butler, and yours is to pretend to be a robot pretending to be you. Then probably you'll be my dad, and I'll be his dad, and then you'll be me. Get it?"

He moved the dog's tail like a lever, and the casing opened. "Would you like some ice cream? It's okay with me, only nobody else gets none."

The boy nodded. The upstairs maid, pretty as ever, came in with a Presidential sundae. The boy looked at her and his scowl almost turned to a smile.

"Mom?"

I Tell You, It's True

by Poul Anderson

Poul Anderson sold his first science fiction story in 1944 and has not looked back since. He is almost a prototype of the ideal science fiction writer with a degree in physics to back up a masterful story telling technique—plus an enviable capacity for food and beer as well as the ability to speak Danish. Some of his stories are light entertainment. Others are grimly complete in their examination of the possibilities of a technological innovation, and this is one of them.

The mansion stood on the edge of Ban Pua town, hard by the Nan River. Through a door open to its shady-side verandah, you saw slow brown waters and intensely green trees beyond that flickered in furnace sunlight. Somewhere monkeys chattered. A couple of men in shabby uniforms stoically kept watch. Their rifles looked too big for them. George Rainsdon wondered if they had personally been in combat against his countrymen.

He brought his attention back to the interior. *Now,* he thought. The sweat that plastered his shirt to him felt suddenly cold. Yet this room, stripped of the luxuries that the landlord owner had kept, was almost serene in its austerity. The four Thais across the table were much more at ease than the five Americans.

Rainsdon knew what implacability underlay those slight, polite smiles. Behind Chukkri hung portraits of Lenin and Ho Chi Minh.

Attendants brought tea and small cakes.

Rainsdon made a sitting bow. "Again I thank Your Excellency for agreeing to receive our delegation," he said with the fluency that years as a diplomat in Bangkok had given him. "Believe me, sir, the last thing my government wishes is a repetition of the Vietnam tragedy. We desire no involvement in the conflict here except to act as peacemakers." He laid on the table the box he was carrying. "In token, we beg that you accept this emblem of friendship."

"I thank you," the leader of the Sacred Liberation Movement answered. "The solution of your difficulty is quite simple. You need merely withdraw your military personnel. But let us see the gift you graciously bring."

He opened the package and took forth a handsome bronze statuette in an abstract native-derived style. Its plaque held soft words. One of his generals frowned. Chukkri flashed him a sardonic glance that might as well have said aloud, *Not even the Americans are stupid enough to imagine that assassinating us will halt the advance of our heroic troops.* "Please thank your President on my behalf," he uttered.

The warmth of his touch completed the activation of a circuit.

Rainsdon leaned forward. *Go for broke!* His slight giddiness passed into a feeling that resembled his emotions when he had led infantry charges in Korea in his long passed youth. The rehearsed but wholly sincere words torrented from him:

"Your Excellency. Gentlemen. Let me deliver, at this private and informal conference, the plain words of the United States Government. The United States has no aggressive intentions toward the people of Thailand or any other country. Our sole desire is to help Thailand end the civil war on terms satisfactory to everyone. The first and most essential prerequisite for peace is that your organization accept a cease-fire and negotiate in good faith with the legitimate government to arrange a plebiscite. Your ideology is alien to the Thai people and must not be forced on them. However, you will be free to advocate it, to persuade by precept and example, to offer candidates for office. If defeated, they must accept with grace; if victorious, they must work within the existing system. But we do not want you to renounce your principles publicly. If nothing else, you can be valuable intermediaries between us and capitals like Hanoi and Peking. Thereby you will truly serve the cause of peace and the liberation of the people."

They sat still, the short, neat Asian men, for a time that grew and grew. Rainsdon's back ached from tension. Would it work? Could it? *How* could it? He had said nothing they hadn't heard a thousand times before and scorned as mendacious where it was not meaningless. They had fought, they had lost friends dear to them, they were ready to be slain themselves or to fight on for a weary lifetime; their cause was as holy to them as that of Godfrey of Bouillon had been to him—though it was no mere Jerusalem they would rescue from the infidel, it was mankind.

Finally, frowning, a fist clenched beside his untasted cup of tea,

132

Chukkri said, very low and slow: "I had not considered the matter in just those terms before. Would you explain in more detail?"

Rainsdon heard a gasp from his aides. They had not expected their journey would prove anything except a barren gesture. Glory mounted in him. *It does work! By God, it works!*

He got busy. The circuitry in the statuette would fuse itself into slag after three hours. That ought to be ample time. The CIA had planned this operation with ultimate care.

The laboratories stood on the peninsula south of San Francisco, commanding a magnificent view of ocean if it were possible to over-look the freeway, the motels, and the human clutter on the beach. The sanctum where Edward Sigerist and Manuel Duarte had brought their guests made it easy to ignore such encroachments. The room, though big, was windowless; the single noise was a murmur of ventilators blowing air which carried a faint tinge of ozone; fluorescent panels threw cold light on the clutter of gadgetry burying the workbenches around the walls, and on the solitary table in the center where six men sat and regarded a thing.

Fenner from MIT spoke: "Pretty big for that level of output, isn't it?" His tone was awed; he was merely breaking a lengthy silence.

"Breadboard circuit," Sigerist answered, equally unnecessarily considering what a jumble of wires and electronic components the thing was. "Any engineer could miniaturize it to the size of your thumb, for short-range work, in a few months. Or scale it up for power, till three of them in synchronous satellites could blanket the Earth. If he couldn't do that, from the cookbook, he'd better go back to chipping flints." He was a large, shaggy, rumpled man. His voice was calm but his eyes were haunted.

"Of course, he'd need the specs," said his collaborator, lean, intense, dark-complexioned Duarte. His glance ranged over the visitors. Fenner, physicist, sharp-featured beneath a cupola of forehead; Mottice, biochemist from London, plump and placid except for the sweat that now glistened on his cheeks; tiny Yuang of the Harvard psychology department; and Ginsberg of Cal Tech, who resembled any grocer or bookkeeper till you remembered his Nobel Prizes for quantum field theory and molecular biology. "That's why we brought you gentlemen here."

"Why the secrecy?" Yuang asked. "Our work has all been reported in the open literature. Others can build on it, as you have done. Others doubtless will."

"N-n-not inevitably," Sigerist replied. "Kind of a fluke, our success. This isn't a big outfit, you know. Mostly we contract to do R and D on biomedical instrumentation. I'm alone in having a completely free hand, which is how come I get away with studying dowsing. I was carrying on Rocard's investigations, which were published back in the mid-'60's and never got the attention they deserved."

Receiving blank stares: "Essentially, he gave good theoretical and experimental grounds for supposing that dowsing results from the nervous system's response to variations in terrestrial magnetism. I was using your data too, Dr. Mottice, Dr. Ginsberg. Then at the Triple-A-S meeting three years ago, I happened to meet Manuel at an after-hours beer party. He was with General Electric . . . He called to my notice the papers by Dr. Yuang and Dr. Fenner. We both took fire; I arranged for him to transfer here; we worked together. Kept our mouths shut, at first because we weren't sure where we were going, later because we made a breakthrough and suddenly realized what it meant to the world." He shrugged. "An unlikely set of coincidences, no?"

"Well," Ginsberg inquired, "what effects do you anticipate?"

"For openers," Duarte told him, "we can stop the war in Thailand. Soon after, we can stop all war everywhere."

The room was long, mirrored, ornate in the red plush fashion of Franz Josef's day. The handful of men who sat there were drab by contrast, like beetles.

Not a bad comparison, thought the President of the United States. *For Party Secretary Tupilov, at least. Premier Grigorovitch seems a bit more human.*

He made the slight, prearranged hand signal. His interpreter responded by nervously tugging his necktie. It energized a circuit in what appeared to be a cigarette case.

"First," said the President, "I want to express my appreciation of your cooperativeness. I hope the considerable concessions made by the United States, especially with regard to the Southeast Asia question, seemed more than a bribe to win your presence here. I hope they indicated that my government genuinely desires a permanent settlement of the conflicts that rack the world—a settlement such that armed strife can never occur again."

While his interpreter put it into Russian, he watched the two overlords. His heart thumped when Grigorovitch beamed and nodded. Tupilov's dourness faded to puzzlement; he shook his big bald head as if to clear away an interior haze.

134

His political years had taught the President how to assume sternness at will, however more common geniality was. "I shall be blunt," he continued. "I shall tell you certain home truths in unvarnished language. We can have no peace until every nation is secure. This requires general nuclear disarmament, enforced by adequate inspection. It requires that the great powers join to guarantee every country safety, not against overt invasion alone, but also against subversion and insurrection. Undeniably, every nation that we Americans label 'free' is not. Many of their governments are tyrannical and corrupt. But liberation is not to be accomplished through violent revolution on the part of fanatics who, if successful, would upset the world balance of power and so bring us to the verge of the final war.

"Instead, peace requires that the leading nations cooperate to make available to the people of every country the means for orderly replacement of their governments through genuinely free elections. This presupposes that they be granted freedom of speech, assembly, petition, travel, and worship, in fact as well as in name.

"Gentlemen, we have talked too long and done too little about democracy. We must begin by putting our own houses in order. You will not resent my stating that your house is in the most urgent need of this."

For the only time on record, Igor Tupilov wept.

"I find it hard to believe," Mottice whispered. "That fundamental a change . . . from a few radio quanta?"

"We found it hard to believe, too," Sigerist admitted, grimly rather than excitedly. "However, your work on synergistics had suggested that the right combination of impulses might trigger autocatalytic transformations in the synapeses. It doesn't take a lot, you see. These events happen on the molecular level. What's needed is not quantity but quality: the exact frequencies, amplitudes, phases, and sequences."

"Our initial evidence came from rats," Duarte said. "When we could alter their training at will, we proceeded to monkeys, finally man. The human pattern turned out to be a good deal more complex, as you'd expect. Finding it was largely a matter of cut-and-try . . . and, again, sheer luck."

Yuang scowled. "You still don't know precisely what the chemistry and neurology are?"

"How could we, two of us in this short a time? Our inducer ought to make quite a research tool!"

"I am wondering about possible harm to the subject."

"We haven't found any," Sigerist stated, "and we didn't just use volunteers for experimentation, we took part ourselves. Nothing happens except that the subject believes absolutely what he's told or what he reads while he's in the inducer field. There doesn't seem to be decay of the new patterns afterward. Why should there be? What we have is nothing but an instant re-educator."

"Instant brainwasher," Ginsberg muttered.

"Well, it's subject to abuse, like all tools," Fenner said. They could see enthusiasm rising in him. "Imagine, though, the potentialities for good. A scalpel can kill a man or save his life. Maybe the inducer can save his soul."

The agent of the Human Relations Board smiled across his desk. "I think our meeting has a symbolic value beyond even what we hope to accomplish," he said.

Hatred smoldered back at him from dark eyes under a bush of hair. One brown fist thumped a chair arm. The bearded lips spat: "Get with it, mother! I promised you an hour o' my time for your donation to the Black Squadron, and sixty minutes by that clock is what you're gonna get, mother."

The local head of Citizens for Law and Order turned mushroom pallid. His dull-blue eyes popped behind their rimless glasses. "What?" he exclaimed. "You . . . gave government funds . . . to that gang of . . . of nihilists——?"

"You will recall, sir," the Human Relations agent replied, mildly, "that you agreed to come after I promised that the investigation of the assault on Reverend Washington would be dropped."

He pressed a button on his desk. "Ringing for coffee," he said, repeating his smile. "I suspect we'll be here longer than an hour."

He leaned forward. As he spoke, passion transfigured his homely features. "Sirs," he declared, "you are both men whose influence goes well beyond this community. Your power for good is potentially still greater than your power for evil. A moderate solution to the problems which called forth your respective organizations must be found . . . before the country we share is torn apart. It can be found! If not perfect satisfaction, then equal and endurable dissatisfaction. If not utopia, then human decency. The white man must lay aside his superiority complex, his greed, his indifference to the suffering around him. The black man must lay aside his hatred, his impatience, his unrealistic separatism. We must work and sacrifice together. We must individually strive to give more than we get, in order that our children may inherit what is rightfully theirs: freedom, equality, and well-being

136

under the law. For we are in fact all equals, all Americans, all brothers in our common humanity."

He spoke on, and his visitors looked from him to each other with a widening gaze, and at last, slowly, their hands reached forth to clasp.

"And if a mistake is made," Duarte answered Fenner in a sarcastic tone, "why, you give the patient a jolt of inducer and straighten him out again." He grinned. "Sig and I actually got to playing with that. He made me a Baptist. I retaliated by making him a vegetarian."

"How'd it feel?" Yuang inquired, sharp-voiced.

"M-m-m . . . hard to describe." Sigerist rubbed his chin and leaned back in his chair till he looked at the ceiling. "We knew what was going on, you see, which our test subjects didn't. Nevertheless, vegetarianism seemed utterly right. No, let me rephrase that: it *was* right. I'd think of what I've read about slaughterhouses and —— We foresaw this, naturally. We stuck by our promises to return next day and be, uh, disillusioned, told we'd been forced into a channel, that our prior beliefs and preferences were normal for us. I thought I could make the comparison later, having then experienced both attitudes, and decide objectively which was better. But right away, when Manuel spoke to me, after the slight initial fogginess of mind had cleared, right away I decided what the hell, I do like steak."

Duarte sobered. "For my part," he said, "frankly, I miss God. I've considered going back to religion. Might have done so by now, except I realize certain faiths are . . . well, easier to hold, and I'd be sensible to investigate first."

Penny twisted a strand of blonde hair nervously between her fingers. Her bare foot kicked an old copy of the *Tribe* against a catbox ammoniacally overdue for changing, with a dry rustle and a small puff of flug. Sunlight straggled through the window grime to glisten off bacon grease on the dishes which filled the sink in one corner of her pad.

"Like, talk," she invited. "Do your thing."

"I hope you don't consider me a busybody," said the social worker in the enormous hat. She sighed. "You probably do. But with your unemployment compensation expiring——"

Penny sat down on the mattress which served for a bed, lit a cigarette, and wished it were a joint. "I'll get along."

The social worker raised a plump arm to point at Billy, playing contentedly with himself in his playpen. At eighteen months, his face had acquired enough individuality that Penny had felt sure Big Dick was the father. She often wondered where Big Dick had gone.

"I'm concerned about him," the social worker proceeded. "Don't you realize you're creating a misfit?"

"This is a world he ought to fit into?" Penny drawled. "Come off it." The smoke was pleasantly acrid in her nostrils.

"Do listen, darling." The social worker gripped her big purse, almost convulsively, squeezing together the brass knobs on its clasp. "You're throwing away his life as well as your own."

For a moment the peace emblem drawn on the wall wobbled. *Damn tobacco,* Penny thought. *Cancer.* She stubbed out the cigarette on the floor. It occurred to her that she really must unplug the bathtub drain, or anyway wash her feet in the sink . . . Oddly hard to concentrate. The woman in the enormous hat droned on:

"—you'll move in with yet another man, or he'll move in with you. Don't you realize that a kiss can transmit syphilis? You could infect your little boy."

Oh, no! Horror struck. *I never thought about that!*

"—You say you are protesting the evil and corruption of society. What evil? What corruption? Look around you. Look at the Thailand Peace, the Vienna Détente, the Treaty of Peking. What about the steady decline of interracial violence, the steady growth of interracial cooperation? What about the new penological program, hundreds of prisoners let out of jail every day, going straight and staying straight?"

"Well," Penny stammered, "well, uh, yeah, I guess that's true, like I seen it in the papers, I guess, only can you trust the kept press?"

"Of course you can! Not that the press is kept. This is a free country. You have your own newspapers of dissent, don't you?"

"Well, we got a lot to dissent about," Penny said. The way the visitor talked and acted, she had to be a person who'd understand. "I don't work on one myself, though. Like, that's not my bag. I'm not the kind that wants to kill pigs or throw rocks, either. I mean, a pig's human too, you know? Only when my friends keep getting busted or clubbed, like that, I can't blame they get mad. See what I mean? If we could all love each other, the problems would go away. Only most people are so uptight they can't love, they don't know how, and the problems get worse and worse." Penny shook her head, trying to clear out the haze. *But things* are *getting better like she said!* "Maybe they've finally begun to learn how in the establishment?"

"They have always known, my dear," the social worker answered. "What they have found at last is practical ways to cure troubles. We have a wonderful future before us. And violence, dropping out, unfair criticism is not what's bringing it. What we need is cooperation within the system.

"You're not with it, Penny. I'll tell you where it's at. Law is where it's at; the police aren't your enemies, they're your friends, your protectors. Cleanliness is where it's at, health, leaving dope alone, regular habits, regular work; that's how you contribute your share to the commune. And marriage. You simply don't know what love is till you're making it with one cat, the two of you sharing your whole lives, raising fine clean bright children in a country you are proud of——"

I . . . I never saw . . . never understood. . . .

Finally Penny cried on the large bosom, in the comforting circle of the plump arms. The social worker soothed her, murmured to her, breathed in her ear, "You don't have to give up your friends, you know. On the contrary. Help them. Help me call them together for a rally where we can tell them——"

"What happens to the person who operates the inducer, hands out the propaganda?" Fenner wondered.

"Oh, the impulses can be screened off," Sigerist replied. "You can easily imagine how. We used a grounded metal-mesh booth. Manuel's since designed a screen in the form of a net over the head, which could be disguised by a wig or a hat. For weak short-range projections, anyhow. Powerful ones, meant to cover a large area, would doubtless continue to require a special room for the speaker." He hesitated. "We haven't established whether psychoinduction occurs with more than one type of radio input. If it does, perhaps a shield against a given type can be bypassed by another."

"I tried to lie, experimentally, while under the field myself," Duarte said. "And I couldn't. I'd try to convince a volunteer that, oh, that two and two equals five. Right off, I'd get appalled and think, 'You can't do that to him! It isn't a fact!' Of course, fiction or poetry or something like that was okay to read aloud, except I got some odd looks from our subjects when I kept explaining at length that what they were hearing was untrue."

"So we'd either speak our lies from the booth," Sigerist put in, "or we'd tell them things we knew . . . believed . . . were real. That's another funny experience. Reinforcement in the brain, I suppose. At any rate, you grow quite vehement, about everything from Maxwell's equations on up. We confined ourselves to that sort of thing with the volunteers, understand. First, we'd no right to tamper with their minds. Second, we didn't want to give the game away. They were always told this was a study of how the tracings on a new kind of three-dimensional EEG correlate with verbal stimuli. Our falsehoods were neutral items. 'Have you heard Doc Malanowicz is trying to use the

Hilsch tube in respiratory function measurements?' Next day we'd disabuse them, always in such a fashion that they didn't suspect. We hope. The spectacular lies we saved for each other." His chuckle was not too happy a sound. "I'm a Republican and Manuel's a Democrat. When we were experimenting, both of us under the inducer field—the temptation to make a convert grew almighty strong."

"Ladies and gentlemen, the President of the United States."

"My fellow Americans. Tonight I wish to discuss with you the state of the nation and of the world. Our problems are many and grave. You know them both by name and by experience—international turmoil; cruel ideologies; subversion; outright treason; lawlessness; domestic discord, worsened by the unfair criticism of certain so-called intellectuals—a small minority, I hasten to add, since by and large the intellectual community is firmly loyal to the American ideal.

"What is that ideal? Let me tell you the eternal truths on which this country is founded, for which it stands. We believe in God. We believe in country; we stand ready to fight and die if need be, in the conviction that America's cause is always just. We believe in the democratic process, and therefore in the leaders which that process has given us——"

Ginsberg whistled. "If this gadget fell into the wrong hands—— Help!"

"Would it necessarily?" Fenner asked. His glance flickered around the table. "I know what you're thinking," he said in a hurried voice. "'The H-bomb's not in a class with this.' Right? Well, let me remind you that thermonuclear fusion is on the point of giving us unlimited power . . . clean power, that doesn't poison air or soil. Let me remind you of lives saved and knowledge gained through abundant radionuclides. And the big birds haven't flown yet, have they?" He drew breath. "If this, uh, inducer is as advertised, and I see no reason to doubt that, why, can't you see what it'll mean? Research. Therapy. Yes, and securing the world. I don't mind admitting I'd turn it on some of those characters who're destroying the ecology that keeps us all alive. Why not? Why can't the inducer be used judiciously?"

"One problem is, when you have the specs, this is an easy thing to build, at least on a small scale," Sigerist replied. "Now when in history was perfect security achieved? You can't reach the entire human race, you know. You may broadcast 'Love thy neighbor' while flooding the planet with inducer waves. But what of the guy who doesn't tune you in? Suppose he happens to be reading *Mein Kampf* instead? Or is down in a mine or driving through a tunnel? Or simply asleep?

"Is everyone who's to be given any knowledge of the inducer's existence . . . will everybody be dragooned first into a mental Janissary corps? I don't see how that can be practical. Their very presence and behavior would tip off shrewd men. And then there are ways . . . burglary, assassination, duplication of research. . . . And once the fact is loose——"

Pidge had to stand a minute and fight his nerves after he stepped out of the car. What if something went wrong?

The suburban street (trees, hedges, lawns, flowers, big well-built houses, under afternoon sunlight that brought forth an odor of growth and a chorus of birdsong) pressed him with its alienness. He was from the inner city, tenements, dark little stores, bars and poolhalls that smelled of urine, smog and blowing trash and thundering trucks and gray crowds. This place was too goddamn quiet. Nobody around except a couple of kids playing in a yard, a starchy nurse pushing a stroller down the sidewalk, a dog or two.

Pidge squared his narrow shoulders. *Don't crawfish now! After the casing you've done, the money you've laid out——* He rallied resentment. *You're not doing a thing except claiming your share. The rich bitches have pushed you around too goddamn long.*

And he wasn't drawing any attention here. He was sure he wasn't. White, and small, not like those bastards who'd shoved him out of their way through his whole life, oh, he'd show them how brains counted. . . . Shave, haircut, good suit, conservative tie, shined shoes, Homburg hat (the wires and transistors beneath his wig enclosed his scalp like claws), briefcase from the Goodwill and car borrowed but you couldn't tell that by looking. And he'd spent many hours in this neighborhood, watched, eased into conversation with servants; everything was known, everything planned, he'd only to go through with his program.

And They wouldn't appreciate his backing out. He'd had a tough time as was, wheedling till They let him in on the operation—the set of operations—he'd gotten wind of. Buying in had cost him all he could scrape together and a third of the haul when he was finished. And it had demanded he do his own legwork and prove he had a good plan.

Well, sure, they'd had plenty of trouble, expense, and risk beforehand, to make these jobs possible. Finding out what was being done in the jails that turned so many guys into squares, hell, into stoolies;

finding guards who could be bought; arranging for an apparatus to be smuggled out and stuff to be left behind so the fuzz would think it'd simply been busted; getting those scientific guys to copy the apparatus. And of course it couldn't be used more than for maybe a week, on the scale that they intended. Though people were awful stodgy, un-alert, these days—those that watched the speeches on TV or read the papers; don't ever do that, Pidge—the cops wouldn't be too dumb to understand what had happened. Then the apparatus wouldn't be good for anything but hit-and-run stuff.

If Pidge screwed up now, They would be mad. Probably They'd make an example of him.

He shivered. His shoes clacked on the sidewalk.

The doorbell of his target sounded faintly in his ears. He tried to wet his lips, but his tongue was too dry. The door swung noiselessly open. A maid said, "Yes, can I help you?"

Pidge pressed the clasp of his briefcase the way he'd been taught. "I have an appointment with Mr. Ames," he said.

For an instant she hesitated. His heart stumbled. He knew the rea-son for her surprise; he'd studied this layout plenty close. The in-dustrialist always spent Wednesdays at home, seeing no one except people he liked. He could afford to.

The maid's brow cleared. "Please come in, sir."

After that, it was a piece of cake. Ames got on the phone and man-aged to arrange the withdrawal of almost two million in bills, certi-fied checks, and bearer bonds without causing suspicion. He thought Pidge was giving him a chance to make a killing. His wife and staff made no fuss about waiting in an offside room, when Pidge whispered to them that national security was involved.

Naturally, the Brink's truck took a couple of hours to arrive. Pidge had himself a bonus meanwhile. Ames' daughter came back from high school, and she was a looker. Not expert in bed, you couldn't expect that of a virgin, but he sure made her anxious to please him. Pidge had never had a looker before. He was tempted to bring her along. But no, too risky. With his kind of money he'd be able to have whatever he wanted. He would.

After the armored truck was gone and the haul had been trans-ferred in suitcases to Pidge's car, he told the people of the house that life was worthless and an hour from now they should let Ames shoot them. Then the man should do himself in. Pidge drove off to his ren-dezvous with Their representative, who held his ticket and passport.

"Oh, you can raise assorted horrors," Fenner argued, "but to be

142

alive is to take chances, and I don't see any risks here that can't be handled. I mean, the United States Government isn't a bloc, it's composed of people, mostly intelligent and well-meaning. Their viewpoints vary. They're quite able to anticipate a possible monolith and take precautions."

"Tell me, what is a monolith?" Sigerist retorted. "Where does rehabilitation leave off and brainwashing begin? What are the constitutional rights of Birchers and militants? Of criminals, for that matter?"

"You're right," Mottice said. The sweat was running heavily down his face; they caught the reek of it. "This must never be used on humans without their prior consent and full understanding."

"Not even on those who're killing American boys and Thai peasants?" Sigerist asked. "Not even to head off nuclear war? Given such an opportunity to help, can you do nothing and live with yourself afterward? And once you've started, where do you stop?"

"You can't keep the secret forever," Duarte said. "Believe me, we've tried to think of ways. Every plausible consequence of the inducer's existence that we've talked about involves the destruction of democracy. And none of the safety measures can work for the rest of eternity. The world has more governments, more societies than ours. Maybe you can convert their present leaders. But the fact of conversion will be noticed, the leaders will have successors, the successors could take precautions of their own and quietly instigate research."

In his last years George Rainsdon always had a headache. He was old when the mesh was planted beneath his scalp, and the technique was new. The results were therefore none too good in his case; and the doctors said that doing the job over would likely cause further nerve damage. As a rule the pain was no worse than a background, never completely outside his awareness. Today it was bad, and he knew it would increase till he lay blind and vomiting.

"I'm going home early," he told his secretary, and rose from the desk.

Penelope Gorman's impeccable façade opened to reveal sympathy. "Another sick spell?" she murmured.

Rainsdon nodded, and wished he hadn't when the pain sloshed around his skull. "I'll recover. The pills really do help." He attempted to smile. "The cause is good, remember."

Her lips tightened. "Good? Only in a way, sir. Only because of the Asians, the radicals, the criminals. Without them, we wouldn't need protection."

"Certainly not," Rainsdon agreed. The indoctrination lecture, required of every citizen before implantation was performed, had made that clear. (A beautiful ceremony had evolved, too, for the younger generation: the eighteen-year-old candidates solemn in their new clothes, families and friends present, wreaths of flowers on the inducer, religious and patriotic exhortations that stirred the soul.) To be sure, crime and political deviancy were virtually extinct. Yet they could rise again. Without preventive measures, they would, and this time the inducer would let them wreck America. Eternal vigilance is the price of liberty.

Tragic, that indoctrination of the whole world had not been possible. But in the chaos that followed the Treaty of Peking, the breakup of the Communist empires after Communism was renounced . . . a Turkoman adventurer somehow welding together a kingdom in Central Asia, somehow obtaining the inducer, probably from a criminal . . . the United States too preoccupied with Latin America, with inculcating those necessary bourgeois virtues that the pseudointellectuals used to sneer at . . . and suddenly the Asians had produced nuclear weapons, insulating the helmets for everybody, their domain expanded with nightmare speed, soon they too were in space and could cover the Western Hemisphere with inducer signals, turning all men into robots unless defenses were erected, civilian as well as military—Rainsdon forced his mind out of that channel. Truth was truth; still, people did tend to get obsessed with their righteous indignation.

"You knock off too, Mrs. Gorman," he said. "I've no chores for you till I recover." The small advisory service—international investments—that he had founded after leaving a diplomatic corps that no longer needed many personnel used public data and computer lines. His office was thus essentially a one-man show.

"Thank you, sir. I appreciate your kindness. I'm snowed under by work in the Edcorps."

"The what?" he asked, having scarcely heard through a fresh surge of migraine.

"Educational Corps. You know. Volunteers, helping poor children. The regular schools teach them to honor their country and obey the law, of course. But schooling can't overcome the harm from generations of neglect, can't teach them skills to make them useful and productive citizens, without extra coaching." Mrs. Gorman rattled her speech off so fast that it must be one she often gave. Repetition didn't seem to lessen her earnestness. *Sexual sublimation?* Rainsdon wondered. He'd had occasion to visit her apartment. Aside from photographs of her late husband, it might almost have been a cell in a convent.

144

They left together. She matched her pace to his shuffle. The elevator took them down and they emerged on Fifth Avenue. Sunlight spilled through the crisp autumn air that could blow nowhere but in New York. Pedestrians strode briskly along the sidewalks. How wise the government had been to phase out private automobiles! How wise the government was!

"Shall I see you home, Mr. Rainsdon? You look quite ill."

"No, thank you, Mrs. Gorman. I'll catch a bus here and——"

The words thundered forth.

PEOPLE OF AMERICA! CLAIM YOUR FREEDOM! YOUR DIABOLICAL RULERS HAVE ENSLAVED YOU WITH LIES AND SHUT YOU AWAY FROM THE TRUTH BY WIRES IN YOUR VERY BODIES. EVERYTHING YOU HAVE BEEN FORCED TO BELIEVE IS FALSE. BUT THE HOUR OF YOUR DELIVERANCE IS AT HAND. THE SCIENTISTS OF THE ASIAN UNION HAVE FOUND THE MEANS TO BREAK OPEN YOUR MENTAL PRISON. NOW HEAR THE TRUTH, AND THE TRUTH SHALL MAKE YOU FREE! HELP YOUR FRIENDS, YOUR LIBERATORS, THE FREE PEOPLE OF THE ASIAN UNION, TO DESTROY YOUR OPPRESSORS AND EXPLOITERS! RISE AGAINST THE AMERICAN DICTATORSHIP. DESTROY ITS FACTORIES, OFFICES, MILITARY FACILITIES, DESTROY THE BASIS OF ITS POWER. KILL THOSE WHO RESIST. DIE IF YOU MUST, THAT YOUR CHILDREN MAY BE FREE!

Down and down the skyscraper walls, from building after building, from end to end of the megalopolis, the voices roared. Rainsdon knew an instant when there flashed through him, *Megaphone-taper units, radio triggered, my God, they must've planted them over the whole country, a million in New York alone, but they're small and cheap, and somewhere beyond that bright blue sky a spacecraft is beaming—* Then he knew how he had been betrayed, chained, vampirized by monsters of cynicism whose single concern was to grind down forever the aspirations of mankind, until the Great Khan had been forced to draw his flaming sword of justice.

Penny ripped apart her careful hairdo. Graying blonde tresses spilled, Medusa locks, over her breasts while she discarded gown, shoes, stockings, corset, the stifling convict uniform put on her by a gaoler civilization. Her shriek cut through the howl of the crowd in the only words of protest she knew, remembered from distant childhood. *"Fuck the establishment! Freedom now!"*

Rainsdon grabbed her arm. "Follow me," he said into her ear. His headache was nearly gone in a glandular rush of excitement, his thoughts leaped, it was like being young again and leading a charge in Korea, save that today his cause was holy. "Come on." He dragged her back inside.

She struggled. "What you at, man? Lemme go! I got pigs to kill."

"Listen." He gestured at the human mass which seethed and bawled outside. "You'd be trampled. That's no army, that's a mob. Think. If the Asians can develop an inducer pattern that gets past our mesh, be sure the kept American technicians have imagined the possibility. Maybe they've developed a shield against it. They'd have sat on that, hoping to keep secret—— Anyway, they'll have made preparations against our learning the truth. They'll send in police, the Guard, tanks, helicopters, the works. And these buildings, they probably screen out radiation, they must be full of persons who haven't had the slave conditioning broken. Penelope, our best service is to find that voice machine and guard it with our lives. Give more people a chance to come out where the truth can reach them."

They located the device in an office and waited, deafened, tormented, stunned by its magnitude of sound. Hand in hand, they stood their prideful watch.

But no one disturbed them for the hour or two that remained, and they never felt the blast that killed them.

The Asians knew that American missile sites were insulated against any radio impulses that might be directed at the controllers. They counted on those missiles staying put. For what would be the point of an American launch, when Washington could no longer govern its own subjects? At the agreed-upon moment, their special envoy was offering the President the help of the Great Khan in restoring order; at a price to be sure.

The Great Khan's advisors were wily men. However, being themselves conditioned, they did not realize they were fanatics; and being fanatics, they did not have the empathy to see that their opponents would necessarily resemble them.

In strike and counterstrike, the big birds flew.

"Well, that's certainly a hairy bunch of scenarios," Fenner admitted after a long discussion. "Are you sure things would turn out so bad?"

"The point is," Sigerist replied, "do we dare assume they wouldn't?"

"What do you propose, then?" Mottice asked.

"That's what we've invited you here to help decide," Duarte said.

146

Ginsberg shifted his bulky body. "I suspect you mean you want us to ratify a decision you've already made," he said, "and its nature is obvious."

"Suppression—— No, damn it!" Fenner protested. "I admit we need to exercise caution, but suppressing data——"

"Worse than that," Sigerist said most softly. "As the recognized authorities in your different fields, you'll have to steer your colleagues away from this area altogether."

"How will we do that?" Yuang demanded. "Suppose I cook an experiment. Somebody is bound to repeat it."

"We're big game, you know," Mottice put in. "A new-made Ph.D. who found us out would make a name for himself. Which would reinforce him in pursuing that line of work."

"The ways needn't be crude," Sigerist said. "If you simply, without any fuss, drop various projects as 'unpromising,' well, you're able men who'll get results elsewhere; you're leaders, who set the fashion. If you scoff a bit at the concept of neuroinduction, raise an eyebrow when Rocard is mentioned . . . it can be done."

He paused. Drawing a breath, rising to his feet, he said, "It must be done."

Ginsberg realized what was intended and scrabbled frantically across the table at the device. Sigerist pinioned his arms. Duarte pulled an automatic from his pocket. "Stand back!" the younger man shouted. "I'm a good target shooter. Back!"

They stumbled into a corner. Ginsberg panted, Fenner cursed; Mottice glared; Yuang, after a moment, nodded. Duarte held the gun steady. Sigerist began crying. "This was our work too, you know," he said through the tears. He pressed a button. A vacuum tube glowed and words come out of a tape recorder.

Five years afterward, Sigerist and his family tuned in a program. Most educated persons did, around the world. The Premier of the Chinese People's Republic had announced a major speech on policy, using and celebrating the three synchronous relay satellites which his country had lately put into orbit. Simultaneous translation into many languages would be provided.

Considering the belligerence of previous statements, Sigerist joined the rest of the human race in worrying about what would be said. He, his wife, the children who were the purpose of their lives, gathered in a solemn little group before the screen. The hour in Peking was well before dawn, which assured that India was the sole major foreign country where live listening would be inconvenient. Well, the eastern Soviet Union too, not to mention China itself; but there would be rebroadcasts, printed texts, commentaries for weeks to come.

When the talk was over, Sigerist's wife sought his arms and gasped with relief. He held her close and grinned shakily across her shoulder at the kids. The Premier's words had been so reasonable, so unarguably right. They had opened his eyes to any number of things which had not occurred to him before. For a moment during those revelations he'd wondered, been afraid . . . and then, actually quite early in the speech, the Premier had smiled with his unmatched kindliness and said: "The enemies of progress have accused us of brainwashing, including by electronic methods. I tell you, and you will believe me, nothing of the sort has ever happened."

And I Have Come Upon This Place by Lost Ways

by James Tiptree, Jr.

It is with some pride that I say I printed this author's first story just a few years ago. He reluctantly admits that he spent most of World War II in a Pentagon sub-basement, and wonders what war it was he watched go by in Shanghai when he was ten years old. Other facts about him are hard to come by, other than the vital fact that he can write stories such as this one—that purports to be about the far future, but is about all science at the same time.

It was so beautiful.

Evan's too-muscular stomach tightened as he came into the Senior Commons and saw them around the great view port. Forgetting his mountain, forgetting even his ghastly vest he stared like a layman at the white-clad Scientists in the high evening sanctum of their ship. He still could not believe.

A Star Research Ship, he marveled. A Star Science Mission and I am on it. Saved from a Technician's mean life, privileged to be a Scientist and search the stars for knowledge——

"What'll it be, Evan?"

Young Doctor Sunny Isham was at the bevbar. Evan mumbled amenities, accepted a glass. Sunny was the other junior Scientist and in theory Evan's equal. But Sunny's parents were famous Research Chiefs and the tissue of his plain white labcoat came from god knew where across the galaxy.

Evan pulled his own coarse whites across his horrible vest and wandered toward the group around the port. Why had he squandered his dress credit on Aldebaranian brocade when all these Star Scientists came from Aldebtech? Much better to have been simple Evan Dilwyn the general issue Galtech nobody—and an anthrosyke to boot.

To his relief the others ignored his approach. Evan skirted the silence around the lean tower of the Mission Chief and found a niche behind a starched ruff belonging to the Deputy, Doctor Pontreve. Pontreve was murmuring to the Astrophysics Chief. Beyond them was a blonde dazzle—little Cyberdoctor Ava Ling. The girl was joking with the Sirian colleague. Evan listened to them giggle, wondering why the Sirian's scaly blue snout seemed more at home here than his own broad face. Then he looked out the port and his stomach knotted in a different way.

On the far side of the bay where the ship had landed a vast presence rose into the sunset clouds. The many-shouldered Clivorn, playing with its unending cloud-veils, oblivious of the alien ship at its feet. *An'druinn,* the Mountain of Leaving, the natives called it. Why "leaving," Evan wondered for the hundredth time, his eyes seeking for the thing he thought he had glimpsed. No use, the clouds streamed forever. And the routine survey scans could not——

The Deputy had said something important.

"The ship is always on status go," rumbled the Captain's voice from the bevbar. "What does the Chief say?"

Evan's gasp went unnoticed; their attention was on the Research Chief. For a moment the high Scientist was silent, smoke of his THC cheroot drifting from his ebony nostrils. Evan gazed up at the hooded eyes, willing him to say no. Then the smoke quivered faintly: *Affirmative.*

"Day after next, then." The Captain slapped the bar.

They would leave without looking! And no ship would ever survey this sector again.

Evan's mouth opened but before he could find courage Sunny Isham was smoothly reminding the Deputy of the enzyme his bioscan had found. "Oh, Sunny, may I touch you?" Ava Ling teased. And then a glance from the Chief started everyone moving toward the refectory, leaving Evan alone by the port.

They would process Sunny's enzyme. And they should, Evan told himself firmly. It was the only valid finding the computers had come up with on this planet. Whereas his mountain . . . he turned wistfully to The Clivorn now sinking behind its golden mists across the bay. If once he could see, could go and feel with his hands——

He choked back the Unscientism. *The computer has freed man's brain,* he repeated fiercely. Was he fit to be a Scientist? His neck hot, he wheeled from the port and hurried after his superiors.

Dinner was another magic scene. Evan's mood softened in the glittering ambience, the graceful small talk. The miracle of his being

150

here. He knew what the miracle was: his old uncle at Galcentral fighting for an outworld nephew's chance. And the old man had won. When this ship's anthrosyke fell sick, Evan Dilwyn's name was topmost on the roster. And here he was among Star Scientists, adding his mite to man's noblest work. Where only merit counted, merit and honesty and devotion to the Aims of Research——

Ava Ling's glance jolted him out of his dream. The Captain was relating an anecdote of Evan's predecessor, the anthrosyke Foster.

"——hammering upon the lock with these wretched newt-women hanging all over him," the Captain chuckled. "Seems the mothers thought he was buying the girls as well as their boxes. When he wouldn't take them in they nearly tore him apart. Clothes all torn, covered with mud." His blue eyes flicked Evan. "What a decon job!"

Evan flushed. The Captain was bracing him for the numerous decontaminations he had required for field trips out of seal. Each decon was charged against his personal fund, of course, but it was a nuisance. And bad form. The others never went out of seal, they collected by probes and robots or—very rarely—a trip by sealed bubble-sled. But Evan couldn't seem to get his data on local cultures that way. Natives just wouldn't interact with his waldobot. He must develop the knack before he used up all his fund.

"Oh, they are beautiful!" Ava Ling was gazing at the three light-crystal caskets adorning the trophy wall. These were the "boxes" Foster had taken from the newt people. Evan frowned, trying to recall the passage in Foster's log.

"Soul boxes!" he heard himself blurt. "The boxes they kept their souls in. If they lost them the girls were dead, that's why they fought. But how could——" His voice trailed off.

"No souls in them now," said Doctor Pontreve lightly. "Well, what do we say? Does this wine have a point or does it not?"

When they finally adjourned to the gameroom it was Evan's duty to dim the lights and activate the servobots. He kept his eyes from the ports where The Clivorn brooded in its clouds, and went out to the laughter and flashes spilling from the gameroom. They were at the controls of a child's laser game called Sigma.

"Turning in?" Little Ava Ling panted brightly, momentarily out of the game. Evan caught her excited scent.

"I don't know," he smiled. But she had already turned away.

He stalked on, hating his own primitive olfactory reflexes, and pushed through the portal of the command wing of the Laboratories. Sound cut off as it closed behind him. The corridor gleamed in austere silence. He was among the high-status Labs, the temples of Hardsci-

151

ence. Beside him was the ever-lighted alcove holding the sacred tape of Mission Requirements in its helium seal.

He started down the hall, his nape as always pricklng faintly. Into these Laboratories flowed all the data from the sensors, the probes, the sampling robots and bioanalysers and cyberscans, to be shaped by the Scientists' skills into forms appropriate to the Mission Requirements and fit to be fed finally into the holy of holies, the Main Computer of the ship, which he was now approaching. From here the precious Data beamed automatically back across the galaxy into the Computer of Mankind at Galcentral.

By the entrance to the Master Console a sentry stood, guarding against Unauthorized Use. Evan tensed as he crossed the man's impassive gaze, tried to hold himself more like a Scientist. In his bones he felt himself an imposter here; he belonged back in Technician's gray, drudging out an anonymous life. Did the sentry know it too? With relief he turned into the staff wing and found his own little cubby.

His console was bare. His assistant had dutifully cleaned up his unprofessional mess of tapes and—embarrassing weakness—handwritten notes. Evan tried to feel grateful. It was not Scientific to mull over raw findings, they should be fed at once into the proper program. *The computer has freed man's brain,* he told himself, tugging at a spool rack.

From behind the rack fell a bulging file. That stupid business he had tried of correlating a culture's social rigidity with their interest in new information, as represented by himself and his waldobot. The results had seemed significant, but he had no suitable computer categories into which he could program. An anthrosyke had twenty-six program nouns. . . . Sunny Isham had over five hundred for his molecular biology. But that was Hardscience, Evan reminded himself. He began to feed the worthless file into his disposer, idly flicking on his local note-tapes.

"——other mountains are called Oremal, Vosnuish, and so on," he heard himself say. "Only The Clivorn has the honorific *An* or *The.* Its native name *An'druinn* or The Mountain of Leaving may refer to the practice of ritual exile or death by climbing the mountain. But this does not appear to fit the rest of the culture. The Clivorn is not a taboo area. Herdsmen's paths run all over the slopes below the glaciation line. The tribe has a taboo area on the headland around their star-sighting stones and the fish-calling shrine. Moreover, the formal third-person case of the word *Leaving* suggests that it is not the natives who leave but some others who leave or have left. But who could that be? An invading tribe? Not likely; the inland ranges are uninhabited and all travel is by coracle along the coasts. And the terrain beyond *An'druinn* seems imp——"

These were his notes made before he began to search the survey scans of The Clivorn for something to explain its name—a cave or cairn or artifact or even a pass or trail. But the clouds had been too dense until that day when he had thought he'd seen that line. *Seen!* He winced. Did he hope to do Science with his feeble human senses?

"——transistorized tar pits of the galaxy!" said a hoarse voice.

Evan whirled. He was alone with the tape.

"Computer of mankind!" sneered the voice. Evan realised it was the voice of his predecessor, the anthrosyke Foster, imperfectly erased from the old tape beyond his own notes. As he jumped to wipe it Foster's ghost-voice said loudly, "A planetary turd of redundant data on stellar processes on which no competent mind has looked for five hundred years."

Evan gasped. His hand missed the wiper, succeeded only in turning the volume down.

"Research!" Foster was cackling drunkenly. "Get their hands *dirty?*" A blur of static; Evan found himself crouching over the console. Horrified he made out the words. "Shamans! Hereditary button-pushing imbeciles!" More blur, and Foster was mumbling something about DNA. "Call that *life?*" he croaked, "the behavior of living beings? . . . In all the galaxy, the most complex, the most difficult . . . our only hope . . ." The voice faded again.

Evan saw the spool was almost finished.

"Scientific utopia!" Foster guffawed. "The perfectly engineered society. No war. We no longer need study ourselves, because we're perfect." A gurgling noise blotted out the words. Foster had been drinking alcohol in his Laboratory, Evan realized. Out of his mind.

"And I'm their court clown." There was a long belch. "Learn a few native words, bring back some trinkets . . . good old Foster. Don't rock the boat." The voice made indistinct groaning noises and then cried clearly, "On your hands and knees! Down on the stones, alone. Simmelweiss. Galois. Dirty work. The hard lonely work of——"

The spool ran out.

Through the whirling in his head Evan heard brisk heel-taps. He stood up as his door opened. It was Deputy Pontreve.

"Whatever are you up to, Evan? Did I hear voices?"

"Just my—local notes, sir."

Pontreve cocked his head.

"On that mountain, Evan?" His voice was dry.

Evan nodded. The thought of their leaving flooded back upon him.

"Doctor Pontreve, sir, it seems such a pity not to check it. This area won't be surveyed again."

"But what can we conceivably hope to find? And above all, what has this *mountain* to do with your specialty?"

"Sir, my cultural studies point to something anomalous there. Some —well, I don't exactly know what yet. But I'm sure I got a glimpse——"

"Of the mythical Time Gate, perhaps?" Pontreve's smile faded. "Evan. There is a time in every young Scientist's life which crucially tests his vocation. Is he a Scientist? Or is he merely an *over-educated Technician?* Science must not, will not betray itself back into phenomenology and impressionistic speculation. . . . You may not know this, Evan," Pontreve went on in a different tone, "but your uncle and I were at PreSci together. He has done a great deal for you. He has faith in you. I would feel it deeply if you failed him."

Evan's heart shrank. Pontreve must have helped his uncle get him here. Appalled, he heard himself saying:

"But Doctor Pontreve, if Uncle has faith in me he'd want me to have faith in myself. Isn't it true that useful discoveries have been made by men who persisted in what seemed to be only a—hunch?"

Pontreve drew back.

"To speak of idle curiosity, which is all you really suffer from, Evan, in the same breath with the inspired intuition, the serendipity of the great Scientists of history? You shock me. I lose sympathy." He eyed Evan, licked his lips. "For your uncle's sake, lad," he said tightly, "I beg of you. Your position is shaky enough now. Do you want to lose everything?"

An acrid odor was in Evan's nostrils. Fear. Pontreve was really frightened. But why?

"Come out of this now, that's an order."

In silence Evan followed the Deputy down the corridors and back into the Commons. No one was in sight except three scared-looking Recreation youngsters waiting outside the gameroom for their nightly duty. As he passed Evan could hear the grunting of the senior Scientists in final duel.

He slammed on into his quarters, for once leaving the view opaque, and tried to sort the nightmare. Pontreve's pinched face roiled with Foster's drunken heresy in his brain. Such fear. But of what? What if Evan did disgrace himself? Was there something that would be investigated, perhaps found out?

Was it possible that a Scientist could have been *bribed?*

That would account for the fear . . . and the "miracle."

Evan gritted his jaw. If so, Pontreve was a false Scientist! Even his warnings were suspect, Evan thought angrily, twisting on his airbed in vain search of something tangible to combat. The memory of Ava Ling's fragrance raked him. He slapped the port filters and was flooded with cold light.

The planet's twin moons were at zenith. Beneath them the mountain loomed unreal as foam in the perpetual racing mists. The Clivorn was not really a large mountain, perhaps a thousand meters to the old glaciation line, but it rose from sea level alone. Torchglows winked from the village at its feet. A fish-calling dance in progress.

Suddenly Evan saw that the clouds were parting over The Clivorn's upper crags. As only once before, the turrets above the glacier's mark were coming clear. The last veils blew by.

Evan peered frantically. Nothing . . . No, wait! And there it was, a faintly-flickering dead level line around the whole top. Say two-hundred meters below the crest. What could it be?

The clouds closed back. Had he really seen anything?

Yes!

He leaned his forehead against the port. Pontreve had said, *there comes a time in every Scientist's life . . .* in a million barren planets he might never have another such chance. The knowledge of what he was about to do grew in his guts and he was scared to death.

Before he could lose courage he flung himself back and slammed his sleep-inducer to full theta.

Next morning he dressed formally, spent a few minutes with his Terms of Grant codex and marched into Pontreve's office. The appointment ritual went smoothly.

"Doctor Deputy-Administrator," Evan's throat was dry. "As accredited Anthrosyke of this Mission I hereby exercise my prerogative of ordering an all-band full sensor probe of the terrain above five hundred meters indicated by these coordinates."

Pontreve's pursed lips sagged. "An all-band probe? But the cost——"

"I certify that my autonomous funds are adequate," Evan told him. "Since this is our last on-planet day, I would like to have it done soonest, sir, if you would."

In the full daylight bustle of the Labs, before the ranked Technicians, Apprentices and Mechs, Pontreve could say no more. Evan was within his rights. The older man's face grayed and he was silent before ordering his aide to produce the authorization forms. When they were placed before Evan he stabbed his finger on the line where

155

Evan must certify that the scan was relevant to his Requirements of Specialization.

Evan set his thumbprint down hard, feeling the eyes of the Tech-staff on him. This would take the last of his fund. But he had seen the Anomaly!

"Sir, you'll be interested to know I've had more evidence since— since our meeting."

Pontreve said nothing. Evan marched back to his lab, conscious of the whispers traveling through the wing. The probe would not take long once the sensor configuration was keyed in. He told his assistant to be ready to receive it and settled to wait.

Endless heartbeats later his man came back holding the heavily-sealed official cannister before him in both hands. Evan realized he had never touched an original before; all-band scans were in practice ordered only by the Chief and then rarely.

He took a deep breath and broke the seals. It would be a long decoding job.

At shiftover he was still sitting, stone-faced at his console. Noon-break had sounded, the Labs had emptied and filled. A silence grew in the staff wing, broken finally by Pontreve's footsteps down the hall. Evan stood up slowly. Pontreve did not speak.

"Nothing, sir," Evan said into the Deputy's eyes. "I'm . . . sorry."

The eyes narrowed and a pulse twitched Pontreve's lip. He nodded in a preoccupied manner and went away.

Evan continued to stand, mechanically reviewing his scan. According to every sensor and probe The Clivorn was an utterly ordinary mountain. It rose up in rounded folds to the glaciation limit and then topped off in strikingly weathered crags. The top was quite bare. There were no caves, no tunnels, no unusual minerals, no emissions, no artifacts nor traces of any sort. At the height where Evan had seen the strange line there was perhaps a faint regularity or tiny shelf, a chance coincidence of wind-eroded layers. The reflection of moon-light on this shelf must have been what he'd seen as a flickering line.

Now he was finished as a Scientist.

For an anthrosyke to waste his whole fund on scanning a bare mountain was clear grounds for personality reassessment. At least. Surely he could also be indicted for misuse of Ship's Resources. And he had defied a Deputy-Administrator.

Evan felt quite calm, but his mind strayed oddly. What would have happened, he wondered, if he had found a genuine Anomaly? A big alien artifact, say; evidence of prior contact by an advanced race. Would it have been believed? Would anyone have looked? He had always believed that Data were Data. But what if the wrong person found them in the wrong, Unscientific way?

Well, he at any rate was no longer a Scientist.

He began to wonder if he was even alive, locked into this sealed ship. He seemed to have left his cubby; he was moving down the corridors leading to the lock.

Something was undoubtedly going to happen to him very soon. Perhaps they would begin by confining him to quarters. His was an unheard-of malfeasance, they might well be looking up precedents.

Meanwhile he was still free to move. To order the Tech-crew to open the personnel lock, to sign him out a bubble sled.

Almost without willing it he was out in the air of the planet.

Delphis Gamma Five, the charts called it. To the natives it was simply the World, *Ardhvenne*. He opened the bubble. The air of *Ardhvenne* was fresh. The planet was in fact not far from the set of abcissae Evan knew only as terranormal.

Beneath his sled the sea arm was running in long salty swells lit here and there by racing fingers of sunlight. Where the sun struck the rocks the spray was dazzling white. A flying creature plummeted past him from the low clouds into the swells below, followed by a tree of spray.

He drove on across the bay to the far shore by the village and grounded in a sandy clutter of fishnets. The sled's voder came alive.

"Doctor Dilwyn." It was Pontreve's voice. "You will return immediately."

"Acknowledged," said Evan absently. He got out of the sled and set the autopilot. The sled rose, wheeled over him and fled away over the water to the gleaming ship.

Evan turned and started up the path toward the village, where he had come on his field trip the week before. He doubted that they would send after him. It would be too costly in time and decontamination.

It felt good to walk on natural earth with the free wind at his back. He hunched his shoulders, straining the formal labcoat. He had always been ashamed of his stocky, powerful body. Not bred to the Scientist life. He drew a lungful of air, turned the corner of a rock outcrop and came face to face with a native.

The creature was his own height with a wrinkled olive head sticking out of a wool poncho. Its knobby shanks were bare, and one hand held a club set with a soft-iron spike. Evan knew it for an elderly pseudo-female. She had just climbed out of a trench in which she had been hacking peat for fuel.

"Good day, Aunt," he greeted her.

"Good three-spans-past-high-sun," she corrected him tartly. Temporal exactitude was important here. She clacked her lips and turned to stack her peat sods. Evan went on toward the village. The natives of *Ardhvenne* were one of the usual hominid variants, distinquished by rather unstable sex morphology on a marsupial base.

Peat smoke wrinkled his nose as he came into the village street. It was lined by a double file of dry-rock huts, thatched with straw and set close together for warmth. Under the summer sun it was bleak enough. In winter it must be desolate.

Signs of last night's ceremonials were visible in the form of burnt-out resin brooms and native males torpid against the sunnier walls. A number of empty gourds lay in the puddles. On the shady side were mounds of dirty wool which raised small bald heads to stare at him. The local sheep-creatures, chewing cud. The native wives, Evan remembered, would now be in the houses feeding the young. There was a desultory clucking of fowl in the eaves. A young voice rose in song and fell silent.

Evan moved down the street. The males' eyes followed him in silence. They were a taciturn race, like many who lived by rocks and sea.

It came to him that he had no idea at all what he was doing. He must be in profound shock or fugue. Why had he come here? In a moment he must turn back and submit himself to whatever was in store. He thought about that. A trial, undoubtedly. A long Reassessment mess. Then what? Prison? No, they would not waste his training. It would be CNPTS, Compulsory Non-Preferred Technicians Service. He thought about the discipline, the rituals. The brawling Tech Commons. The dorms. End of hope. And his uncle heartbroken.

He shivered. He could not grasp the reality.

What would happen if he didn't go back? What if the ship had to leave tomorrow as programmed? It couldn't be worth sterilizing this whole area just for him. He would be recorded as escaped, lost perhaps after a mental breakdown.

He looked around the miserable village. The huts were dark and reeked inside. Could he live here? Could he teach these people anything?

Before him was the headman's house.

"Good, uh, four-spans-past-high-sun, Uncle."

The headman clicked noncommittally. He was a huge-limbed creature, sprawled upon his lounging bench. Beside him was the young male Parag from whom Evan had obtained most of his local information.

Evan found a dry stone and sat down. Above the huts streamed the unceasing mist-veils. The Clivorn was a shadow in the sky; revealed, hidden, revealed again. A naked infant wandered out, its mouth sticky with gruel. It came and stared at Evan, one foot scratching the other leg. No one spoke. These people were capable of convulsive activity, he knew. But when there was nothing urgent to be done they simply sat, as they had sat for centuries. Incurious.

With a start Evan realized that he was comparing these scraggy hominids to the Scientist at ease in their ship. He must be mad. The ship—the very symbol of man's insatiable search for knowledge! How could he be so insane, just because they had rejected his data—or rather, his non-data? He shook his head to clear the heresy.

"Friend Parag," he said thickly.

Parag's eyes came 'round.

"Next sun-day is the time of going of the sky ship. It is possible that I-alone-without-co-family will remain here."

The chief's eyes came open and swiveled toward him too.

Parag clicked I-hear.

Evan looked up at the misty shoulders of The Clivorn. There was sunlight on one of the nearly vertical meadows cradled in its crags. It was just past *Ardhvenne*'s summer solstice, the days were very long now. In his pocket was the emergency ration from the sled.

Suddenly he knew why he was here. He stood up staring at The Clivorn. *An'druinn*, The Mountain of Leaving.

"An easy homeward path, Uncle." He had inadvertently used the formal farewell. He began to walk out of the village on the main Path. Other trails ran straight up the mountain flank behind the huts; the females used these to herd their flocks. But the main Path ran in long straight graded zigzags. On his previous trips he had gone along it as far as the cairn.

The cairn was nothing but a crumbled double-walled fire hearth, strewn with the remains of gourds and dyed fleeces. The natives did not treat it as a sacred place. It was simply the lower end of the Path of Leaving and a good place to boil dyes.

Beyond the cairn the Path narrowed to eroded gravel, a straight scratch winding over The Clivorn's shoulders to the clouds. The dead and dying were carried up this way, Evan knew, and abandoned when they died or when the bearers had had enough. Sometimes relatives returned to pile stones beside the corpse, and doubtless to retrieve

159

the deceased's clothing. He had already passed a few small heaps of weathered rocks and bones.

Up this path also were driven those criminals or witches of whom the tribe wished to be rid. None ever returned, Parag told him. Perhaps they made it to another village. More likely, they died in the mountains. The nearest settlement was ninety kilometers along the rugged coast.

He topped the first long grade over the lowest ridge, walking easily with the wind at his back. The gravel was almost dry at this season though The Clivorn was alive with springs. Alongside ran a soppy sponge of peat moss and heather in which Evan could make out bones every few paces now.

When the Path turned back into the wind he found that the thin mists had already hidden the village below. A birdlike creature soared over him, keening and showing its hooked beak. One of the tenders of The Clivorn's dead. He watched it ride off on the gale, wondering if he were a puzzle to its small brain.

When he looked down there were three olive figures ahead of him on the Path. The native Parag with two other males. They must have climbed the sheep-trails to meet him here. Now they waited stolidly as he plodded up.

Evan groped through the friends-met-on-a-journey greeting.

Parag responded. The other two merely clicked and stood waiting, blocking the Path. What did they want? Perhaps they had come after a strayed animal.

"An easy home-going," Evan offered in farewell. When they did not stir he started uphill around them.

Parag confronted him.

"You go on the Path."

"I go on the Path," Evan confirmed. "I will return at sun-end."

"No," said Parag. "You go on the Path of Leaving."

"I will return," insisted Evan. "At sun-end we will have friendly speech."

"No." Parag's hand shot out and gripped Evan's jacket. He yanked.

Evan jumped back. The others surged forward. One of them was pointing at Evan's shoes. "Not needful."

Evan understood now. Those who went on this Path took nothing. They assumed he was going to his death and they had come for his clothing.

"No!" he protested. "I will return! I go not to Leaving!"

Scowls of olive anger closed in. Evan realized how very poor they were. He was stealing valuable garments, a hostile act.

160

"I go to village now! I will return with you!"

But it was too late. They were pawing at him, jerking the strange fastenings with scarred olive claws. Dirty hair-smell in his nose. Evan pushed at them and half his jacket ripped loose. He began running straight up the hillside. They started after him. To his surprise he saw that his civilized body was stronger and more agile than theirs. He was leaving them behind as he lunged up from sheep-track to track.

At the ridge he risked a look back and shouted, "Friends! I will return!" One of them was brandishing a sheep-goad.

He whirled and pounded on up the ridge. Next moment he felt a hard blow in his side and went reeling. The sheep-goad clattered by his legs. His side—they had speared him! He gulped air on a skewer of pain and made himself run on. Up. No track here but a smooth marsh tipped skyward. He ran stumbling on the tussocks, on and up. Mist-wraiths flew by.

At a rock cornice he looked back. Below him three misty figures were turning away. Not following, up The Clivorn.

His breathing steadied. The pain in his side was localized now. He wedged his torn sleeve between arm and ribs and began to climb again. He was on the great sinew that was The Clivorn's lowest shoulder. As he climbed he found he was not quite alone in the streaming wraith-world; now and then a sheep bounded up with an absurd *kek-kek-kek* and froze to stare at him down its pointed nose.

He was, he realized, a dead man as far as the village was concerned. A dead man to the ship, a dead man here. Could he make the next village, wounded as he was? Without compass, without tools? And the pocket with his ration had been torn away. His best hope was to catch one of the sheep-creatures. That was not easily done by a single man. He would have to devise some sort of trap.

Curiously uncaring of his own despair he climbed on. The first palisades were behind him now. Before him was a steep meadow moist with springs of clear peat water, sprigged with small flowers. Great boulders stood, or rather hung here, tumbled by the vanished batteries of ice. In the milky dazzle their cold black shadows were more solid than they. The sun was coming with the wind, lighting the underside of the cloud-wrack above him.

He clambered leaning sideways against the wind, his free hand clutching at wet rocks, tufts of fern. His heart was going too fast. Even when he rested it did not slow but hammered in his chest. The wound must be deeper than he'd thought. It was burning now and it hurt increasingly to lift his feet. Presently he found that he had made no progress at all but marched in place drunkenly for a dozen steps.

He ground his teeth, gasping through them. The task was to focus on a certain rock ahead—not too far—and push himself up into the sky. One rock at a time. Rest. Pick another, push on. Rest. Push on. Finally he had to stop between rocks. Breath was a searing ache. He wiped at the slaver on his jaw.

Make ten steps, then. Stop. Ten steps. Stop. Ten steps. . . .

A vague track came underfoot. Not a sheep-track, he was above the sheep. Only the huge creatures of the clouds ranged here. The track helped, but he fell often to his knees. On ten steps. Fall. Struggle up. Ten steps. On your knees in the stones, someone had said. There was no more sunlight.

He did not at first understand why he was facing rocky walls. He looked up, stupid with pain, and saw he was against the high, the dreadful cliffs. Somewhere above him was The Clivorn's head. It was nearly dark.

He sobbed, leaning on the stone flanks. When his body quieted he heard water and staggered to it among the rocks. A spouting stream-let, very cold, acid-clear. The Water of Leaving. His teeth rattled.

While he was drinking a drumming sound started up in the cliff beside him and a big round body caromed out, smelling of fat and fur. A giant rock-coney. He drank again, shivering violently, and pulled himself to the crevice out of which the creature had come. Inside was a dry heathery nest. With enormous effort he got himself inside and into the coney's form. It was safe here, surely. Safe as death. Almost at once he was unconscious.

Pain woke him in the night. Above the pain he watched the stars racing the mists. The moons rose and cloud-shadows walked on the silver wrinkled sea below him. The Clivorn hung over him, held him fast. He was of The Clivorn now, living its life, seeing through its eyes.

Over the ridgeline, a hazy transience. Moon-glints on a forest of antlers. The beasts of Clivorn were drifting in the night. Clouds streamed in and they were gone. The wind moaned unceasing, wreathing the flying scud.

Moonlight faded to rose-whiteness. Cries of birds. Outside his den a musky thing lapped at the stream, chittered and fled. He moved. He was all pain now, he could not lie still. He crawled out into the pale rose dawn hoping for warmth, and drank again at Clivorn's water, leaning on the rock.

Slowly, with mindless caution he looked around. Above the thrumming of the wind he heard a wail. It rose louder.

An opening came in the cloud stream below. He saw the headland beyond the bay. On it was a blinding rose-gold splinter. The Ship. Thin vapor was forming at its feet.

While he watched it began to slide gently upwards, faster and faster. He made a sound as if to call out, but it was no use. Clouds came between. When they opened again the headland was empty. The wailing died, leaving only the winds of Clivorn.

They had left him.

Cold came round his heart. He was utterly lost now. A dead man. Free as death.

His head seemed light now and he felt a strange frail energy. Up on his right there seemed to be a ledge leading onto a slanting shield of rock. Could he conceivably go on? The thought that he should do something about killing a sheep troubled him briefly, died. He found he was moving upward. It was like his dreams of being able to soar. Up—easily—so long as he struck nothing, breathed without letting go of the thing in his side.

He had reached the slanting shield and was actually climbing now. Hand up and grasp, pull, foot up, push. A few steps sidling along a cleft. The Clivorn's gray lichened face was close to his. He patted it foolishly, caught himself from walking into space. Hand up, grasp. Pull. Foot up. How had he come so high? Handhold. Left hand would not grip hard. He forced it, felt warm wet start down his side. Pull.

The rocks had changed now. No longer smooth but wildly crystalloid. He had cut his cheek. Igneous extrusion weathered into fantastic shelves.

"I am above the great glaciation," he muttered to the carved chimney that rose beside him, resonating in the gale. Everything seemed acutely clear. His hand was caught overhead.

He frowned up at it, furious. Nothing there. He wrenched. Something. He was perched, he saw on a small snug knob. Wind was a steady shrieking. Silver-gold floodlights wheeled across him; the sun was high now, somewhere above the cloud. One hand was still stuck in something above his head. Odd.

He strained at it, hauling himself upright.

As he rose, his head and shoulders jolted ringingly. Then it was gone and he was spread-eagled, hanging on The Clivorn, fighting agony. When it ebbed he saw that there was nothing here. What was it? What had happened?

He tried to think, decided painfully that it had been an hallucination. Then he saw that the rock beside his face was sterile. Lichenless. And curiously smooth, much less wind-eroded.

Something must have been shielding it slightly for a very long time. Something which had resisted him and then snapped away.

An energy-barrier.

Bewildered he turned his head into the wind-howl, peered along the cliffs. To either side of him a band of unweathered rock about a meter broad stretched away level around The Clivorn's crags. It was overhung in places by the rocks above. Invisible from a flyer, really.

This must be the faint shelf-line he had found on the scans. The effect of long shielding by an energy-barrier. But why hadn't the detectors registered this energy? He puzzled, finally saw that the barrier could not be constant. It must only spring into existence when something came near, triggered it. And it had yielded when he pushed hard. Was it set to allow passage to larger animals which could climb these rocks?

He studied the surfaces. How long? How long had it been here, intermittently protecting this band of rock? Millennia of weathering, above and below. It was above the ice-line. Placed when the ice was here? By whom?

This sourceless, passive energy was beyond all human technology and beyond that of the few advanced aliens that man had so far encountered.

There rose within him a tide of infinite joy, carrying on it like a cork his rational conviction that he was delirious. He began to climb again. Up. Up. The barrier was fifty meters below him now. He dislodged a stone, looked under his arm to see it fall. He thought he detected a tiny flash, but he could not see whether it had been deflected or not. Birds or falling stones would make such sparkles. That could have been the flickering he had glimpsed.

He climbed. Wetness ran down his side, made red ropes. The pain rode him, he carried it strongly up. Handhold. Wrench. Toehold. Push. Rest. Handhold. "I am pain's horse," he said aloud.

He had been in dense clouds for some time now, the wind-thrum loud in the rock against his body. But something was going wrong with his body and legs. They dragged, would not lift clear. After a bit he saw what it was. The rock face had leveled. He was crawling rather than climbing.

Was it possible he had reached The Clivorn's brow?

He rose to his knees, frightened in the whirling mists. Beside him was a smear of red. My blood with Clivorn's, he thought. On my knees in the stones. My hands are dirty. Sick hatred of The Clivorn washed through him, hatred of the slave for the iron, the stone that outwears

164

his flesh. The hard lonely job. . . . Who was Simmelweiss? "Clivorn I hate you," he mumbled weakly. There was nothing here.

He swayed forward—and suddenly felt again the gluey resistance, the jolting crackle and release. Another energy-barrier on Clivorn's top.

He fell through it into still air, scrabbled a length and collapsed, hearing the silence. The rocks were wonderfully cool to his torn cheek. But they were not unweathered here, he saw. It came to him slowly that this second barrier must have been activated by the first. It was only here when something pushed up through the one below.

Before his eyes as he lay was a very small veined flower. A strange cold pulse boomed under his ear. The Clivorn's heartbeat, harmonics of the gale outside his shield.

The changing light changed more as he lay there. Some time later, he was looking at the stones scattered beyond the little plant. Water-clear gold pebbles, with here and there between them a singular white fragment shaped like a horn. The light was very odd. Too bright. After a while he managed to raise his head.

There was a glow in the mist ahead of him.

His body felt disconnected, and inexplicable agonies whose cause he could no longer remember bit into his breath. He began to crawl clumsily. His belly would not lift. But his mind was perfectly clear now and he was quite prepared.

Quite unstartled, as the mist passed, to see the shining corridor—or path, really, for it was made of a watery stonework from which the golden pebbles had crumbled—the glowing corridor-path where no path could be, stretching up from The Clivorn's summit among the rushing clouds.

The floor of the path was not long, perhaps a hundred meters if the perspective was true. A lilac-blue color showed at the upper end. Freshness flowed down, mingled with The Clivorn's spume.

He could not possibly get up it just now. . . . But he could look.

There was machinery, too, he saw. An apparatus of gelatinous complexity at the boundary where the path merged with Clivorn rock. He made out a dialed face pulsing with lissajou figures—the mechanism which must have been activated by his passage through the barriers, and which in turn had materialized this path.

He smiled and felt his smile nudge gravel. He seemed to be lying with his cheek on the tawny pebbles at the foot of the path. The alien air helped the furnace in his throat. He looked steadily up the path. Nothing moved. Nothing appeared. The lilac-blue, was it sky? It was flawlessly smooth. No cloud, no bird.

Up there at the end of the path—what? A field perhaps? A great arena into which other such corridor-paths converged? He couldn't imagine.

No one looked down at him.

In his line of sight, above the dialed face was a device like a translucent pair of helices. One coil was full of liquid coruscations. In the other were only a few sparks of light. While he watched, one of the sparks on the empty side winked out and the filled end flickered. Then another. He wondered, watched. It was regular.

A timing device. The read-out of an energy bank perhaps. And almost at an end. When the last one goes, he thought, the gate will be finished. It has waited here, how long?

Receiving maybe a few sheep, a half-dead native. The beasts of Clivorn.

There are only a few minutes left.

With infinite effort he made his right arm move. But his left arm and leg were dead weights. He dragged himself half his length forward, almost to where the path began. Another meter . . . but his arm had no more strength.

It was no use. He was done.

If I had climbed yesterday, he thought. Instead of the scan. The scan was by flyer, of course, circling The Clivorn. But the thing here couldn't be seen by a flyer because it wasn't here then. It was only in existence when something triggered the first barrier down below, pushed up through them both. Something large, warm-blooded maybe. Willing to climb.

The computer has freed man's brain.

But computers did not go hand by bloody hand across The Clivorn's crags. Only a living man, stupid enough to wonder, to drudge for knowledge on his knees. To risk. To experience. To be lonely.

No cheap way.

The shining Ship, the sealed Star Scientists had gone. They would not be back.

He had finished struggling now. He lay quiet and watched the brilliance at the end of the alien timer wink out. Presently there was no more left. With a faint no-sound the path and all its apparatus that had waited on Clivorn since before the glaciers fell, went away.

As it went the winds raged back but he did not hear them. He was lying quite comfortably where the bones of his face and body would mingle one day with the golden pebbles on The Clivorn's empty rock.

166

The Ergot Show

by Brian W. Aldiss

*The mainstream world of letters has at last discovered Brian Aldiss
after the publication of his uproarious, hyperrealistic comic novel,*
Hand-Reared Boy. *We have happily known for years both him and
the dazzling pyrotechnics he displays here as he leads us by the hand
through the prophesied McLuhanesque global village of the future.*

Church interior: not very inspiring but very lofty, walls faced with
mottled brown marbling, light dim, frescoes hardly recognizable. Organ case, with clock perched slenderly on its arch, is a fine and elegant
work, if a little crushed between gallery and ceiling. It now peals forth
with a flamboyant rendering of the toccata from Georgi Mushel's
"Suite for Organ," as the congregation genuflect and depart, laughing.

Pagolini emerges with his friend and fellow-artist, Rhodes, and
genially rubs his hands as they descend the steps.

"A dinky service. I attend only for the sake of the departed. Things
are bad enough for them without our neglect. Why should the living
cut them dead? Live and let live, I say."

He is a tall and well-built man, rugged, a very tough fifty, still with a
thatch of faintly pink fair hair. Nothing eccentric, but when you've
met him, you know you've met him.

Rhodes merely says, "*Coffin* is a word with a beautiful period fla-
vor. Like *gutta percha* and *rubric.*"

Rhodes is also large, no signs of debauchery about him. He is forty-
six, his face still fresh, his eyes keen behind heavy glasses. He makes
love only to Thai women, and then only in the *soixante-neuf* position.

The viewpoint moves back faster than the two men move forward,
revealing more and more of the church behind. It is recognizable as
Pennsylvania Station in New York, U.S.A., no longer used for rail
traffic and hired by Pagolini for the occasion. The organ still plays.

167

Most of the congregation are holding hands as they emerge, stranger smiling at stranger. There are people everywhere.

Pagolini and Rhodes cross to a public transport unit, but a moment later we see them driving across sand in Rhodes' Volvo 255S. The organ is still playing. The car filming them lies behind, occasionally drawing level for a side-shot. Some areas of the beach are crowded with people. Fortunately nobody is killed, or not more than one might expect.

Now the music pealing forth is—surely we recognise it with a thrill —the Byrnes theme, "All That We Are." All that we are happened so long ago. Envelops us like a bath full of fudge.

Rhodes punches the cassetteer as he steers. Naked women swim up in the holovision and dance on the dashboard. He enlarges them until they fill the windscreen and the car is zooming through their thighs. Then he flips off. "Shall we go to Molly's as invited?"

"Feel holy enough?"

Rhodes shrugs. So Pagolini picks up the radiophone and dials Molly. Yeah, it would be dobro to see them. Come on up. Have they fixed on the two films yet? No, but they are going ahead and shooting the first one anyway. Isn't that kinda complicated? The men look at each other. Gutta percha, coffin, complicated, says Rhodes.

Now we are following one of Rhodes' muscle-planes as it gathers background footage over what may be regarded as a typical city of the teens of the new century: the Basque seaside tourism-and-industry center of San Friguras. Siesta is over, the streets are crowded with people. The evening is being passed in the usual way with plenty of demo, agro, and proto. The demo is by local trade unions demonstrating against poor working conditions and bad leisure pay. The proto is by tourists protesting against poor holiday facilities—when you have to spend a month holidaying abroad each year to support economically depressed areas, doll, you need adequate recompense! The agro is by local yobs aggravating anyone who looks too pleased with himself.

The muscle-plane takes it all in, the five rowers straining at their wings as the cameraman, Danko Brankic, a Croat, peers through his sights. Machine-powered planes are forbidden over most Mediterranean holiday resorts. The shadow of wings flutters over the crowd. Brankic points his instrument elsewhere, eschewing obvious symbolism.

Throughout this shot, Molly is still conversing in brittle fashion over the radiophone. Despite her millions, hers is the voice of the crowd, as the demo-argo-proto footage may perhaps indicate.

Back-and-forth dissolve to Molly's place, where some three hundred people loll on the sunlit terraces or stroll through the shadowy rooms. She managed to pick up an old Frankfurt tube alloy factory cheap in the nineties. Gutted and plastic-laminated in black, yellow, and gamboge, it contrasts well with the replica of a Nubian palace already *in situ*.

Molly herself is rather a disappointment amid all this trendy splendor, which looks as if it were designed by Pagolini himself, although he laughed sharply when she suggested as much. The ample bust which won her the qualifying round as Mrs. Ernstein-Diphthong the Third still supports her almost as well as she supports it, but the essentially shoddy bone structure of her cheeks is beginning to show through.

We catch a guest saying, "In five years' time, give or take the give-and-take of a year either way, her chin will begin to cascade."

A female guest replies, "She's as high as Brankic's muscle-plane," for all the world as if she caught the last sequence—in which we are still involved in the back-and-forth dissolve.

"*And* absorbs as much man-power."

Molly is coming forward to greet Pagolini and Rhodes as they alight from their plane. A close-up of their expressionless faces shows rugged Adriatic scenery in the background, with the sea glinting in an old-fashioned key of blue. The camera, turning with them to greet their hostess, reveals the familiar peak of the Matterhorn towering behind her mock-palace. Maybe it is just a phallic symbol.

"You two gorgeous men! Things were getting just a little bit boring until you came. Don't think I really mind but, Cecil, do we have to have your camera team tracking you all the time?"

"It's only my number two camera team," he apologized.

"Catatonic!" she enthused.

While they are talking, the scene has been growing dark, until it fades to a living black. No sound. An excerpt from Jacob Byrnes' book, *The Amphibians of Time,* appears:

Again we face a time of historical crisis, which I call clock-and-gun time. Such crises have occurred before, notably towards the end of the Thirteenth Century, when towns were growing rapidly, creating new human densities which foreshadowed the Renaissance. Guns and clocks were invented then, symbolizing the outward and inward aspects of Western man. New densities have always created new levels of consciousness.

A verge-escapement with foliot, ticking, ticking. Growing in the center of it, the ravaged and mountainous visage of Jacob Byrnes himself.

Byrnes is talking to Rhoda, who is still in her air-drop outfit. She brushes her hair as she listens. Hint of theme song on a solitary violin.

"Although I could say that the globe is my habitation, I don't share the contemporary restlessness. You know I'm just a relic from last century, doll. But I could live anywhere, and the Amoy ranch would suit me dandy for my declining years. That does not bug me one bit."

"Dobro! Then don't let it occupy you!" She still has her superb leonine hair, unchanged now for thirty years, and it fills the screen.

"It occupies me only to this extent. Should I sell up the Gondwana estates here in the States before I move out?"

She made an impatient gesture. She loved him, had loved him, because he was not the sort of man who needed to ask questions in order to make up his mind. When he asked, it was because he had possession of the answers.

"Rhoda, you know Gondwana means a lot to me—but it is always insanity to own land. I have the essential Gondwana inside me. I'll sell —unless you want it all. If you want it all, it's all yours."

"What about Rhodes? Is he going to film any more here?"

He crossed the room with its drab Slavonic curtains at the tall windows. He was as stocky as ever, slightly too heavy. His legs were painful. He had taken to limping.

Flinging open the end door, he gestured into the writing room, which had been converted into a projection room a few months before. She looked over his shoulder.

"I know."

Cans of holofilm were stacked here, standing on tables and floor. Some cans were not even labeled.

"Maybe they'll be back."

She looked at him.

"No two people ever really understand each other, Jake. Give about yourself. Do you resent the tricks Rhodes and Pagolini are playing with your book?"

He grinned. "We used to have trouble about finding where our real selves lay. Remember? That was a long time ago. We never solved the mystery. It was simply one of the fictitious problems of the twentieth century."

"Answer my poxing question, will you?"

He picked up one of the holofilms out of the can and slid it into the projector. "There's a logic in their illogic. Even their mode of expression is outmoded now, with sense-verity arriving. So my book is doubly outmoded. At least they appear to be transmitting the basic message, that we are reaching an epoch where literacy is a handicap. Now give me a decision on what we do about Gondwana. . . ."

He has flipped the power and drive switches, and the last words are played out against a three-dimensional view of the star, Quiller Singh, in a Ford-Cunard Laser 5, driving into Lasha during the first stage of the Himalayan Rally, closely followed by two I.B.M. Saab Nanosines. Cheering llamas. A yak stampeding up a side street. Singh turns into the pits for a quick change of inertia baffles. The cube fills with bent bodies of mechanics. Steam and smoke rise in the chill sunlight.

Singh raises his goggles and looks across at Rosemay Schleiffer. Theme music, a husky voice singing, "All that we are Happened so long ago—What we may be, That is deciding now. . . ." The vantage point swings up to the monasteries clinging to battlements of the mountains and, above them on the real heights, the curly-eaved palaces of the revenant Martian millionaires.

Dissolve into interior shot of one of the curly-eaved palaces.

Antiseptic Asian light here, further bleached by hidden fluorescents. They can never get enough light, the revenants. Gravity is another matter. Old barrel-chested Dick Hogan Meyer wears reflecting glasses and leg braces, walks with a crutch attached to his right lower arm. He points the crutch at Pagolini.

"Listen to me, I may own half of Lasha now, but when I first shipped out to Mars as a youngster, I was just a plain stovepipe welder, what they called a plain stovepipe welder. Know what that is, Mister, 'cos they don't have them any more?"

Pagolini took a drink and said, "Whenever you talk, Meyer, I begin to think of a certain tone of green."

"You do? Well, you listen to me, I was one of the guys that laid the water pipes right across half of Mars, you know that?"

Very murky landscape, like a close-up shot of a boulder sparsely covered by lichen. Land and sky split the screen between them. Nothing to see except the odd crater and the depressions of the ground. Emptiness that was never filled, desolation that was always deserted. Habitable, sure, but whatever came to inhabit it would be changed in the process.

Slowly the vista moves. The machines come into view. Dexion lorries, designed to come apart and make up into different vehicles when needed. They carry giant-bore water pipes. Two excavators, a counterbalanced pipe-laying caterpillar. Down in the thousand-mile ditch, a couple of men work, welding the sleeves of the pipes together. The lorry's engine splutters, feeding in power on a thin sad note.

All the time, Dick Hogan Meyer's voice continues, although it also is thin and sad, as if attenuated by weary planetary distances.

"Men did that, working kilometer by kilometer, one hundred lengths of pipe to the kilometer. They hadn't the machines like on Earth, they hadn't the machines to do it, Mister. So we did it. Mind you, the pay was great or I wouldn't have been there, would I? But, by Christ, it was hard slogging, that's what it was, Mister! We lived dead rough and worked dead rough. Such a wind used to blow out of them dinky pipes, you wonder where it come from."

"Catatonic! It's the green of a Hapsburg uniform perhaps."

"If so happen I'm boring you, you'll tell me? All I'm saying is I were just a stovepipe welder on Mars, that's how I made my jam, so what you want you'll have to spell out to me simple, so I can understand, just a simple stovepipe welder at heart."

Mars was gone, though still reflected in Meyer's reflecting lenses as Shackerton, smart young aide to Pagolini, came forward through the brightness of the great room saying, "Right, right, right, Mr. Meyer, my name's Provis Shackerton but never mind that—I won't bother you with irrelevancies—let's just say my name's Jones or Chang, as you prefer, and I will proceed to explain the deal in words of one syllable suited to those who carved their pile out of stovepipe welding, right?" He genuflected with something between a bow, a curtsy, and an obscene gesture.

"Mister Cecil Rhodes is the world's number one film-maker, right? He is not present here. Mister Pagolini is world's number one film-designer, right? Stands beside you. Used to be world's number one environment-designer, right? Designed, in fact, this Lasha and all that therein, from what was once a fairly unpromising stretch of the Andes. Rhodes and Pagolini now work together, right? Now Mister Pagolini makes a film based loosely on the masterwork *Amphibians of Time* by Jake Byrnes—don't worry if you haven't heard of *him,* Mister Meyer, because very many rich revenant Martian stovepipe-laying millionaires are in the same ignominious position—besides he's only the greatest prophet of our pre-post-literate age—and, at the same time, Mister Rhodes will make a film of Pagolini making his film, right? All we ask of you is the loan of x million credits to recreate the nineteen-seventies, for an agreed percentage of the gross of both holofilms."

Sneak close-up of Pagolini laughing. He adopts an English accent to say to himself, "The poor old sod is so ignorant he thinks parthenogenesis means being born in the Parthenon."

"Yeah, well, dobro, only what you going to do with the nineteen-seventies when you get them?" Some tendency of the old mouth to sag open. Could be the effect of Earth-gravity.

"Shoot them!" View over the busy busy idle guests. "Shoot them all, that's what I'd like to do!" Molly says, twinkling up at the heavy glasses and the light beard of Rhodes. "Now you come with me some place where we can talk."

"Mind if I take a fumigant?"

"Let me show you to your suite. How about you, Pagolini, doll, darling?"

He is talking to a tall bare-bummed girl in an Oriental mask, and sipping a treacley liquid through a straw. She has a straw in the same liquid and is—significantly, one supposes—not yet sipping.

"I'll be around here, Molly."

"Cataleptic, doll!"

She takes Rhodes' arm and leads him slowly away. Dappled light and shade as of sun through lightly foliaged trees—the poplars of Provence perhaps—play over their faces as they move through the long room among the droves of elegant bodies. The expression on their faces is pleasant. Here and there, a man or woman stands naked among the other guests. One such woman is being absent-mindedly fingered by a man and wife as she plays with a little toy clown.

Molly and Rhodes enter the dance room, where strobe lights burn to the beat. The stop-start-stop-start movements of dance are abstract. Limbs are dislocated in the microseconds of dark.

"A friend of mine had epilepsy in here last week. Some sort of an illness."

"Coffin, gutta percha, illness."

She laughed, sagging against him. "Dobro! Must have been hell back in the old centuries. Too few people to go around. . . ."

Rhodes' beard trembles with emotion as he speaks.

"Old Byrnes was right, a true prophet. I met him—I told you, over at his ranch in the States, big ranch. Gondwana. We did some filming there. Not too good. He perceived that the essential *differentness* of humanity to other species is our interdependence, one on another. Sometimes we call it love, sometimes hate, but it is always *interdependence*. So societies built up, always just too elaborate for the average solitary consciousness to comprehend. It's the building up, the *concentration*, that accounts for man's progress. We make ourselves forcing houses. Greater concentrations precede *major cultural advances.* Byrnes grasped many years ago that——"

He emphasizes what he is saying with forceful gestures, in a manner unlike his usual cool speech. He is shouting to compete with the insistent beat that rivals the strobes in punching sensibilities. So part of this crucial speech is lost, and is drowned out finally before completion as the camera gets snarled in dancers and loses Molly and her guest in the melee.

Instead we get an almost subliminal shot of Quiller Singh snarling up a series of hairpins, with Rosemay beside him in the red Laser 5.

Instead we have to put up with the bare-bummed girl smiling her beautiful best and whispering to Pagolini, "They say she really does change her cars whenever the ashtrays are full."

He is looking pensive. "Probably so, but you must remember that she has cut down her smoking considerably."

She is taking his hand and saying, "Ride with me in an ashtray-powered automobile and we will all the pleasures prove that stately mountain, hill, and grove. . . ."

He is running with her down a long flight of steps, saying, "Isn't it 'We will all the pleasures disprove . . . '?"

When she dives into the lake, he follows, and they sink down and down deeper, smiling at each other. All That We Are Happened so long ago—What we may be. . . . A cascade of harps. At the bottom of the sea, a little Greek temple with fish fluttering like birds among the pillars. They drift towards it, hand in hand.

"This is the green again, the exact green I want," he tells her. "We are all moving towards a new level of human consciousness! It's the green of *Macbeth.* You know *Macbeth?*"

"Was that the guy who swam all the way from Luna to Earth a few years back?"

"No, that was Behemoth or some such name. *Macbeth* is a Shakespeare film. That's the green I want."

"Rigor mortis, man! Isn't any old green green enough?"

"Not if you are an artist. Are you an artist?"

It was all white inside the temple, white and Macbeth green.

"Ask me another."

"Will you let me lie with you for, say, forty-three minutes?"

She looks up startled from the treacley liquid which she has now begun to sip, almost as if his fantasy disrupted her own line of thought. "What was that?"

He stares at his watch, studying the minute, second, and microsecond hand. "Maybe it's not worth the bother. I was wondering if you would lie with me for around forty-one and a half minutes."

Meyer's wife is running about the place screaming. She has a long Asian axe in her hands. A sub-title reads: LIKE AN ORDINARY AXE, BUT SHARPER. She is smashing up things.

"What is she doing?" Shackerton asks.

"She's smashing up things," Meyer says.

"Right, right, right!" He goes over to Pagolini, who is leaning out of one of the windows looking down at the monastery roofs. "Mrs. Meyer has gone mad. Very revenant. Hadn't we better leave, right?"

"She's not mad," Meyer explains, scratching his ear by way of apology. "It's the ergot in the bread, that's what they tell me. Ergot in the bread—makes you mad."

"How cataleptic to find ergot here," Pagolini says. The view shows rows of terraced houses stretching east and west; crowning Mount Everest is a big sign reading "LOTS" visible several hundreds of miles away—and even farther than that when Earth is on the wane and you are standing in Luna City with a pair of good binoculars. "Ergot has played a major part in influencing human history. The French character, so I have heard, has been moulded——"

"Moulded, right, right, right!" says Shackerton, screaming with laughter at the pun.

"——by various outbreaks of ergot throughout the centuries. The Ottoman Empire would have fallen two centuries before it did had not the armies of Peter the Great, which were marching south to defeat the Turks, been afflicted with madness caused by ergot. It stopped them in Astrakhan. Make a note of that title, Shackerton—possible song there. You don't know when you are mad——"

While he is speaking, Mrs. Meyer has been drawing nearer, carving her way through the paneling, furniture, and light fixtures as she comes.

"I know when I'm mad! And I'm good and mad now!"

"Right, right, right!"

"Catatonic!"

"She does know, too, she does!"

Meyer runs to a huge gamboge sofa that would hold ten, swivels it round, and reveals an escape chute. They take it. Mrs. Meyer comes after them, axe in hand. As they pick themselves up in the snow, she runs past them and begins to chop up the Pagolini helicopter.

"She likes a good whirley-bird when the fit takes her, does my Mary," Meyer says, with just a touch of complacency to his sorrow.

"Coffin, complicated, gutta percha, whirley-bird," collects Pagolini. He appears somewhat impatient.

"Figgle-fam, then," says Meyer, sulkily. He is caught at a disadvantage. He goes over to where one of the rotor vanes lies, stoops, holding the small of his back as he bends, and retrieves a shattered vane.

"I suppose I'd better agree to financing the nineteen-seventies," he says. People can change Without any why or how, Powers will emerge Building behind your brow. . . .

The axe comes flying and catches Shackerton on the glutea maxima. He falls, screaming.

Blood fills the screen. A notice appears:
FOR THE BENEFIT OF THOSE WHO WOULD CARE TO LEAVE THIS THEATER NOW
It hangs there in the void before giving way to its completion, and the dissolve is so slow that the two ends of the sentence intermix irritatingly before the end can be read.

The screams of Shackerton fade as the theme emerges again. WE ANNOUNCE THAT THE REST OF THE FILM IS NON-VIOLENT

"Isn't it a bit of a muddle?" Rhoda asked, as Byrnes switched off.

"Life?"

"The Rhodes epic."

"To a degree."

"Come on, Jake. It's a load of bullshit!"

"Life?"

"He isn't making one connection with your book, not one little connection, right?"

"Right, right, right!" He laughed. "Let's go and get an old-fashioned alcoholic drink, the kind that these holofilm guys don't use any more."

As they padded back into the rather old-fashioned living area, where an alligator dozed with open eyes beside an ivory pool, he said, "No, honey, Rhodes has made the connection okay. He is second generation to my book. He finds the book kind of fuddy-duddy simply because the message got across to him so long ago that he acts on it well nigh instinctually."

She smiled, curling her long legs beneath her as she settled by the pool and started fondling the drugged reptile. " 'Well nigh.' Coffin, gutta percha, whirley-bird, what was the other thing?"

"*Literacy*. The mass-psychosis of the nineteen-seventies was

176

merely a build-up for the breakthrough into a higher level of human consciousness. That's what we're witnessing now. Rhodes' epic would hardly be intelligible a few years ago. And he has seen that literacy has to go, just as I predicted."

She accepted the drink he poured her and set the clouded glass down on the alligator's head.

"You explained to me before about why literacy has to go, but I still don't get it. It's to do with needing more dimensions, isn't it?"

"The linear business, yes. More importantly, we are going to regain senses by sloughing off literacy. Those who could write ruled the world for—what?—ten thousand years. Very powerful minority, but only a minority in almost any culture you care to name. They were the clerks, and they shaped civilization. Now Rhodes, and more especially the generation after him—the true inheritors of this alien new century—they are shaking off the stultifying effects of literacy and getting back all the senses that have to be sacrificed to master a printed page and the cultures of the printed page."

Rhoda sipped her drink and then began to slide into the pool.

"And this sloughing of literacy, as you call it, is the result of computerization?"

"I'd put it this way—and how lovely you look!—the result of man's still-developing mind. We have never been satisfied with our limited senses. The earliest men painted and developed weapons to extend his psychesphere. But some senses we were born with got lost in the upward battle, just as Meyer lost all potentiality in his fight for brute cash. Now that computers take most of the load, we reclaim many old freedoms. . . ."

She smiled up at him as he stripped.

"You hairy old ape! Come in with me. Drag Horace in!"

"You and I, Rhoda, my eternal love, we are the first man and woman on this planet." And he blundered down into the water beside her.

"Ah, the female element!"

The number two camera crew are sitting on the wide landing outside Rhodes' suite, drinking stepped-milk and eating chickwiches. The landing is lumbered with Molly's signature motifs, bright and outrageous confections inspired by Khmer art, burial ornaments, and the morphology of insects. The boys munch and chatter.

"Wonder how Danko and his gang are getting on. . . ."

"Yeah. . . ."

"Think they'll let us sleep here?"

"You know the Commo-capitalist system, boy—you'll be sacking out on the beach tonight."

"What beach? The mountains, you mean!"

"Get phased! You're on the wrong dinky set."

"Alpha, I was getting muddled. . . ."

"What's she doing in there with Cecil, anyway? Not being Thai, she'll get no change out of him!"

Beyond his moving mouth, before the chickwich comes up again, we see the door open and Molly emerge. We glide through the door before she can close it.

Rhodes is polishing his spectacle lenses; without them, he has a deceptively mild look.

"Gun-and-Clock Time . . ."

He kicks off his boots.

There is an array of screens in the hall of his suite. He pads over to them and turns them on. Views of packed humanity everywhere, long distance or swooping to close-ups revealing skin texture as he twiddles the controls. He fiddles the volume at the same time, so that noise comes and goes. We see Meyer running through the snow, weeping, pursued by his wife who still wields the axe. Shots from Pagolini's fantasy, swimming down to the temple—what he dreamed, someone else acted out in reality because the Earth is so crowded that coincidence is one with coffin and complicated. Shots of Danko Brankic still flying noiselessly in and out of choking Mediterranean alleys. Byrnes, belly upwards, floating beside an alligator and a blonde. Quiller Singh, his Laser 5 belting triumphantly into Katmandu.

Rhodes laughs.

"Great old prehistoric man, Byrnes! We've left him behind. Left them all behind. . . . New human beings are coming up."

Flicking over switches with decision, he hurries back into the adjoining room among plastic insect bodies and adjusts monitor and scanner so that he can stand and see himself burning solid in the screen. He begins to 'act,' reciting rather than speaking.

"Earth swarms with people—crawls with people. It's full up with people, but there's still room for more. Byrnes saw it first—this film is our tribute to him while he still lives. He saw that the population explosion was a positive thing, born from our love of children, of more and more life. He saw that great pressure of population was necessary for man to be forced into his next stage of being, a new level of awareness, a greater integration. From the mass-psychosis of the twentieth century, a new sanity is being born. Now that we have entire control

178

of population build-up, and can feed our glad new mouths, we need fear nothing except the old fears. . . ."

Then he burst out laughing.

"Cut! I'm talking twentieth century rhodomontade! One foot in the past, that's me—but we'll get there. One more generation, psyche striking sparks off psyche. . . . It needs seeing. . . ."

His voice tails off inaudibly. He goes over to the interior omnivision and switches on. Room after room of Molly's palace is revealed, many untenanted, many bare of furnishing. Some are packed with human activity. He hits on one room where there is a monitor screen burning. He sees himself in it.

The woman viewing his image looks up, startled but smiling. She waves, her lips move, but Rhodes has the volume too low to hear. He flicks on. He is searching searching for a nest of Thai girls. Molly must have one somewhere in her castle.

He flips on to the terraces, zooms in on Pagolini just getting up to go, holding the hand of his bare-bummed girl.

"Ever see a movie called *Kid Auto Races in Venice?*"

"Is that a movie?"

"Quite an historic one."

Rhodes is fiddling with the volume. Their voices are enormously loud, echoing through the room, growing louder as Pagolini and the girl retreat from the eye of the camera.

Pagolini is talking to Byrnes and Rhoda in a cathedral. They walk up and down. It is an unusual cathedral, very heavy—possibly the cathedral in Saragossa, Spain.

"This is where we intend to start recreating the nineteen-seventies. This cathedral is not used any more, except for the benefit of tourists —they get about fifty thousand through the turnstiles on an average day in the high season. I have bought it. A performance of *Macbeth* was given here some years ago which I stage-managed. I like the coloring."

"Maybe we should holiday near here and watch you shoot," Rhoda said.

"You know what a Macbeth green is?"

"Sure, it's the place where the witches three shacked up."

"You are a lady of the old culture."

"You must get in my point about cities as a symbol of the death of the old human psyche, Signor Pagolini. The Romantics are the sickening point. Their cities slowly sink underground. Remember Kublai Khan's pleasure dome, and the subterranean passages in Poe . . .

Partly they were the effect of opium, but only in part." As he speaks, he stops to study some intricate stucco ornamentation, not noticing that Pagolini has walked on with Rhoda. "In later writers, the psyche fades lower still. The writings of Cocteau and Asimov provide examples. Asimov has whole underground planets, if one may so say . . . Psychic death before rebirth. Dark before renaissance . . ."

There is a beautiful shot of Pagolini and Rhoda as they pause far down the patterned aisle under the high windows. She hesitates, as if wishing to go back to Jake. Jake's voice is lost. Before Pagolini can turn to her, a girl appears in the main entrance, framed in light from outside. She may be the girl he is later to discover on Molly's terraces. She wears a long simple dress of frail material which might have been designed from a Walter Crane drawing. When Pagolini sees her, he in his turn hesitates, looking back to see what Rhoda is doing. People caught in light, transfixed, transformed. All this in long shot, viewed from Byrnes' pillar.

Rhoda makes a slight gesture. Pagolini interprets it as one of assent. With a slight bow to her, he turns toward the door, the daylight, the girl framed there. Beyond her, the crowded square can faintly be discerned. The camera crew is there, ready to record the moment of splendor when Pagolini emerges. Is that Rhodes, sitting on a camera dolly?

The organ is playing part of Georgi Mushel's "Suite for Organ"— something of a second-rate piece of music.

Almost subliminal shot of Pagolini manifesting himself in the doorway from outside. The cathedral is Pennsylvania Station.

Another cathedral facade—or at least a monstrous building. Shadow of the muscle-plane over it. The plane lands. While the five rowers slump over their oars, Rhodes and Brankic jump nimbly out.

Rhodes walks along the promenade by the sea, head down, hands clasped behind his back in a somewhat dejected fashion.

DON'T WORRY—ALL ENDS HAPPILY

Brankic trudges behind, lugging cans of film.

OR CEASES ON A NOT UNHAPPY NOTE, LET'S SAY

"We also have to bring in the dear departed. Where would we all be without the countless past generations copulating away for our sakes?"

Brankic chuckles. "You don't really want to make a holo. You want to recreate life itself."

Rhodes also chuckles. "Right, right, right!" he quotes.

On the snow-covered cliffs above them are running figures. We see Mrs. Meyer, axeless now that the madness has passed. She weeps as she flees, pursued by her husband, who is wielding the axe. Some day we'll evolve so far, We'll become All That We Are. . . . Louder and louder, till drowned by the ticking of a clock. Last chance to study a verge-escapement with foliot before the house-lights come up.